TROPHIES AND DEAD THINGS

Also published in Large Print
by Marcia Muller:

The Cheshire Cat's Eye
Games to Keep the Dark Away

TROPHIES AND DEAD THINGS

Marcia Muller

G.K.HALL&CO.
Boston, Massachusetts
1991

Published in Large Print by arrangement with
Mysterious Press, a division of
Warner Books, Inc.

G.K. Hall Large Print Book Series.

Set in 18 pt. Plantin.

Library of Congress Cataloging-in-Publication Data

Muller, Marcia.
   Trophies and dead things / Marcia Muller.
      p.   cm.—(G.K. Hall large print book series)
    ISBN 0-8161-5134-2 (lg. print)
    1. Large type books. I. Title.
  [PS3563.U397T75   1991]
  813'.54—dc20   91-9001

For Liz Alexander

TROPHIES
AND
DEAD
THINGS

One

On summer mornings San Francisco is often shrouded by a heavy fog. It billows through the Golden Gate and moves insidiously about the city, transforming familiar places and ordinary objects into things of beauty, mystery, or—in certain cases—evil. It hangs thick outside windows, slips under doors, and permeates the consciousness of those on the raw edge of waking. An untroubled rest will then degenerate into tossing and turning; pleasant dreams grow nightmarish. When the fog's victims open their eyes, they are already aware of a curious deadening of spirit, even before they face the gray day.

I was one of those victims on a Saturday morning in July. Long before my alarm was due to go off at the unholy hour of seven I woke and lay contemplating the shadows that gathered in the corners of my bedroom. Finally I reached for the rod that controlled the mini-blinds on the window above my head and turned it. The light that entered

1

was murky; I sat up, saw mist decorating the branches of my backyard pine trees like angel's hair.

I sighed, turned off the alarm before it could ring, and flopped back against the pillows. The flat, dull feeling I'd awakened with deepened. There had been a dream . . . of what? I couldn't remember, but its aura persisted—distinctive, depressing.

I focused on the day ahead, but its prospects weren't too cheerful, either. Hank Zahn, senior partner at All Souls Legal Cooperative, where I am staff investigator, had asked a favor: that I help him clear out the flat of a client who had been killed in one of a recent rash of random street shootings. Although it was not the way I cared to spend my Saturday, I'd agreed because I sensed that Hank—one of my oldest and closest friends—needed my presence. And there *was* one bright spot: he'd bribed me with the promise of lunch; that plus Hank's good company was a winning combination.

Lord knew I could use some good company. This morning's low-grade depression might be mostly fog-induced, but the last month had been lonely and bleak, the five before it not much better. I had to find some way out of these emotional doldrums—

The doorbell rang.

Uneasiness stole over me, the way it does when doorbells or phones ring at times when they're typically not supposed to. I got up, grabbed my robe, belted it securely as I went down the hall. When I got to the door, I peered through its peephole.

Jim Addison, the man I'd been seeing up until a month ago, stood on the steps—and he was drunk. At a little after seven in the morning, he was obviously drunk.

I opened the door and stared. Jim listed against the porch railing, a foxy little gleam in his blue eyes. His sandy hair was tousled, his clothing was rumpled, and he reeked of cigarette smoke.

He said, "All-night jam session." Jim was a jazz pianist who played on weekends with a group at a small club near the beach. "Can I come in?"

I hesitated, wondering how quickly and easily I could get rid of him, then decided humoring him was the best approach. (Get rid of him . . . humor him . . . What had once been a pleasant relationship had come down to that.)

"For a few minutes." I let him in and led him down the hall to the kitchen, where I went directly to the coffeemaker and filled

3

it with water. He went directly to the refrigerator and looked inside.

"Got any wine?"

"There's half a bottle of Riesling on the shelf in the door." While I whirled beans in the coffee grinder with one hand, I reached into the cupboard with the other and passed him a glass. I'd become used to Jim winding down his day while I was just beginning mine, although he didn't often unwind to such excess.

When I got the coffee going and turned, I saw he was just standing there, holding the empty wineglass and frowning. "You hate me, don't you?" he said.

I sighed. "Of course not." It was the same question he'd asked when I'd told him I didn't want to see him anymore—and in each of his numerous and persistent phone calls since then. My answer was true, although I'd long ago wearied of reassuring him. Jim was a nice man with a good sense of humor, a talented and dedicated musician, and I liked him a great deal. In fact, it was liking him so much that had made me decide to end the relationship. It's unkind to use someone you care for to get over someone else whom you think you love.

He regarded me for a moment and then

his lips twisted disgustedly. "Sensible and rational as ever, aren't you?"

"What's that supposed to—"

"You're always right, you always know what's best for me, for you, for the whole fucking world!"

"That's not true." If I were so sensible and rational, would I allow myself to go on missing a man whom I hadn't heard from for over six months? Would I have allowed myself to fall in love with that particular man in the first place?

Jim slammed the wineglass down on the counter so hard that it shattered. My gaze jumped to the gleaming shards and then to his face, mottled with rage. It was the first time I'd ever seen him angry.

"What do I have to say to get through to you?" he demanded.

"We've said it all before."

"No, I don't think so. Not yet, we haven't!" Abruptly he turned and went down the hall; the front door opened and slammed behind him.

"Great," I said. "Just great. What else can go wrong today?"

I expelled a long breath and leaned back against the counter; behind me the coffee-maker wheezed and burbled. For a moment

I considered whether Jim—this new angry Jim whom I didn't know—had a potential for violence. Well, I decided, we all did, didn't we? I'd have to wait and see what he did next. And on that less than encouraging note, I went to turn on the shower.

While I was washing my hair, the dream I'd had came back to me. I'd been driving to meet Hank at his client's flat in the Inner Richmond district, but after I crested Buena Vista Heights and descended into the Haight-Ashbury, I found that Stanyan, the northbound street on the edge of Golden Gate Park, had disappeared. In my confusion I made a series of turns that led me deep into unfamiliar territory, then suddenly I arrived at the top of the hill again. Over and over I'd driven down into the Haight. Over and over I'd found no trace of Stanyan Street.

Such frustration dreams—repeatedly dialing a phone and hitting the wrong buttons, missing a plane because I couldn't get packed in time—were nothing new to me. I'd recently read a paperback on the subject and learned that they're an indication that the dreamer is of two minds about reaching the destination, completing the call, or making the plane trip. But in this case, despite the depressing nature of the task ahead, I couldn't understand why I should feel such strong ambivalence—or why the dream had left such an unpleasant, lingering aura.

Superstitiously I crossed my shampoo-slick fingers against the possibility of the dream being a bad omen.

By nine o'clock I'd had three cups of coffee and done the *Chronicle* crossword, and my spirits had risen somewhat. By nine-thirty, when I arrived in the Inner Richmond (Stanyan Street still being there after all), I felt reasonably cheerful.

The Richmond is a solidly middle-class district on the northwest side of Golden Gate Park, consisting mainly of single-family homes and multi-flat buildings set close together on small lots. Once it was heavily populated by members of the city's Russian and Irish communities, but in the past couple of decades it has become the neighborhood of choice for upwardly mobile Asians. While the Catholic churches and Irish pubs and the Russian Orthodox cathedral on Geary Boulevard remain, everywhere there are signs of the new residents.

As I drove along Clement Street, the district's busy shopping area, I noted eight

Asian restaurants within two blocks: one Thai, one Japanese, one Burmese, two Vietnamese, and three different types of Chinese. Produce stands with outdoor bins full of bok choy and daikon radish, groceries with smoked ducks and barbecued pork ribs hanging in their windows, banks and insurance agencies with signs in both English and various Asian characters—all these stood side by side with such longtime institutions as Green Apple Books, Churchill's Pub, Woolworth's, and Busvan Bargain Furniture. Eight out of ten faces that I spotted were Asian—reflecting the same ethnic mix as the restaurants, and ranging from stooped old people pulling shopping carts to young couples emerging from Japanese-model sports cars. Clement Street, I thought, was the perfect embodiment of the changing cultural patterns of San Francisco.

Unfortunately, it is also one of the worst examples of the city's congested parking and traffic. The area was built up at a time when no one envisioned today's large population of both people and cars, and consequently there are too few parking lots and garages. Even at that relatively early hour, all the metered spaces were taken and trucks double-parked while making deliveries. Cars

8

moved slowly, their drivers looking for vacancies at the curbs; other irate drivers made U-turns, slid through stop signs, and endangered pedestrians in the crosswalks. I waited behind an exhaust-belching Muni bus as it unloaded passengers, tapping my fingers on the steering wheel of my MG and giving mental thanks to Hank for remembering to tell me it was okay to park in the driveway of the house on Third Avenue— should I ever reach it.

After five more minutes of creeping along Clement, I rounded the corner onto Third and found the address Hank had given me: one of those two-flat buildings with a garage and illegal in-law apartment on the ground floor. Its facade was bastardized Victorian, mint green with mauve and tangerine trim —a combination that would cause even a person of minimal taste to cringe. Hank's Honda stood in the driveway, blocking the sidewalk. I looked around, saw that most of the residents had left their cars in a similar fashion, except for one enterprising soul who had pulled up parallel to the curb on the sidewalk itself. So much for parking regulations, I thought as I pulled in beside the Honda.

As soon as Hank came to the door of the

downstairs flat, I was glad I'd agreed to help him. There were lines of strain around his mouth, and when he took his horn-rimmed glasses off to polish their thick lenses on the tail of his maroon corduroy work shirt, I saw that his eyes were clouded. Hank is a man who cares deeply for his clients—too deeply, perhaps, to maintain the distance needed when dealing with their problems. It's not that it renders him ineffectual; it just causes him more pain than he deserves.

I smiled reassuringly at him and stepped inside. The flat was chilly; Hank probably didn't want to waste the estate's money by turning up the heat. A narrow hallway ran the length of the building; at its end was a door through which I could see a kitchen table and refrigerator. To my left was a small living room with a bay window overlooking the street. I went in there and started to take off my suede jacket. Then I stopped; I might soil it while hefting cartons and furniture, but I'd be too cold without it.

Hank sensed my predicament. "I've got coffee on," he said, "and you can wear one of Perry's sweaters."

"Thanks." I followed him down the hall and into a bedroom that was even smaller than the living room. He rummaged through a pile of clothing that lay on the double bed, then tossed me a heavy green cardigan with a hole in one elbow and a raveled right cuff. When I put it on, it came down to my knees; I rolled up the sleeves to wrist length. Perry Hilderly, the deceased client, had been a big man.

Hank was already on his way to the kitchen. By the time I got there he'd poured coffee and was holding out a mug. I took it, then peered through a door to the left. It led to a dining room with a fireplace and built-in leaded-glass cabinets—standard for this type and vintage of flat. The room contained no furniture, nothing but cardboard boxes with the name BEKINS stenciled on them.

I looked at Hank, eyebrows raised inquiringly.

"It's the stuff Perry moved here years ago, after his divorce," he said. "He wasn't much of a homebody. Accountants never are, I guess."

It was one of those blanket statements Hank sometimes makes—bald assumptions with little or no basis in fact. They always startle me, considering the variety of individuals with full complements of quirks that he's seen wander through the door of All Souls year after year. Such typecasting of his

11

fellow man is a product of his early environment—his mother is quite adamant in her pronouncements about others—and since he never allows it to cloud his judgment, I can put up with it without comment.

I went over to the refrigerator to look at a color snapshot that was held up there by a magnet. It showed a tall, lanky man with curly blond hair and granny glasses; he wore a Giants sweatshirt and was flanked by two similarly attired blond boys who were only tall enough to reach to his waist. "This is Hilderly, right?"

"Uh-huh. It's an old photo; his boys are in their teens now."

I examined it more closely. "He doesn't look all that different from the way he did in the nineteen sixty-five picture that they ran in the *Chron* the morning after he was shot. Of course, his hair was long and wild back then."

Perry Hilderly had been one of the founders of the Free Speech Movement at U.C. Berkeley in the 1960s. Although I'd still been in high school then, I'd taken a great interest in the changing mood on the campuses—probably because I was the white sheep in a family of rebels and envied both my siblings' and the students' ability to blatantly challenge authority. My impressions of Hilderly were somewhat vague, but I recalled television coverage of the protests in which he could be seen clowning around on the periphery.

Hank said, "Do you remember him?"

"Some."

"I'm surprised."

I sat down at the kitchen table with him. "Why?"

"Well, you were just a baby then."

I smiled. Hank is only six years older than I, but he has always taken a paternalistic stance toward me. Partly this is because when we met at Berkeley—years after Hilderly had passed from that scene—he was a world-weary law student with the horrors of Vietnam behind him, while I was an undergrad whose toughest battles had been fought in the trenches of the department store where I'd worked in security before deciding to go to college. Over the years the balance of world-weariness has shifted more to my side, but Hank persists in the notion that he must watch out for and guide me. I know, although we've never discussed it, that this persistence is fueled by the fact that our friendship has never been endangered by romantic entanglement. Hank's paternalism is designed to preserve the status quo.

"Still, I remember him," I said, "even if he never received as much media attention as Mario Savio."

"Well, few people had Mario's charisma. Perry's comedic style was a bit like Abbie Hoffman's, but not nearly as outrageous. And there were a lot of lesser luminaries hogging the limelight." Hank's smile was reminiscently wry.

I knew what he was thinking; as a friend of mine once put it, not many of the sixties people have "held up." Few went on to achieve the heights that those on the sidelines expected of them. But for a time such visionaries as Mario Savio had captured the imagination of a generation. Mario, who one fall day in 1964 respectfully removed his shoes before climbing atop a police car that had been entrapped by some three thousand students protesting the arrest of a civil-rights worker on the Cal campus. Mario, who seized a microphone and involved others in the crowd in a thirty-hour spontaneous public dialog that forever changed the university, the youth of America, the nation itself. No, Perry Hilderly hadn't held a safety match to Mario Savio's incandescence, but he had brought humor to a basically humorless movement, had defused potentially dangerous situations with his wit.

As I recalled, in the late sixties Hilderly had vanished from the Berkeley scene. By the time I arrived there, most of his compatriots had disappeared, too. I'd once listened to a news analyst on KPFA discussing how many of the former leaders of the FSM had become frustrated by their lack of tangible progress and gone underground with the Weathermen. Now it seemed that Hilderly, at least, had become an accountant—and died many years later in a senseless street shooting on Geary Boulevard, two blocks from his apartment.

I said to Hank, "You were still an undergrad at Stanford in the sixties. How come you knew Hilderly? Or did that come later?"

"Later. I met him in 'Nam in nineteen seventy. Perry'd been thrown out of Cal and gone to work for a leftist magazine. He went to 'Nam to report on the war for them, but they folded shortly after he got there. When I met him, he was living with a family near Cam Ranh Bay. He had a baby boy by one of the daughters. He was lonely for American company, so he hung out at a bar with some of us liberals from the base, talking

15

about the war and what was going down back home. Then his woman and son were killed in the mortar shelling. Right after that, Perry went back to California."

"And then?"

Hank shrugged. "He enrolled in S.F. State and got his degree in accounting. Married again, had two more boys. Was divorced about ten years ago, lived alone in this flat, and worked at Geary and Twenty-second, for one of those tax firms that's a cut above H&R Block."

"How'd you come to be his attorney?"

"I ran into him at Churchill's Pub one night about five years ago. Recognized him right off—as you pointed out, he hadn't changed much except for having short hair. After that he came to see me about a minor legal problem, and we started to meet fairly frequently, always at Churchill's."

"Were you close friends?"

"Not really. Why?"

"I just wondered about him becoming an accountant. And living like this." I gestured around the plain, conventional-looking kitchen. "It doesn't fit with his past."

"No, it doesn't. But the few times I tried to ask him about it, he just changed the subject."

16

"What did you usually talk about?"

"My work. All Souls. He was interested in the workings of a low-cost legal services plan. Sports; he was a Giants fan. And old movies—he watched a lot of them, mostly from the thirties and forties. But I had the feeling that anything more personal was off limits."

"What do you suppose happened to make him that way?"

"I don't know, but I sensed it in 'Nam, too. He wasn't quite as closed off then, but if anybody got on the subject of the old days at Berkeley, Perry all of a sudden remembered someplace else he had to be." Hank looked at his watch. "But enough—we'd better get busy. I've only got today free to work on clearing this place out, and the landlady wants to start showing it on Monday."

I drained my coffee mug and stood. "What do you want me to do?"

"You could box up the books and videotapes and other stuff in the living room. The Salvation Army'll pick up everything on Monday."

"You mentioned Hilderly's sons—won't they want any of it?"

"Their mother said no. Apparently he wasn't close to the boys. She remarried a

17

long time ago, and they live over in Blackhawk—that fancy development near Danville. But the kids are provided for in the will; Perry inherited a substantial amount from his mother a few years after the divorce. It's to be divided equally between the boys."

"I see. Well, I'd better get to it." I started for the door.

"Shar," Hank said.

I turned.

"Thanks for helping. This is easily the worst part about being executor of an estate."

"No problem."

He added, "Even though Perry and I weren't all that close, his death has really upset me. You know?"

I nodded. "Probably because of the way he died. These snipings. If they hadn't been spread out over more than three months, the city would be in a panic right now—like when the Zebra killings were going on."

"You're probably right. I find myself getting paranoid. I worked late a couple of nights last week, and when I left I could have sworn there was someone lurking around outside All Souls."

"Nerves."

"Typical urban ailment."

I went down the hall to the front room and dragged a carton over to the brick-and-board bookcase opposite the bay window. Perry Hilderly's books were mainly texts on accounting, tax law, math, statistics, and investing. The number of them and their presence didn't surprise me, but what did was the absence of any lighter reading material such as magazines, novels, or nonfiction that didn't relate to his profession. Finally on the bottom shelf I found a few volumes on film: guides to serials, crime movies, and *film noir*, plus a few books about old TV series such as "Perry Mason." I boxed them all, then turned to the videotapes.

There were hundreds of them, stacked against the wall behind the TV: Bogart, Tracy and Hepburn, Barbara Stanwyck, William Powell, Cary Grant; a full run of Charlie Chans and Mr. Motos and the Topper series; westerns, comedies, drama. Not one of them had been produced later than the mid-fifties. It made me wonder if Hilderly hadn't been trying to pretend the sixties and seventies and eighties had never happened.

After I boxed the tapes, I looked around for what Hank had called "the other stuff."

There wasn't much of it. A water-stained lobby card for a Bogart movie called *All Through the Night*, framed but with badly cracked glass. A carved wooden box, the kind you find at Cost Plus, containing two sets of worn playing cards. A set of Capiz-shell coasters. A silver-plated table lighter, nonfunctional. A brass bowl, also Cost Plus quality, containing nothing but a paper clip and some dust. I put the smaller items into a carton and left it and the lobby card on the cracked vinyl recliner that faced the TV. Then I unplugged the TV, unhooked the VCR, and shoved the stand over by the ugly plaid couch. The act held a depressing finality.

When I went down the hall, I found Hank in the bedroom. He was folding the clothing that lay on the bed and stuffing it into a big plastic trash bag, where it immediately became unfolded and jumbled. One look at his woebegone face made me say, "Let me do that while you get started on the kitchen."

He nodded, looking grateful, and gently set down the sweater he held.

I'd never had to dispose of a dead friend's possessions, but I guessed the clothing must be the most difficult task of all. Even though I hadn't known Hilderly personally, I also

20

found myself smoothing and folding each item before placing it in the bag; somehow it seemed a negation of the person to toss his garments in there like so many rags.

As I worked I could hear Hank clinking dishes in the kitchen, but after a while the sounds stopped, and I feared he'd become discouraged again. I finished with the clothing, stripped the bed, checked to make sure there was nothing in the bureau or nightstand drawers. Then I went back there.

Hank was sitting at the table, a sheaf of papers spread before him. When I came in, he looked up at me, his face a study in shock and bewilderment.

"What's wrong?" I asked.

"These were in a plastic bag in the freezer." He gestured at the papers. "Perry told me to look for his important documents there—said it was a good fireproof place, and cheaper than a safe-deposit box."

I looked closer at what lay before him. There were stock certificates, an automobile pink slip, a number of savings-account passbooks, and some other papers. "So?"

"This," he said, fingering a document with a pale blue cover sheet, "is a copy of the will I drew up for him four years ago. I had the original in the All Souls safe, and

21

I've already entered it into probate. But this"—he held up a page covered in cramped handwriting—"is a second will, superseding the first one."

"Is it legal?"

"Yes. It's a holograph, and he did it properly. It's dated three weeks ago."

"And?"

"It's totally different from the first. Cuts out his kids entirely and makes no explanation of why. He leaves his money to be divided equally among four people—and damned if I know who they are, or what they were to him."

Two

Hank handed me the sheet of paper, and I scanned it quickly. From the legal terminology, I gathered that Hilderly had copied it from his original will, changing only the names under the section headed "Specific Bequests." The conditions for the executor and disposal of personal effects were as Hank had described them, but instead of Hilderly's sons, four individuals were to share equally in "all cash, securities, and other financial assets": Jess Goodhue, Thomas Y.

Grant, Libby Heikkinen, and David Arlen Taylor. Hilderly did not specify their relationship to him, but he did state that he was making no provision for his former wife and children. The will didn't look as official as the typed copy from All Souls, but if Hank said it was legal, it had to be.

My fingers touched something attached to the other side of the sheet. I turned it over, found one of those yellow stick-on memos. On it Hilderly had written, "Hank: You'll know how to contact Goodhue and Grant, but you'll have to trace Heikkinen and Taylor. Sorry for the inconvenience." I peeled the memo off and handed it to Hank.

He read it and grimaced in annoyance. "Sure, Perry. I've never heard of any of these people!"

"You must know who Jess Goodhue is."

"Why the hell would I?"

"She's a co-anchor on the KSTS evening news."

"You forgot—I don't watch broadcast news."

"Oh, right." For as long as I've known him, Hank has been a news snob; he prefers his information written—in depth, and in quantity. Every day he reads at least five papers: the *San Francisco Chronicle* and *Ex-*

aminer, the *New York Times,* the *Wall Street Journal,* and the *Los Angeles Times.* Every week he pores over the newsmagazines, regardless of their political orientation, and when he runs out of those he's likely to be found with his nose stuck in *Business Week, Sports Illustrated,* or a legal journal. But one place he is never found is in front of the TV at six or eleven in the evening.

"Well," I said, "that's who Jess Goodhue is."

"Tell me more about her."

"She's one of these up-and-coming media stars. Young, in her early to mid twenties. I'm willing to bet that by the time she's thirty she'll be anchoring for one of the networks. You know the type: good-looking, poised, superprofessional."

"I can't imagine Perry even knowing someone like that."

"But he must have. Are you sure you don't know this Thomas Y. Grant? According to Hilderly's note, he assumed you do."

Hank thought for a moment, then snapped his fingers. "Son of a bitch, I bet it is," he said softly.

"Who?"

"Another local attorney." His lip curled slightly, but he didn't elaborate.

24

I spotted a directory lying on the counter beneath the wall phone. "Heikkinen's not a very common name." I set the will down and went to look under the *H*'s. "No listing," I said after a few seconds, "but that's not surprising. Just because the first two are local doesn't mean the others have to be. Besides, she might have married and changed her name." I flipped to the *T*'s. There was more than a page of Taylors, including two with just the initial *D* and two Davids with no middle initial. "No David Arlen Taylor, either."

"That could be a tough one."

"Not really—the middle name's distinctive." I moved back toward the table. "I suppose this one's going to end up on my desk."

"Unless you want to turn it over to Rae." Rae Kelleher was my rapidly-becoming-indispensable assistant.

"No, I've kind of loaded her down lately. Maybe I'll have her do some of the preliminary work, but I'll handle the rest personally." I didn't want to tell Hank that Rae had become so good at her job I really hadn't had much to do recently. It had taken far too many years for the All Souls partners to give me the go-ahead to hire an assistant, and I wasn't about to sow any seeds of doubt as to the wisdom of that action. I also didn't want to admit that nowadays I had a lot of empty hours that I'd prefer to fill with work, for fear that such a confession would provoke a solicitous—and unwelcome—inquiry about my private life.

"Well, handle it however you want. In the meantime I'll have to stop probate of the other will. And inform Perry's ex-wife that the kids aren't going to inherit." Hank took off his glasses and rubbed his eyes. "There are times when I hate my work, and this is one of them." Then he stood abruptly, replacing the glasses. "Come on, let's get out of here for a while, have some lunch, clear the cobwebs."

I trailed him to the front door, shrugging off Hilderly's big sweater and grabbing my jacket and bag. On the sidewalk I lengthened my stride to match Hank's. He walked with his head bent, hands shoved in his pockets, obviously preoccupied. I steered him toward Clement. Earlier I'd noticed a *dim sum* place—the Fook Restaurant, of all things— and now the idea of steamed dumplings and pork buns appealed to me.

As we turned onto Clement, I realized that the fog had lifted, and observed a phenomenon that has always interested me: the line of demarcation between blue and gray sky stopped in the middle of Arguello Boulevard, bisecting the city in a north-south line. To the west, in the largely bland residential avenues that stretch toward the sea, the day would remain overcast; to the east, in such diverse areas as North Beach, downtown, Noe Valley, Hunters Point, and my own little neighborhood near the Glen Park district, the weather would turn sunny. It is a peculiarly San Francisco phenomenon, and one that outsiders have difficulty grasping. As a New York friend once told me, "There's something very odd about a city where people move across town just to get better weather."

Hank seemed oblivious to where we were going, so I steered him into the restaurant. It was noisy and crowded, but we were quickly shown to a table against one of the walls. He blinked and looked around like a rudely awakened sleepwalker as I ordered jasmine tea. The nearby tables—round ones with lazy Susans in their centers—were mainly occupied by Asian families; restaurant employees moved slowly among them, pushing stainless-steel carts loaded with delicacies and hawking their wares in Chinese.

When the first cart arrived at our table, I pointed to plates of pork buns and barbecued spareribs. Hank recovered from his preoccupation and gave the nod to shrimp in fluted rice wrappers.

As I picked up my chopsticks I said, "Is Hilderly's ex-wife going to be upset that the kids won't inherit?"

"Hard to say."

"How much is the estate worth?"

"Quite a bit. Perry inherited roughly a quarter of a million dollars some seven, eight years ago. From time to time he'd mention investments to me—mostly conservative stuff like municipal bonds, T-bills, blue chips. But every now and then he'd take a flier on one of the glamour stocks like Genentech. I'd estimate that he was worth at least a million."

"He didn't live like a millionaire."

"Perry wasn't into money. The investing was a game to him, matching his wits against the market. If he made a profit, that was fine, because it would mean there was more to leave to his boys. But he didn't care about it for himself, and he spent very little."

"Well, what about those four people named in the new will? What *were* they to him, that he'd cut out his own kids and leave them that much money?"

"Damned if I know. He never so much as mentioned a one of them to me. Two of them he himself didn't know how to contact."

"You say Thomas Grant is an attorney?"

Hank nodded, biting into one of the shrimp dumplings. After he swallowed he said, "A real sleazebag. Around fifty, I'd say. He turned up here in the mid-seventies, went into divorce work—for men only, taking a very aggressive 'to hell with the wife and kids' stance. Advises his clients on how to get around the community-property laws, and not always in legitimate ways."

"Sounds like a sweetheart."

"He doesn't have too many scruples, or much humanity. Grant latched on to an idea whose time—unfortunately—had come, due to the backlash against the women's movement. Now he's got branch offices—franchises is actually a better description—throughout the Bay Area, and is looking to expand further."

"The fast-food chain of divorce lawyers."

"Right."

I looked over at a cart that had paused by our table. There was a plate of oddly shaped

29

objects coated in a golden crust. I pointed at it with my chopsticks. "What're those?"

The waitress said, "Duck feet."

"Duck . . . *feet?*"

She nodded, smiling at my reaction.

"How about some of that chicken? And a plate of pearl balls?"

She set the plates down, marked our check, and departed.

Hank was grinning. "I thought, as you're fond of proclaiming, that you have no food prejudices."

"I don't."

"Then why not try the duck feet?"

"Well, it's just that . . . they probably don't have much meat on them."

"Uh-huh."

"Well, it's true—you saw them. And I *don't* have any prejudices; I'll eat what's set before me. People who are picky or won't try new things drive me crazy."

"That's why you wouldn't eat Larry's tofu in chili sauce last week." Larry Koslowski, an All Souls partner, is a health-food nut.

"I couldn't help that. It looked like . . . I don't think we should discuss it while we're eating. Anyway, back to Hilderly. He never talked to you about wanting to change his will?"

30

"No."

"I wonder why he made a holograph? Why not ask you to draw up the new will?"

"I suspect because he was afraid I'd try to talk him out of it. Or insist on knowing what those people were to him and why he wanted to make them his heirs."

"Makes sense."

We ate in silence for a few minutes. A dessert cart went past, and I spied the little yellow custard pies I'm fond of. I'd eaten too much to even entertain the thought of having one now, but I'd noticed a take-out counter off the restaurant's lobby; I'd stop there and buy a few of the pies for later.

Hank was looking preoccupied again, fiddling with his chopsticks.

"What's wrong?" I asked.

"Just brooding. I keep thinking how unlike Perry this is. He wasn't close to those kids, but he loved them and always carried out his responsibilities."

"Then he must have had a strong reason for disinheriting them. Maybe when we locate the beneficiaries they can explain it."

"It isn't really any of our business," Hank said. "As Perry's executor, I'm bound to carry out his wishes, not to snoop into something he clearly didn't care to explain to me."

31

"No, it's not our business, but I wonder . . ."

"Wonder what?"

I pushed my plate away toward the others that littered the table, then took my teacup in both hands and stared down into it, trying to put the feeling of wrongness that I was experiencing into words. "When someone makes a major change in his will and conceals it from his attorney, isn't there a possibility of undue influence or duress?"

"A possibility, yes."

"And when the person dies violently, as Perry did—"

"Shar," Hank said patiently, "you've read the papers. His killing was a random shooting. The bullet matched those found in the bodies of the sniper's other victims, all of whom were unrelated."

That was true. Still . . . "Hank, does any of this feel right to you?"

". . . No."

"Then let's see if we can't find an explanation for Perry's actions."

There was no way I could start a skip trace on either Heikkinen or Taylor on a Saturday. When we returned to Hilderly's flat and I checked the phone directory, I found that

32

neither Grant's nor Goodhue's home number was listed. I called Grant's law office and reached the answering service; the operator at KSTS-TV told me Goodhue was off until Monday. In the end I decided to go through the boxes in Hilderly's dining room, which Hank said had been sitting untouched since he'd moved to the flat nearly ten years before; they might contain something that would explain his connection to his four heirs.

The boxes held fairly commonplace items: household goods such as a fondue pot and yogurt maker that Hilderly had apparently had no use for; high-school yearbooks from a town I'd never heard of; photograph albums with pictures of his boys and a plump brown-haired woman, as well as of a younger Hilderly and a couple I took to be his parents; 45-rpm records that had been hits in the fifties; a collection of baseball cards that by now would be quite valuable; a catcher's mitt; a set of Hardy Boys mysteries; a high-school diploma. Like the flat itself, the boxes contained no memento of his rebellious college days; it was as if he had never attended Cal or participated in the Free Speech Movement. There were no journals, personal letters, or address books that might contain telling information.

I was about to give up when, at the bottom of the last carton, under a folded athletic jacket that showed Hilderly had lettered in high-school baseball, I found a heavy leather drawstring pouch. The object inside had the distinctive shape of a gun.

I lifted the pouch from the carton and loosened its drawstrings. Inside, my fingers touched metal. When I took the gun out, I saw it was a .38 Special of German manufacture, with a two-inch barrel—a reasonably powerful weapon that is easy to conceal on one's person. I examined it more closely and found that someone had attempted to remove the serial number, probably with acid. The number was indecipherable, but a forensics laboratory would be able to bring it out with chemicals.

There was something else in the pouch, something lighter. I reached for it, expecting ammunition. It was a pendant of sorts—a gray pot-metal chain with two small letters attached to it, a *K* and an *A*. A curving edge encased the *A*, but the *K* was jagged, as if the fragment had been broken off a larger object. A clip-like piece of metal protruded from the back of it.

A piece of junk that ended up in the pouch by mistake? I wondered. Or something that mattered enough to Hilderly that he took the trouble to separate it from his other mementoes?

I got up from the floor and carried the gun and pendant into the kitchen, where Hank was emptying a cupboard. "I found a couple of odd things," I said, "but I can't even tell what one of them is."

He turned, saw the gun, and frowned. "Is that Perry's?"

"Must be. It was in one of the boxes in the dining room. Someone's removed the serial number from it."

"That's odd."

"It could have been done by someone who had possession of it previously, and Perry bought the gun illegally—on the street, for instance. Or he could have done it himself because he—or someone close to him—was the registered owner, and he didn't want that fact to come out."

Hank looked down at a blue pottery bowl he held, then set it carefully on the counter, as if he were afraid he'd drop it. "And if the latter is the case, what it implies is that he used it or intended to use it for some illegal purpose."

35

I nodded.

"Jesus. I came here this morning with one conception of Perry, and I'll be going away with a completely different one."

"Don't jump to conclusions," I warned. "There are other possibilities. He could have taken this off someone and put it away for safekeeping. He could have found it. You don't know."

"I don't know *what* I know anymore." He glanced at the pendant. "What's that on the chain?"

"A pair of letters." I handed it to him.

He examined it, fingering the rough edges as I had. "Every weekend hippie had a chain like this, but it usually had a peace symbol attached."

I smiled and took it from his outstretched hand. "*I* even had one. We weren't allowed to wear them to school, but on weekends we'd dress up in our bell-bottoms and tie-dye and love beads. There was this store in Laguna Beach that sold beads—fantastic hand-painted ones, all colors and sizes and shapes. We'd drive all the way up there from San Diego to buy them." I still had some of the prettier ones, unstrung now, in my jewelry box.

"You were a regular little hippie child,

weren't you?" Hank said. "I never would have guessed. When I met you at Berkeley, you struck me as such a . . . well, cheerleader."

"I was. Captain of the high-school squad my senior year. The hippie stuff was strictly masquerade; it made us feel with-it and wicked. I hardly ever smoked dope until I got to Cal, and I only attended one feeble peace march. Then, when I was in college, the energy had kind of gone out of the Movement, and besides, I was too busy studying and working to have the time." I'd put myself through the university, working nights and weekends as a security guard, poring over my textbooks during the long, fallow hours.

Hank nodded, his gaze far away, seeing —what? The young man and woman we'd been? The idealists with all of life ahead of us? And was he comparing those people to the ones we'd become: in his case, the disillusioned but ever-hopeful dreamer; in mine, the realist whose cynicism was thus far untainted by bitterness?

I said, "Can I keep the gun and this . . . whatever it is?"

He roused himself from his reverie. "Sure. I doubt the Salvation Army would want the whatsis, and we'd better hang on to the gun for a while, until . . ." He let his words trail off, unsure what that eventuality might be.

"I'll put it in the strongbox where I keep my own gun. It'll be safe there. By the way, before they pick up the furniture and boxes, you ought to look through the ones I've set aside in the dining room. There's a lot of personal stuff, plus a fairly valuable baseball-card collection. It would be nice if Hilderly's kids had the cards, plus other things to remember their father by."

"You're right. I'll see that they get them."

I helped Hank clear the remaining cupboards, then offered to drop the keys at the landlady's, since he'd mentioned she lived in my neighborhood. He said he'd take care of it, then added, "I meant to tell you, I'm cooking chili at my flat Monday night, in honor of Anne-Marie's birthday. Jack and Ted'll be there, and Rae and Willie. I'd like you to come, too."

"Rae and Willie—that's getting to be a pretty steady thing, isn't it?"

"Appears that way. Do you disapprove?"

Since she'd started seeing Willie Whelan some months before, I'd harbored certain reservations about my assistant's new relationship, mainly because I know Willie's

38

myriad faults altogether too well. He is a friend of Hank's from his Vietnam days, and a former fence who—as he puts it—has "gone legit." What started as a small discount jewelry store on Market Street had turned into a gold mine for him, with branches all over the Bay Area, and he takes great pride in the fact that he—like his arch-competitor at the well-known Diamond Center—performs his own television commercials. On late-night TV you can usually see him luring the young and gullible to acquire gems that they don't need, to establish credit histories that will set the stage for future judgments against them, and—if by some miracle they don't default—to surrender a good portion of their lifetime earnings to Willie Whelan.

Willie is, in many respects, a great guy—provided you don't buy anything from him or take him too seriously. But I couldn't for the life of me figure out why my bright, young, recently divorced assistant was seeing him.

I said to Hank, "It's not my place to approve or disapprove. I just hope she doesn't get hurt."

"Would be a shame, so soon after she got rid of Doug-the-asshole, as she's so fond of calling her ex. But what about it—will you come for dinner?"

I checked my mental calendar. I'd planned to suggest to Anne-Marie Altman, Hank's wife, that I take her to lunch to celebrate her birthday, but with this new investigation, there might not be time for that. "Okay," I said, "you can count me in."

"If you want to bring Jim—"

Jim, I thought, feeling a sinking sensation. I'd almost forgotten his unwelcome early-morning visit.

"No, I'll come by myself." I hadn't yet told Hank that I'd broken it off, and I was in no mood to discuss it now. Quickly I started down the hall, trying to remember where I'd tossed my bag and jacket on the way in.

Hank followed me. "Shar, is something wrong between—"

"Everything's fine," I lied. "And I'd better get going because I have a date tonight."

Hank looked both relieved and pleased. Every time I become irritated with his nosiness, I have to remind myself that it's not his fault that he loves me and wants me to be happy.

I'd been looking forward to a quiet evening

at home, but when I got there, my little brown-shingled earthquake cottage—one of some four thousand built as emergency housing after the quake and fire of '06, and lovingly added onto by a succession of owners, including me—seemed less of a haven than it usually did. One reason, I knew, was the unsettling effect of Jim's visit. Another was that my fat black-and-white-spotted cat, Watney, had died in his sleep two months before, and I hadn't replaced him, didn't think it possible to replace him. But the chief reason was that the man who might have become the love of my life was living in Palo Alto to be near his estranged, mentally ill wife, whose fragile emotional balance had been toppled as a result of my own bad judgment during a particularly complex investigation. Never mind that my lover, George Kostakos—who is a psychologist and ought to know—didn't blame me for her collapse. Never mind that he said it had been long in the making. *I* blamed myself, and I went about clad in the proverbial hair shirt, insulated by it against disappointment and loneliness.

But even self-created hair shirts could itch and chafe sometimes. And resentment could occasionally flare against a former lover who was uncondemning, caring, and honorable.

And after years of Wat's curmudgeonly companionship, a house without my cat was not a home.

I stowed the pouch containing Hilderly's gun in the strongbox, then went to the fridge and put away the little custard pies I'd bought at the restaurant. For a moment I considered a glass of wine, but drinking alone in the kind of mood I was in could lead to dangerous introspection. There was a new comedy I'd been wanting to see at the Northpoint, and if I hurried I could catch the early show. Quickly I took a shower to wash away the dust of Hilderly's apartment, then donned my soft old faded jeans and a sweater.

Before I left the house, however, I looked into my jewelry box at the love beads I'd kept there for more than twenty years. They glimmered in the day's fading light—opalescent blue and pink and green and yellow symbols of an era that perhaps was never as joyful or innocent as some of us remember it.

Three

The first thing Monday morning I called Rae Kelleher at All Souls and briefed her on the Hilderly investigation. She said she'd get started immediately on the skip traces on Heikkinen and Taylor.

"I take it you're not coming in for a while," she added.

"No. I'm going to see what I can find out from Grant and Goodhue, and I'm also going to stop by the SFPD, talk about Hilderly's death with the detective in charge of these random shootings."

"The detective?" Her voice was a shade sly.

I sighed. "Okay—Greg Marcus."

"You mentioned you'd had dinner with him a couple of weeks ago. Are you seeing him again?"

"We've been going to lunch or dinner together ever since we got over being bitter about our breakup. It's no big deal."

"Amazing how you manage to stay on good terms with your former boyfriends."

I started to say, "Except for Jim," but thought better of it. Rae had introduced me to him last winter, and she'd been disappointed when I broke it off. Instead I said, "Staying on good terms with Greg comes under the heading of good police relationships. I'll check in with you later."

Next I phoned the local branch of Thomas Y. Grant Associates; the switchboard operator told me Mr. Grant worked out of his home office and gave me that number. When I called it and requested an appointment, Grant's secretary hastened to caution me that his legal practice was restricted to men. I said my business was personal and concerned a substantial bequest left to him by an All Souls client. That prompted her to put me on hold. When she returned, she said Mr. Grant could fit me in at ten-thirty and gave me a Pacific Heights address on the section of Lyon Street that borders the Presidio.

The final item on my mental list was to try to contact Jess Goodhue at KSTS. The anchorwoman, I was told, would not come into the studio until three or three-thirty. I left my name and number and said that if I didn't hear from her, I'd check back then. After I replaced the receiver in its cradle I stared indecisively at it: should I call Greg for an appointment or just drop in? Finally I opted for setting a definite time and punched out the number for his extension at the Homicide detail of the SFPD. He was there, and sounded pleased to hear from me. When I explained what I wanted to talk with him about, he invited me to lunch.

"We could try the South Park Cafe," he added.

"No," I said quickly. South Park, a curious little street in the newly trendy SoMa district near the Hall of Justice, had figured in the investigation when I'd met and lost George Kostakos; it still held painful memories for me.

". . . Oh, right," Greg said. "Well, there's always Max's Diner."

"Why don't I meet you at your office, and we'll decide then."

He agreed and we hung up.

I went to dress for my appointment with Thomas Grant. After some deliberation I chose a gray wool suit with a short skirt and a long double-breasted jacket—a Chanel knockoff that nevertheless had been outrageously expensive and worth every penny of it. It's the outfit that Anne-Marie has dubbed my "schizoid suit," because it's businesslike and sexy at the same time.

The fog had continued through the weekend

and into that morning. Even the quiet streets of Pacific Heights—where the residents are normally blessed not only with affluence but also with good weather—were finely misted. I parked my MG in front of the address Grant's secretary had given me and got out, shivering slightly from the cold.

The house—one of only a few that backed up on the thickly forested grounds of the Presidio—was a large one. Its brown shingles, leaded-glass windows, and shiny black trim were of an early twentieth-century style that abounds in that part of the city. An arched wooden gate led into a bricked front yard shaded by an acacia tree. The bricks had been swept clean of every leaf. Raised flower beds bordered the small yard at the base of its high wooden fence. The geraniums that grew in them were planted at precise intervals; they looked prim and stiff, as if standing at attention.

Grant's secretary, who greeted me at the door and introduced herself as Ms. Angela Curtis, looked prim and stiff, too. Her blond hair was cropped in a style that immediately suggested the word "efficient"; she wore a plain gray suit, simple gold jewelry, and sensible low-heeled pumps. Although she was around my age, she seemed a much older woman. As I watched her cross the large oak-paneled entry to tell Grant I was there, I tried—and failed—to imagine her running on the beach, or laughing and eating and drinking with friends, or making love, or any of the other things that normal, vital women enjoy doing.

When Ms. Curtis vanished through a closed door to the right of the wide central staircase, I turned and studied my surroundings. The other doors that opened off the room were shut, too, as if Grant sought to separate his professional and personal lives. There was a red Chinese rug on the parquet floor and a large oval table in the center under the brass chandelier, but otherwise there were no furnishings, no decorations, no pictures on the golden-oak walls. An austere man, this Thomas Y. Grant.

Ms. Curtis returned and motioned to me. "Mr. Grant is on the telephone," she said. "If you'll go in and take a seat, he'll be with you shortly."

I thanked her and entered the office. At first glance the room appeared to be a typical lawyer's study, with the obligatory wall of thick tomes, the obligatory mahogany desk and leather-upholstered furniture. I couldn't see Grant because he was swiveled around with the high back of his chair to the desk, talking into the phone in a low voice. Ms. Curtis shut the door behind me.

Then I realized that unlike the typical lawyer's study, the room contained no framed diplomas, certificates, or pictures of the attorney with prominent clients or politicians. I smiled faintly, thinking that this office was also different from Hank's, which contains —among other things—a cigarstore Indian and a poster of Uncle Sam saying, "I want YOU for the U.S. Army." But then I realized Grant had some peculiar objects of his own, and went over to the shelves that flanked the fireplace to have a closer look at them.

They appeared to be a bizarre form of sculpture: strange, twisted, unrecognizable shapes of wood and metal intermingled with feathers and tufts of fur and fragments of bone. I looked more closely at one and saw a pair of yellowed fangs protruding from a strip of reptile skin; another had claws— ragged, broken ones. Some sort of primitive folk art, I supposed, unsettling and quite unpleasant.

Behind me, Grant was still talking. I moved to the other side of the fireplace and examined a piece that sat apart from the rest on a shelf of its own. The framework was a crossed pair of rusted metal spikes, each festooned with mockingbirds' feathers. Stretched between the spikes was a swatch of what resembled—but certainly couldn't be—dried human skin.

I recoiled, and a phrase came to me: *trophies and dead things*. An odd phrase. I couldn't remember where I'd heard or read it.

There was a footfall behind me; I turned. Thomas Grant was approaching, one hand extended. For a moment I wasn't sure if I wanted the possessor of such nasty artworks to touch me.

Grant was handsome in a conventional way. The body clad in the expensive blue suit was trim and well muscled, and I suspected he didn't have to work at keeping in shape. His hair was iron gray, thick, and so well cut that not a lock strayed from its proper place. His strong-featured face, while not totally unlined, was supple and youthful; its only imperfection was a jagged scar on his left cheek that made him look like the romantic lead in a melodrama about male honor. Otherwise it was as if nothing in his life had touched him deeply enough to leave vestiges of pain, sorrow, or even happiness.

As he shook my hand I felt a wave of visceral dislike.

"I see you were looking at my fetishes," he said.

"Is that what they are?"

"In a strict sense, no. But a fetish is a charm, something with magical powers. These certainly do have the power to disturb." His eyes—gray like his hair—remained on mine as he released my hand. Their expression was sly, knowing; he liked the fact that the fetishes had unsettled me.

I moved toward the clients' chairs in front of the desk, set my briefcase on one of them. "Are they some kind of tribal art?" I asked.

"Actually, I make them myself."

I paused in the act of opening the briefcase. "You . . . ?"

"Yes, I have a studio at the rear of the property. Perhaps you'd care to see it sometime, since you seem to be interested in the pieces."

". . . Perhaps. Where do you get your materials?"

He moved around the desk and sat, motioned at one of the client's chairs. "Here and there. I guess you could call me a scavenger. I pick up things on the beach or in the parks."

Things. Meaning dead birds and animals, or parts of them. God knew what he had to do to them to make them usable. I'd recently started—and quickly stopped—reading an article in a magazine in the dentist's office about a Texas woman who created what she termed "road kill art"; the point at which I'd set it aside was where she described the odor in the cave where she left her "art supplies" so flesh-eating beetles could clean them. Rather than commenting on Grant's hobby, I sat and busied myself with the file I'd taken from my briefcase. "Mr. Grant—" I began.

"Please—Tom."

"Tom. Does the name Perry Hilderly mean anything to you?"

I thought I glimpsed a flash of recognition in his eyes, but it was gone so quickly that I might have imagined it. He considered briefly, then shook his head. "I can't say as it does. Angela—Ms. Curtis—mentioned something about a bequest. Is this Hilderman—"

"Hilderly."

"Is he the testator?"

"Yes."

"Why did he make a bequest to me?"

"I don't know precisely that he did. Hil-

51

derly named a Thomas Y. Grant in his will, without indicating what the relationship was. In a note to his attorney, he said that he—the attorney, Hank Zahn—would know how to reach Grant. You are the only Thomas Y. Grant that Mr. Zahn knows of."

Grant's expression became puzzled. "I know Hank Zahn by reputation. I'm surprised he would draw up a will without first ascertaining the client's relationship to his beneficiary."

"He didn't draw up this particular one. It was a holograph superseding an earlier will, written three weeks before Hilderly died."

"When and how was that? His death, I mean."

"Last week, in a random shooting on Geary Boulevard."

"One of those snipings? I remember seeing on TV that there had been another, but none of the details." Grant closed his eyes, as if trying to call forth the news story. When he opened them again, their expression was one of bewilderment. "Ms. . . . may I call you Sharon?"

I nodded.

"Sharon, I'll be damned if I know what this is all about."

"Is it possible that Hilderly was once a client of yours?"

"I have a good memory for my clients. He wasn't."

"Could you have employed him as an accountant at some time?"

"Is that what he was? No, I've always used the same man at the same Big Eight firm."

"Where are you originally from, Tom?"

"Durango, Colorado."

"And you attended college and law school at . . . ?"

"Undergraduate at Boulder, law at Illinois."

"Have you spent much time in Berkeley?"

"I don't believe I've been there more than a dozen times in my life. Is that where Hilderly came from?"

"He attended the university until he was expelled for activities relating to the Free Speech Movement."

"I'm afraid I don't know much about that, other than what I read in the papers a long time ago."

I watched him for a moment. While his eyes seemed candid and his manner was relaxed, I sensed an undercurrent of falsehood in the man. After a bit I asked, "What about the name Libby Heikkinen? Is that familiar to you?"

He shook his head—too quickly, I thought.

"Jess Goodhue? David Arlen Taylor?"

"Neither. Who are these people?"

"The other beneficiaries. Are you sure none of their names rings a bell?"

"Goodhue sounds vaguely familiar."

"She's an anchorwoman with KSTS-TV."

"Right. I think she interviewed me once."

The sense of falsehood still nudged me. I said, "Aren't you interested in the value of your share of Hilderly's estate?"

"I'm more interested in why he named me in his will. But, yes, how large is it?"

"Your share would come to around a quarter of a million dollars—should you be able to prove you are the Thomas Y. Grant that Hilderly intended the money to go to."

Grant's gaze strayed to a window that overlooked another bricked courtyard, and to the eucalyptus groves of the Presidio beyond its wall. He was silent for a long moment, then looked back at me and said, "I'm afraid I can't do that. And frankly, while it's a good deal of money, I don't really need it. I understand the difficult position this places

54

Hank Zahn in; naturally he's bound to do everything he can to carry out his client's wishes. So what I'm going to propose is this: I will sign a document renouncing all claim to this inheritance, in perpetuity."

It was a gesture I hadn't expected—and one that was totally unnecessary. Now I began to suspect that—despite his outwardly cool manner—Tom Grant had known Perry Hilderly and was afraid I'd find out the nature of the relationship.

I said, "Are you sure you want to do that?"

"Yes. Will you ask Mr. Zahn to draw up the paperwork?"

"Certainly. I'll call for an appointment when it's ready." I closed the file and replaced it in my briefcase.

Grant stood. "When you do, ask Angela to schedule it for late in the day; I'd like to show you my studio."

Involuntarily I glanced over at the shelf beside the fireplace, where the mockingbird feathers spread about the dry, taut piece of skin. My feeling of distaste was even stronger now.

"Since you seem so interested in my hobby," Grant added.

On my way through the pristine front courtyard, I suddenly recalled the source of the odd phrase that had popped into my head earlier: it was from the last stanza of a song by the seventeenth-century English playwright John Webster that I'd been required to memorize in one of my high-school literature classes. I could still remember the entire quatrain, more or less accurately.

Vain the ambition of kings
Who seek by trophies and dead things
To leave a living name behind,
And weave but nets to catch the wind.

Four

As it turned out, Greg was forced to cancel our lunch—a fact about which I had mixed emotions. When I arrived at Homicide, one of the inspectors—a man named Wallace, whom I knew slightly—handed me an armful of files and showed me to Greg's cubicle. "The lieutenant said to leave them on the desk when you're finished," he told me.

So I spent what should have been my lunch hour reading through the case files on the random shootings. Four of them, dating back to April, the latest being Hilderly's on July 6. The first was a restaurant employee,

56

returning late to his rooming house in the Outer Mission. Next was a nurse, leaving for her four-to-midnight shift at Children's Hospital in Laurel Heights. The third victim, a veteran on disability, had been unable to sleep and gone outside his home in the Outer Sunset to get some air minutes before he was killed. And then there was Hilderly. The weapon used was a .357 Magnum, and the bullets recovered from the bodies matched ballistically. All the shootings had occurred after ten P.M. and on relatively quiet streets; even Hilderly's had been no exception, since normally busy Geary Boulevard is almost deserted at one-fifty A.M., the hour he'd alighted from an empty Muni bus at the corner of Third Avenue.

There had been no eyewitnesses to any of the killings; the Muni bus, in Hilderly's case, had already driven away. Family, friends, and coworkers of the victims had been interviewed, and the investigators were unable to turn up an enemy or anyone else with a motive for murder. The information in the files showed that the victims had been more or less upright citizens, ordinary people going about their ordinary business. Ordinary people who just happened to be in the wrong place at the wrong time.

As is customary in such cases, the mayor's office had offered a reward for information leading to the apprehension of the murderer. The usual false leads, extortion attempts, and crackpot calls (including one in which the caller claimed the shootings were the work of her husband, who had then flown off in a UFO) had been phoned in to the police hot line. Unlike killers such as Zodiac, the perpetrator did not contact either the press or the police. If the snipings continued, the public outcry would become louder, and panic would ensue; political pressure on the department, already heavy, would increase.

I skimmed the files devoted to each individual, then turned to Hilderly's, curious to see where he'd been on the night of his death. There was a statement from his employer, Gene Carver of Tax Management Corporation, saying that Hilderly had worked late that evening. I frowned; he'd been shot only the week before last, long after the busy income-tax season. Why the late hours? Then I read on; Hilderly and his boss had been preparing for an IRS audit of one of their major clients. Carver stated that he himself had left the office at one A.M. and offered Hilderly a ride home; Hilderly declined, saying he wanted to finish with what he was working on.

I sighed and leaned back in Greg's chair. I could understand why the police had been thus far frustrated by the killings. The only links among the victims of the sniper that they'd been able to establish were the circumstances under which they'd been shot and the matching bullets. Apparently none of them had known one another, and there were few commonalities. Of course, little was known about the restaurant worker, who appeared to be even more of a loner than Hilderly, but the fact he'd been more or less a drifter whose history could not be fully established removed him a step further from his fellow victims. The shootings were random, all right. I didn't envy Greg this one.

After a moment I looked at my watch, saw it was nearly two. Greg—who had been called away to a meeting with his unit's deputy chief—obviously wouldn't be back for some time. I used his phone to check in at All Souls, found there were no messages of any importance, and decided to go grab a burger before running by KSTS-TV. As I hurried through the busy squad room toward the elevators, I waved to Inspector Wallace. He motioned for me to come over, but I shook my head and pointed to my watch. My stomach was making a hollow plaint; if I was to have any lunch at all, I'd better do so quickly.

At close to three I arrived at the TV studio on the Embarcadero, virtually in the shadow of the Bay Bridge, and only blocks from the proposed site for a new downtown athletic stadium. The building was bulky, red brick with a flat roof sporting an antenna and various other broadcast gear—the former plant of a bakery that had gone belly-up in the seventies. Tracks from a railroad spur ribbed the pavement in front of it; across the boulevard that rimmed this side of the city along the bay were three piers—no longer used for shipping, but instead devoted to such enterprises as architects' and real-estate brokers' offices. To their right was the SFFD's fireboat station.

The roar of cars and trucks on the bridge and its approaches drowned out other sounds; the massive concrete facades of the piers all but blocked my view of the water. The day—at least in this part of the city— had turned warmish and sunny. On the wide promenade beyond the fireboat station people sat on benches or leaned against the seawall, looking out toward Treasure Island; joggers pounded along, most of them appearing oblivious to the attractiveness of their surroundings. After I got out of my car I watched one of the harbor pilot's boats churn by, then turned and went into the TV studio's lobby.

The lobby was decorated in high-tech gray and black, with blown-up photos of KSTS personalities on the walls. As I waited for the receptionist—who was answering phones, putting people on hold, getting back to other callers—I studied the picture of Jess Goodhue. The anchorwoman had a pert, almost elfin face, with sleek dark brown hair that swept back from her forehead and ears, its ends curling under just above her shoulders. In spite of her youthful cuteness—which she probably found a liability—the photo exuded a forceful presence. Her eyes met that of the camera candidly; their direct gaze and the set of her mouth showed determination and intelligence. Even before seeing her in person, I sensed Goodhue was a woman who demanded respect—and got it.

The receptionist finished with the last of the waiting callers. "May I help you?" he asked.

I told him I wanted to speak with Goodhue

and handed him one of my cards. He dialed an extension and spoke into the phone, then said to me, "She wants to know what this is in reference to."

I said it was in reference to an inheritance left her by an All Souls client.

He spoke into the phone again, then replaced the receiver. "She says she's got to review a couple more scripts, but if you want to talk afterward, while she's doing her makeup, that's fine with her."

"Fine with me, too."

"Okay, why don't you—" He broke off and waved to a young woman who was entering from the street, bearing a grease-stained bag of what looked and smelled to be Chinese carry-out. "Hey, Marge, would you take this lady back to the newsroom and point her toward Jess?"

Marge nodded and motioned for me to follow her; the receptionist buzzed us through an interior door near his desk. The newsroom was the first on the left off the long hall beyond it.

My initial impression was of noise: voices, telephone bells, the clatter of typewriters, the squawk of police-band radios. A half dozen TV monitors were mounted on one wall, pictures turned on, but sound muted.

Silent spectral images moved across their screens: Woody Woodpecker, a hand-wringing soap-opera heroine, Oprah Winfrey, earnest individuals extolling the virtues of baby diapers and spray wax and deodorant.

Marge said, "First cubicle to the right of the assignment desk," and went back into the hall.

Directly ahead of me was a long desk on a raised platform. Three men and a woman sat at it—talking on phones, scribbling notes, scrutinizing the monitors. I looked to the right and saw a row of modular cubicles. As I started over there I had to dodge a woman who rushed through the door behind me dragging a bulky tote bag by its strap and flashing a victory sign toward the assignment desk.

There were two people in the first cubicle: a dark-haired woman seated in a swivel chair at the desk and a tall, angular man who loomed over her, stabbing his finger at a typewritten page. The woman's face was not visible, but I assumed she was Jess Goodhue. I moved away from the opening of the cubicle and leaned against its wall, idly observing the activity in the newsroom. The woman I'd nearly collided with was at the assignment desk talking with a bald-headed man. After a moment she hurried to one of a row of smaller desks on the far side of the room, plunked her tote bag down, and began rolling paper into a typewriter while still standing. The bald-headed man got up and went to a board that resembled an airline arrivals-and-departures schedule mounted on the wall behind him. He rubbed out a couple of notations with the side of his hand, then used a blue crayon to enter new ones.

A voice came from inside the cubicle—Goodhue's, not so carefully modulated as it was on her newscasts. "No, Marv, that's got to be rewritten. I don't see how we can compare Barbara Bush to Mother Teresa."

Marv said something that I couldn't quite make out.

"No, I am *not* expressing a political bias. This is one I think even Babs would agree with me on."

The man left the cubicle without another word and stalked toward the row of desks on the other side of the room.

"That's a Republican for you," Goodhue said. I glanced into the cubicle, saw she was paging through a script, and stepped back.

After a few more minutes a thin blond-haired woman approached, her step tentative, expression anxious. She stopped a foot from the cubicle's entrance, as if afraid to go further. "Jess? The order of these stories—do you really want the mercy killing moved ahead of the drug busts and the new environmental plan?"

"Yes, I do. It's lost where you had it."

"But—"

"It's an important story, Linda. It's about . . . just reorder it."

Linda remained where she was, silent and indecisive.

Goodhue added, "And when you see Roberta, tell her the lead-in to the drug busts needs more punch—a lot more. I want to see new copy by four-thirty."

Linda turned quickly and walked away.

Goodhue said to herself in a low voice, "You get too abrupt with them on days like this. It's something you've got to work on."

I stepped up to the entrance of the cubicle and saw she had pushed back from her desk, extending her arms in a little stretch. "Ms. Goodhue?"

She looked up, then snapped her fingers. "You're the woman from the law firm . . . what was it?"

"All Souls Legal Cooperative."

"Right. I know of you people. Did a series

65

on alternative legal services back when I was a field reporter. McCone, is it?"

"Sharon McCone."

She stood and came forward, clasping my hand in a strong grip. "Call me Jess, everybody does. Let's go upstairs, huh? I have to make up for the three-fifty-five teaser."

"The . . . ?"

She started through the busy newsroom toward the hall. "A one-minute spot. You've probably seen hundreds of them: 'Coming up on the six o'clock news.'"

"Of course." I trailed her down the hall. Goodhue was not as tall as I—five two or three to my own five six—but her brisk pace made up for her shorter stride. As she clattered down the hall in high-heeled shoes that matched her smart turquoise dress, she kept up a running chatter.

"Sorry I kept you waiting, but things are pretty frantic, and they'll get positively hairy from here on out. I've got to make up, do the spot, go over the scripts again with my co-anchor. You came at the right time, though; nobody, absolutely nobody, bothers me in my dressing room."

At the end of the hallway was a winding iron staircase. Goodhue led me up it, and down another long hall, past other rooms that hummed with activity. "Sports and weather," she said, waving her hand. "They're pretty much autonomous of the newsroom." Close to the end of the hall she opened a door and motioned me inside. "And this," she said, "is where I go when I want privacy."

It wasn't much of a dressing room: a long counter below a bulb-edged mirror; two wicker chairs, both somewhat raveled; a rack with changes of clothes hanging from it; a small adjoining bathroom. The counter was littered with cosmetics. Among them stood a vase of yellow roses that had seen better days.

Goodhue shut the door and grinned wryly at me. "Well, it ain't Broadway, but it's mine."

"I don't think they have it so good on Broadway, either."

"Probably not. You've got to go to Hollywood for the glitzy stuff." She frowned at the browning roses, swept them from the vase, and jammed them into a wastebasket under the counter. "Sit, while I make up," she said, and plunked down onto a stool in front of the mirror. "What's this about an inheritance?"

I sat in one of the wicker chairs—gingerly

at first. "One of our clients has named you as a beneficiary in his will. Perry Hilderly. Do you know him?"

She considered, picking up a bottle of makeup base and beginning to apply it with practiced strokes. "The name's familiar. Who is . . . was he?"

"A tax accountant. Worked for a small firm out in the Avenues."

"Wait a minute!" She snapped her fingers. "Wasn't he the last victim of that sniper?"

"Right."

"Weird. Why would he leave *me* money?"

"I don't know. He made a holograph will—self-written, without the aid of an attorney—and left no explanation."

"I don't get it. Would it be crass to ask how much he left me?"

"Somewhere in the neighborhood of a quarter of a million dollars." More, I reminded myself, if Grant went through with signing the document renouncing his inheritance, since it had been left on a share-alike basis.

Goodhue's hand paused in mid-stroke near her hairline. "Jesus! Why on earth . . . ?"

"I'd hoped you could tell me."

She shook her head, set the makeup bottle

68

down, and opened a compact of blush. After rummaging around on the counter for a brush, she began applying color to her cheekbones. "As far as I know, I never met the man. Tell me more about him."

"Before I do that, I have a few questions. Does the name Thomas Y. Grant mean anything to you?"

"Grant . . . Tom Grant, the attorney?"

"Right."

"I interviewed him for that series on alternative legal services I mentioned. Not that I approve of his particular alternative, but it fit with the theme. Actually, I was surprised to find him quite charming."

It was a temptation to ask what she'd thought of Grant's fetishes, but I merely asked, "What about someone named Libby Heikkinen?"

"No."

"David Arlen Taylor?"

"Uh-uh. Who *are* these people?"

"Your co-beneficiaries. Hilderly divided his estate four ways."

"This Hilderly must have been a wealthy man."

"Not in the usual sense. He inherited

some money, invested well, and didn't have expensive habits."

"And he lived here in the city? Of course he did; I remember that he was shot on Geary, near his apartment. Was he from here originally?"

"I don't know much about his background, just that he was a radical during the Vietnam era, one of the founders of the Free Speech Movement at Berkeley."

"Berkeley!" She spun on the stool, the cosmetic brush falling from her fingers.

"Is that significant?"

She ignored the question. "What else can you tell me about him?"

"He was kicked out of college, worked for a magazine for a while, until they sent him to Vietnam as a correspondent. He stayed there for some time, had a son by a Vietnamese woman. She and the child were killed by mortar fire, and then Hilderly came back to the States. Married, had two more boys, divorced, and lived very quietly in the Inner Richmond until he was shot."

Goodhue was sitting very still now, hands locked together on her lap, makeup brush forgotten on the floor at her feet. "Just think of that," she said after a moment. "I reported the story of his death." There was an

70

odd tremor in her voice, an emotion I couldn't define.

"Are you sure you never met him?"

"Very sure. The Free Speech Movement —that was right around the time I was born."

"It started in the fall of nineteen sixty-four."

Goodhue's focus was inward, searching. After a bit she said softly, "I was born in January of nineteen sixty-five."

I waited, but when she didn't elaborate, said, "I'm sorry, but I don't follow you."

"What I'm trying to say is . . . this Perry Hilderly may have been my father."

Five

The statement came from so far out in left field that it took me a moment to formulate a response. "Why would you think that?" I finally asked.

"Because my mother was at Berkeley then."

"So were thousands of other people."

"But not—" She broke off, looking at her watch. "Dammit! It's a long story, and I don't have much time."

"Why don't you start telling me now. I can wait around for the rest as long as necessary."

"All right." She swiveled back toward the mirror and fussed nervously with her hair. "As I said before, I was born in January of nineteen sixty-five. Out of wedlock." She paused, looking at me in the mirror, as if she was waiting for some reaction. When she didn't get one, she went on. "My mother's name was Jenny Ruhl. She was a campus radical, heavily into the protest movement. Or so I found out later."

"You never knew her?"

Goodhue turned toward me again, backlit by the glow from the bare frosted bulbs around the mirror. It softened the planes and curves of her face and she appeared even younger. When she spoke, her voice was not as crisp and self-assured as before.

"Oh, I knew her. I can even remember her—some. But I'm getting ahead of my story. Anyway, my mother had me on January seventeenth. My father was listed as 'unknown' on my birth certificate. My mother came from a well-to-do Orange County family; I guess a lot of the so-called revolutionaries had affluent, conservative backgrounds. For whatever reason, she

72

never let her people know about me. Instead, she used the allowance they sent her to farm me out to an older couple here in San Francisco who ran a little day-care center and took in kids whose parents couldn't care for them—foster kids from the welfare department, as well as others like me. Ben and Nilla Goodhue. They—"

There was a knock at the door. A woman's voice called, "Jess, you're due on the set. Hurry up!"

Goodhue started. "Jesus, I almost missed the spot! I've got to get my ass upstairs on the double. Do you mind staying here—they don't like strangers on the set."

"Sure. I'll wait."

After she left the minutes passed slowly. I shifted on the wicker chair—which had grown uncomfortable—and tried to fit Goodhue's claim that Hilderly might have been her father into what I already knew. I supposed it was possible that Hilderly had fathered her and written her into his will in a too-late attack of conscience. But that didn't explain the bequest to Tom Grant. And what about Heikkinen and Taylor? Other children he'd failed to acknowledge? Could any young man have been that prolific—even in the sexually free sixties?

When Goodhue came back, her forehead was beaded with moisture. She mopped it with a tissue and set about repairing her makeup. "I've never been that late," she said. "Never. Slid into the chair with only five seconds to spare."

"I shouldn't have let you lose track of the time."

"Not your fault. Look, I have maybe ten more minutes, then I've got to get down to the newsroom and go over the scripts with my co-anchor. Where was I?"

"Ben and Nilla Goodhue."

"Right." The mention of their names banished her preoccupation with the time. A gentle, reminiscent expression stole over her features, and she set down the mascara wand she was using.

"Ben and Nilla. Great people. Loving people. He was English, proper as could be, except when he was rolling around on the rug with us kids. She was Swedish—the Nilla was short for Gunnilla—and she could warm up a room just with her smile. They lived in the Portola district. It was nice there back then—solid working class, a good ethnic mix. Lots of Italian delis and soul-food places and little corner markets. People had vegetable gardens; the man next door to us kept chickens. It's not like that anymore; there's a lot of gang violence, spillover from Bayview and Visitación Valley—" She broke off and picked up the mascara wand again, as if she'd suddenly reminded herself of the shortness of time.

"Anyway," she went on, "that's where I grew up, in this big house on a corner lot with anywhere from two to six other kids. They came and went. I stayed."

"Did your mother visit you?"

"Occasionally, until I was four. I remember her as pretty, but not very warm. When she held me, I always felt she was afraid she might drop and break me. After she left, I would sit on Ben's or Nilla's lap for a long time. I couldn't understand why, if she was my mother, she didn't hold me the way they did."

"What about your father? Did your mother ever talk about him?"

"No, but he visited me once. I was maybe three and a half, close to four. I hoped—or maybe I just imagine I hoped—that they were going to take me away to live with them soon, but then he never came again."

"Can you describe him?"

She shook her head. "I can't. Over the years I've tried to picture him, but it's all cloudy. The only impression I have is that he might have been from the Southwest, because he wore a string tie. I remember sitting on his lap and playing with it, clicking the little metal ends on the strings together."

I made a mental note to find out where Hilderly had originally come from. "You say your mother came to see you until you were around four. What happened then?"

As she'd spoken of her childhood, Goodhue's face had become animated. Now it was as if someone had turned a switch and put out a light. She set down the mascara wand and moved to perch on the edge of the other chair. "She . . . died."

"How?"

"She . . . I didn't know this until a long time after. Nilla and Ben just told me she'd had to go away, but that I shouldn't worry because she loved me and would always be thinking about me. After that they didn't seem to want to talk about her and, frankly, she'd been such a small part of my life that I sort of forgot her. But when I was in sixth grade, I heard a couple of the neighbor kids talking—older kids, who had lived there all their lives. What happened was she got into trouble—something to do with the war protests—and then she killed herself."

76

I felt a stab of sympathy for the sixth grader who had found out an ugly fact in an unpleasant way. "What kind of trouble?"

Goodhue shook her head. "The kids only heard part of the story—picked up snatches of conversation, the way kids do. What they told me was that my mother went out to Ocean Beach one night and shot herself in the head. Ben and Nilla freaked out when they saw it on the news. I went to them with the story, hoping it wasn't true, but they wouldn't talk about it. That was the only time they let me down. Years later, after they were both dead and I didn't feel that I was betraying either of them, I hired an investigator to find out the whole story. He verbally confirmed that it had happened like the kids said it had, and wrote up a report. But—this is the weird part—you know what I did?"

"What?"

"I burned the damned thing without reading it. After all those years of wondering and all the money I'd spent on the investigator, I just didn't want to know."

Reputable investigators, however, kept copies of their reports on file for quite some time. "Do you recall the name of the person you hired?"

"Not offhand, but I'm sure it's somewhere in my records."

"I'd like it, if it's not too much trouble to locate."

Goodhue looked somewhat apprehensive. "Why? Do you need it to establish my claim to the inheritance?"

Given the fact Hilderly had assumed Hank would know who she was, plus the fact that her name was a relatively unusual one, I felt it safe to assume she was the right Jess Goodhue. Still, I replied cautiously, "It would help. And it might also help me to understand why Hilderly wrote the kind of will he did."

"Why is that important to you?"

I hesitated, then opted for the answer that I sensed Goodhue—as a newswoman—would understand. "I'm a truth seeker. I need to know."

She nodded. "You're like me. I'll look for the name tomorrow, and let you know."

She still seemed oblivious to the amount of time that was passing, so I pressed on with my questioning while I could. "After your mother . . . died, what happened to you?"

"Nothing. I stayed on with Ben and Nilla. I was there unofficially; the welfare department had no idea I existed. Neither did my mother's family, and my father obviously didn't care. Ben and Nilla raised me as their own. I took their name. Ben died when I was fifteen, just keeled over of a stroke at the breakfast table. That about killed Nilla, too. She withdrew, closed the day-care center, stopped taking in kids. Finally I was all she had.

"There had never been much money. Without what the welfare department paid for the foster kids, things were rough. I left school at sixteen so I could support Nilla. Got a girl-Friday job at a stationery supply company, and they trained me as a secretary. Nilla died when I was eighteen—it was her heart, in more ways than one. I left the job at the stationery company, and the Portola district. Moved downtown and got a job as a secretary here at KSTS. After a year and a half, I convinced them to let me try my hand as a writer. The field reporting came along pretty quick. And now here I am." She flung her arms out, as if to embrace the shabby dressing room, the entire studio, her successful life. But to me she looked like the little girl whose mother had been pretty but not very warm, reaching out for the surrogate parents who knew how to hold a child.

I said, "Jess, tell me this: do you *want* to know if Perry Hilderly was your father?"

Her hands locked together again, and she compressed her lips. After a moment she said, "You know, I do. At first, after Nilla died, I was wild to find out about my parents. I contacted my mother's family in southern California, but they wouldn't have anything to do with me, wouldn't even believe I was Jenny Ruhl's daughter, claimed my birth certificate was a fake. It was after that that I hired the detective. But then—well, I told you what I did with the report."

"Why is it different now?"

"Because Perry Hilderly left me money. A lot of money. That must mean something."

I wasn't sure. At least not that it meant all the good things she was obviously imagining. Guilt at deeds left undone, I've found, does not necessarily imply love for the wronged party.

Goodhue must have sensed my doubt, because she stood abruptly. "Look, I've got to get down to the newsroom. I'll look for that detective's name, give you a call."

I handed her one of my cards. She pocketed it, checked her makeup a final time, and led me out of the dressing room. On the

80

way downstairs I asked if there was a phone I might use, and Goodhue directed me to one at an unoccupied desk in the newsroom. I called All Souls, found Hank was still there, and reported my day's findings.

"Damned curious," he said when I finished. "It doesn't quite fit with what I know of Perry. I can't see him abandoning his own child."

"Did you break the news to his former wife about the sons not getting their inheritance?"

"Yes. She didn't seem very upset. Apparently she and her new husband are quite well off. She was happy about the personal stuff, though—said what you did about it being nice for the boys, who will have something to remember Perry by."

"I'd like to talk with her. If anyone might know about Hilderly's past, she's the one. Will you give me her new name and number?"

"Sure." There was a pause, and then he read off the information to me. "You're not planning on going out to Danville tonight?"

"If she'll see me."

Hank was silent.

"Oh, Lord, your dinner party for Anne-Marie! I almost forgot."

81

"Look, don't worry about that. Go see Judy Fleming and come by my place later. But just be sure to come."

"I will, I promise. Is Rae around?"

"She left about fifteen minutes ago. Asked me to tell you she's turned up something on Heikkinen; she'll talk to you about it tonight."

"Okay. Keep some chili warm for me." I hung up and placed a credit-card call to Judy Fleming, the former Mrs. Hilderly, in the exclusive East Bay development of Blackhawk. She was cordial and agreed to see me if I didn't mind driving over there in rush-hour traffic. I said I'd be at her house as soon as possible.

As I crossed the newsroom toward the hallway, I glanced at Goodhue's cubicle. The anchorwoman was again seated at her desk, next to her co-anchor, Les Gates. Gates, whom I recognized from countless newscasts, was expounding on a script that lay in front of them. Goodhue nodded and responded, but her expression was distracted. When I passed the cubicle, she looked up, and I felt her gaze upon me all the way to the door.

Six

Blackhawk, the development where Hilderly's former wife and sons now lived, has long struck me as a phenomenon that could only have occurred in the latter decades of the twentieth century. It is an exclusive enclave of custom-built homes nestled in the foothills of Mount Diablo, and insulated from the world by high walls, a private security force, and recreational facilities that ensure no resident need seek pleasure elsewhere. Everything is designed for the ease and comfort of the busy property owners, most of whom are engaged in making fortunes in the industrial parks that cover what used to be farmland near San Ramon. A buyer may purchase a house that is fully furnished and equipped, down to the last teaspoon and guest towel; the local supermarket boasts of clocks that display the time in such global cities as London, New York, and Tokyo—presumably so shoppers can rush home and call their brokers before the stock exchanges close. While Blackhawkians may appreciate and even need these refinements, I find something vaguely depressing about a place where life's edges have been so smoothed and rounded.

After I was admitted past the guard station at one of the gates, I drove through a maze of large homes on spacious lots to the Fleming house. It was mock Tudor, with a big live oak in the front yard. I parked at the curb and went up a flagstone walk that bisected the neatly barbered lawn.

When Judy Fleming answered the door, I recognized her as an older version of the woman in Hilderly's photo album; her short brown hair was now streaked with gray, and she was no longer plump, her face having that gaunt look that comes from frequent dieting. She greeted me pleasantly and led me to the rear of her air-conditioned house, where an informal living room overlooked a swimming pool full of noisy teenagers. The room, a dining area, and the kitchen were all connected, and there was a lived-in feel to the space that had been missing from the more formal rooms we'd passed on the way.

Mrs. Fleming seated me on the couch, offered coffee—which I accepted—and went to pour it from a percolator that stood on the wet bar. She hesitated, then poured a second mug for herself. "I shouldn't," she said. "I drink too much of it. But I'm dieting, and it keeps me going."

She certainly did look tired, I thought as she seated herself in a rocking chair opposite me. Bluish circles under her eyes were more pronounced in the late sunlight that slanted through the glass doors behind her, and her movements were weary, almost leaden. I suspected her fatigue stemmed less from unwise dieting than from her ex-husband's death and altered will.

A roar of laughter—muted by the closed doors—rose from the pool, and the kids began clapping; two boys had just tossed a struggling girl in. Mrs. Fleming smiled and said, "It's good to hear laughter around here. The last week and a half have been grim. My boys weren't close to Perry—by his choice, not mine or theirs—but his death and now this business of the new will have been upsetting."

"Why did he choose to distance himself from his sons?"

"That was his way. It was one of the reasons I divorced him. The main reason, actually." She paused. "I've always loved Perry, though. That's why this business of him disinheriting the boys is so hard to take."

"Hank Zahn had the impression you don't mind about the money."

"About the money, no. It's Perry's lack of caring and the . . . *inexplicableness* of what he did that's disturbing."

"So far I've been able to locate two of Perry's new beneficiaries—Thomas Y. Grant and Jess Goodhue. Did he ever mention either of them to you?"

She shook her head.

"What about a David Arlen Taylor, Libby Heikkinen, or Jenny Ruhl?"

"None of those names is familiar. I'm sure I'd remember if I'd known or heard of them."

"Well, neither of the two I've spoken to claims to have known Perry, or understands why he would name them in his will. Perhaps when I locate Taylor and Heikkinen, they can shed some light on his reasons. The other person I mentioned, Jenny Ruhl, was the mother of Jess Goodhue. Goodhue thought her mother might have known Perry at Berkeley."

"That would have been long before I met him."

"When was that, and where?"

"At S.F. State, after he'd come back from Vietnam. I was only nineteen; he was several years older, and very intriguing to me. A distant, silent, *haunted* man, who had already lost a wife and a child. I thought I could help him, bring him out of himself. That's how naive I was!"

"I take it he remained distant."

"Yes. It wasn't until after my first son, Kurt, was born that I realized how distant. I remember looking at Kurt and wondering which of us he would be more like—Perry or me. And then it came to me that I knew virtually nothing of the man who had fathered him."

"Do you mean what he thought and felt, or actual biographical details?"

"Both. Oh, he'd sketched out a chronology for me when we first met, but it was more like an outline, with none of the substance."

"Where was Perry originally from?"

"Albuquerque."

I thought of the father wearing a string tie who had visited Jess Goodhue. "Did he speak of his childhood?"

"More than any other part of his life. It sounded fairly normal. I never met his father; he died when Perry was in high school. His mother had remarried and they traveled a lot; I only met her once. She was quite outgoing, so wherever he got his remoteness, it wasn't from her."

"And you divorced Perry ten years ago?"

"Ten years next month. Toward the end we were living in Pacifica. We'd bought a house. Perry commuted to the city. He kept long hours—purposely, I thought. It wasn't as if he didn't love the boys or me; he just couldn't cope with the intimacy of family life. Eventually he became more like the fog that drifted in and out, rather than a husband or father. I felt as if I were failing him when I divorced him, but he seemed more relieved than anything else. I guess he'd gotten in over his head emotionally by marrying and having a family."

The kind of uninvolved individual Mrs. Fleming described didn't mesh with the young man who had clowned and laughed his way through the stormy days at Berkeley. Even the man Hank had known in Vietnam had sounded more connected to others. I wondered if it had been the deaths of the woman and child over there that had changed him. But even when they had been alive, Hilderly had been closed off in certain respects.

I asked, "After the divorce, did you see Perry?"

"Very occasionally. He'd pick up the boys on their birthdays to take them to the city to the zoo or a ball game. On Christmas he'd send gifts—usually ones that were inappropriate for their age levels—and call. But that was the extent of it."

I'd been wrong in thinking Judy Fleming knew anything useful about her husband's past. "I know you find Perry changing his will inexplicable," I said, "but I'd like to ask you to think over the contacts you and your sons have had with him in, say, the past year. Was there anything in his behavior that even hinted he might do such a thing?"

She considered, pleating the fabric of her skirt between her fingers. "One occasion comes to mind. Perry was behaving oddly . . . but maybe you'd best talk to Kurt about it. He was there and I wasn't." She went to the glass door and opened it, called out to one of the boys by the pool. He came to the house, toweling himself off as he walked.

At around sixteen Kurt looked quite a bit like early pictures of his father. He was tall and lanky, but possessed of a natural grace; his hair was blond, curly, and somewhat on the long side. He shook my hand and greeted me with a directness unusual in one of his age.

89

The introductions over, Kurt sat down on the raised stone hearth, his long arms wrapped around his bare knees. His mother said, "Tell Ms. McCone about your birthday celebration with Perry." To me she added, "Neither of the boys felt close enough to call him 'Dad.' That's what they call my husband."

Kurt asked, "You mean tell her about the weird stuff?"

Judy Fleming nodded.

"Okay. This was in the middle of June, a Saturday. I went into the city on BART and we took in a Giants game. Perry was kind of quiet. I thought it might be because for my present he'd given me this video game that was really for young kids, and I couldn't work up much enthusiasm over it." Kurt paused, looking at his mother. "He was always doing that. You remember the year he gave me the big stuffed koala bear for Christmas? I was thirteen and into Indiana Jones."

Mrs. Fleming merely smiled.

"Okay," Kurt went on, "after the game we started back here and stopped in Walnut Creek at a Mexican restaurant. Perry got into the margaritas. They make a strong one there—" He glanced at his mother again. "Or so I'm told. Perry had four. After the

90

second he started going on, sort of—what's that word I just learned? Maundering." He seemed to savor the new word; his mouth shaped it as if he were tasting each syllable.

"About what?" I asked.

"All sorts of stuff. He started by asking me if I'd decided on a college yet, but before I could answer, he said that the decisions people make early on are important, that the wrong one can change the whole course of your life. He said that even a right decision can come back at you later, even if you know you did the right thing."

"That sounds like fairly standard father-to-son advice."

"You didn't know Perry. He wasn't much on advice. Anyway, then he started going on about this seminar he'd had to go to for his job a couple of weeks before. He said he hadn't wanted to go, but that it was one of the best things that ever happened to him. 'It's changed my whole life,' he said. 'I know what I have to do to get in touch with my former self.'"

"Those were his exact words?"

"More or less."

"What kind of seminar was it?"

"He didn't say, and I couldn't ask; he was getting *really* weird by that time. Then he started in on . . . well, what he said was, 'You can't beat yourself up for being unable to control the consequences of your actions.' And other stuff along that line."

It sounded to me as if Hilderly had been trying to articulate the preachings of a pop psychologist to his son—and had not done too good a job of it. "Anything else?"

"Well, there was some stuff about ideals. How you should hang on to them, but sometimes you had to dump some in order to live up to the most important of all. And then he got into guilt and atonement. All the time I was trying to eat my enchiladas, he was sucking up margaritas and carrying on like a born-again."

"Maybe he *had* gotten involved in some religion; there's a lot of that going around."

Kurt looked dubious. His mother said, "I can't imagine that. Perry was a lifelong atheist."

"What else did he say?" I asked Kurt.

"Not much that made any sense. It worried me; I'd never seen him that way before. Like Mom says, I wasn't close to Perry, but he was a nice man, and I hated to see him sort of . . . losing it. You think maybe he was cracking up, and that was why he made that weird will?"

92

"Maybe." I made a mental note to ask Hilderly's former employer about the seminar he'd attended late in May.

"Well," Kurt said, "whatever made him do it must have been really something. I know he loved my brother and me, even if he was sort of off on another planet most of the time." Up to now Kurt had sounded almost cavalier about his last dinner with his father, but as he spoke a tremor came into his voice. He turned to his mother. "I wish I could have done or said something—you know, to let him know I cared."

Judy Fleming said, "Kurt, he knew you cared."

"But there should have been *something*. I'm sorry now that all those years I wasn't a better son to him."

Quickly she went to him and put her arms around his shoulders. "You *were* a good son. You were the best you could be, under the circumstances."

She could easily have countered Kurt's feelings of regret by pointing out that Perry hadn't been much of a father, but instead she'd chosen the more difficult option of refusing to degrade her former husband's memory. She may, as she'd said, have let

93

Hilderly down when she divorced him, but now, at the end, she hadn't failed him.

Seven

On the way back to the city I stopped at a K-Mart to buy a birthday card and a hanging fuchsia plant for Anne-Marie. By the time I reached the building she and Hank owned on Twenty-sixth Street in Noe Valley, it was close to ten and a refreshing fog once more enveloped San Francisco. I went up on the front porch, fuchsia dangling from my hand, and surveyed the row of hooks for plants that Anne-Marie had installed in front of the door to her first-floor flat; one was still vacant, and the space was the right size for my gift. I turned, nodding in satisfaction, but something across the street caught my attention. I looked back. There was no one over there, at least no one discernible, and all I heard were distant traffic noises and voices down the block.

In a few seconds I turned away again, remembering the conversation I'd had with Hank on Saturday, when he'd described his paranoid feeling that someone might have been lurking around outside All Souls.

"Nerves," I'd said. "Typical urban ailment," he'd said. Right on both counts. Quickly I went to the door of the upstairs flat and rang the bell.

Anne-Marie and Hank are one of those couples who, once married, discovered they couldn't live together. She's fastidious, he's just plain messy. She values a routine, he thrives on chaos. In the end they solved the problem by occupying separate flats in the same building—far enough apart, but never out of reach.

The buzzer sounded, and I pushed the door open and climbed the narrow flight of stairs. The air was redolent of chili—an aroma that in the past would have made me cringe, because Hank's secret recipe was one he should have carried untried to the grave. But the previous winter Anne-Marie had critiqued it in a fit of anger, I had backed up her damning judgment, and since then Hank had made a concerted and moderately successful effort to improve it. Not that it mattered: nobody went to Hank's for the food. We went for the good talk and company.

I hung my coat and bag on the hall tree and walked to the rear of the flat. Hank had reversed the typical order of the rooms, turning the front parlor into his bedroom and merging the remaining ones into a big space for entertaining that opened off the kitchen. It was back there that I found him and his three remaining dinner guests, scattered on the sectional sofa, coffee or wine to hand.

Anne-Marie sat closest to the door. I went over and plunked the fuchsia and card on her lap. "Happy birthday."

"Thank you! I'm glad you could make it." She examined the plant, then ripped open the envelope. Since I'd last seen her, she'd cut her long blond hair, and the pert new style enhanced the delicacy of her elegant nose and sculpted cheekbones. The haircut was the latest in a series of changes in her life, the most startling of which was taking an extended leave of absence from All Souls to act as consulting attorney to a large coalition of environmentalists. I wondered what had prompted the move, but so far had not found the right opportunity to ask.

Anne-Marie laughed at the card—which likened our lives to the fast lane at the supermarket checkout—and passed it to Hank. He nodded in agreement and handed it to Rae, who sat on the other section of the sofa. Willie Whelan, dressed in his usual leather vest and western wear, sprawled next to her, his head lolling against her shoulder.

I noticed there was something wrong with his face—it looked puffy. He raised a listless hand to me, then let it drop back onto the couch.

Before I could ask what his problem was, Hank stood, insisting I come to the kitchen for some chili. I followed him out there, where a big pot of the stuff still simmered on the stove. While he dished it up I went to the cupboard for a wineglass and looked in the fridge, sighing when I found a mediocre brand of wine-in-a-box that Hank favors because of the convenience factor. As I pressed the rubber spigot and waited for my glass to fill, I said, "I need to discuss the Hilderly case with you."

"Now?"

"Tomorrow morning will do."

"I'll be in court until noon."

"Then I'll catch you afterward—" I broke off as Rae entered the room.

Looking at my assistant tonight, I had to admit that this new liaison with Willie was doing her wonders. Her round, freckled face glowed and her manner was relaxed and easy. When she'd come to work for me the previous year, she'd been a bundle of insecurities; shedding an immature and demanding husband, some therapy, and a new

97

romantic relationship had made her blossom. She'd even begun dressing better—although her everyday wardrobe still ran to thrift-shop jeans and ratty sweaters. Tonight she had on a pair of corduroy slacks whose color exactly matched her auburn hair, and her shirt was a Liz Claiborne.

She noticed my admiring glance and said, "Macy's. I charged it. Willie has convinced me of the ease of living on credit."

"Just so long as he doesn't convince you of the ease of going into bankruptcy. But, really, you look great."

"Thanks. Listen, I started those skip traces."

"Hank said you have something on Heikkinen."

"Yes. I haven't gotten a response from your friend at the DMV yet—she was swamped, and their computers were down for part of the day. But I went by Vital Statistics and came up with a marriage for Heikkinen—to a Glen A. Ross in nineteen seventy-eight. I passed the married name along to your friend, and she said she'd try to have the info by noon tomorrow."

"Good. Nothing on David Arlen Taylor?"

"No. If the DMV files don't show anything, do you want me to widen the search to Vital Statistics in other counties?"

"Yes. Try Alameda, Marin, Contra Costa, and San Mateo for openers. I know that'll mean a lot of travel time for you, but I'll cover at the office."

"I don't think you'll need to, much. My desk is clear, and we seem to be into a slow period. You may have to cover for me with Willie, though."

Hank handed me my bowl of chili and grinned evilly—because it was extra hot, or because of what Rae had just said, I couldn't tell. "What does that mean? What's wrong with Willie, anyway? He looks funny."

Now Rae grinned, too. "Willie had all four wisdom teeth pulled this morning. He called me every hour on the hour all day to whine, and I suspect he'll do the same tomorrow. He's not talking much tonight, though; he couldn't eat his dinner, so he drank it."

"Does that mean he's too sedated to do his renditions of the latest Jewelry Mart commercials?"

"You got it."

"Thank God." Willie gets a bit frenetic on the subject of his television stardom, and

99

has frequently been known to reenact his commercials for captive audiences.

We went back to the living room and I took up my favorite position on the floor by the coffee table, bowl of chili (Hank had done something unfortunate to it—too much Tabasco, I thought) and glass of wine in front of me. I noticed an empty espresso cup to one side, recalled that Jack Stuart, our specialist in criminal law, was a fan of the vile brew, and asked, "Why'd Jack leave so early?"

Hank said, "He had to go to the Hall of Justice. That Iranian client of his got arrested again, shot at a kid who he claims was trying to steal beer from his store. Fortunately, he missed."

"Poor Jack. But what about Ted? Didn't you say he was coming?"

All four faces clouded. Anne-Marie said, "Ted couldn't make it. His friend Harry died."

"Oh, no." I set down my spoon, what little appetite I'd had completely gone. Harry had been our secretary's childhood friend; like Ted, he'd been gay, and he'd died of AIDS. As always when confronted with the horror of the disease, I felt overwhelmed with helplessness and anger. "How's Ted handling it?"

Rae said, "I had a drink with him right after he got the news this afternoon. He's bearing up all right; it wasn't as if it was unexpected. But still . . . You know what he told me? He said he felt disconnected, that Harry's dying was the first major break with his youth. He said it made him feel like he was straddling the gap between the beginning and the end of his life."

"I know what he means," Hank said. "This client of mine, the one whose heirs Shar's trying to locate, makes me feel that way. Perry wasn't that close a friend, but he was a symbol of an era to me."

"Like Abbie Hoffman," Anne-Marie added. "I couldn't believe it when he killed himself. The clown prince of the student revolution, ending up dead in middle age of booze and antidepression drugs. When I heard about Abbie, I knew the sixties were dead, too."

Willie mumbled wistfully, "I missed the sixties, was in 'Nam trying to stay alive. Missed the seventies, too, trying to stay out of jail. Come to think of it, I might of missed the eighties."

Rae said, "I did, too—the sixties, I mean.

Unless being born then counts. Those must have been the days, huh?"

Hank shrugged. "They were, if you judge from all the nostalgia that's being wallowed in lately. They had a reunion of aging militants at Stanford last May. All the folks who sat in at the Applied Electronics Lab in nineteen sixty-nine got together to talk over old times with current campus radicals."

"My God!" I said. "Did you go?"

"Are you kidding? In nineteen sixty-nine—because I'd stupidly joined ROTC, thinking the war would be over before I graduated—I was sitting around with Willie in an army supply depot in Cam Ranh Bay. Besides, even if I'd been in on the protests, the idea of sipping white wine and nibbling on crudités with a bunch of affluent people worried about wrinkles and hair loss turns my stomach."

"Where are your ideals?"

"Oh, they're still around someplace. Trouble is, half the time I can't keep track of *what* I'm supposed to believe these days."

"Yeah, it's tough for an aging leftist to remain politically correct," Anne-Marie said.

"Go ahead—be sarcastic. You're no better

102

than I am. You know what she did last week?" he asked the rest of us.

"Don't you dare tell them about the grapes!"

"We were in Bell Market looking at the grapes, and this asshole who thinks he's the social conscience of Noe Valley sidled up to her and warned her that grapes are still on the boycott list. She couldn't remember whether it was just Thompson seedless or all grapes, and was too embarrassed to ask, so we didn't buy any. But about an hour later I saw her slinking out of the house to go to that little produce stand two blocks away."

"I wanted grapes."

"Yeah—but that guy's produce isn't even organic."

"And organic," Rae said, "is always correct. As is oat bran, anything made out of soybeans, recycling, and taking public transit."

"Great," Hank said. "Just when I finally bought a decent car. I guess I'm politically hopeless: until three months ago I was still calling Asians 'Orientals.' I was corrected by a high-school girl, for Christ's sake. I've now got that one licked, but I still slip up on calling blacks 'African-Americans.'"

Anne-Marie said, "High-school *woman*."

103

"Huh?"

"Woman, not girl."

"Jesus!"

The subject of the conversation was beginning to irritate me, as trendy things—whether on the left or the right of the political spectrum—tend to do. "You know what all of this is?" I asked. "Just trappings. People are finally emerging from the selfishness of the Reagan era, and they want to act socially responsible again, but they don't know how to go about it. And you know what else I think? I think a lot of the people who are into being politically correct are the same ones who took up jogging and Cajun cooking and BMWs with a vengeance. It's something to do, and it makes them feel less guilty about having money."

Willie said, "Nice rant, McCone."

"Thank you."

Rae said, "Well, wasn't it just trappings back in the sixties, too? No, I guess not. The sixties were about peace and love and freedom—"

I interrupted her. "What the sixties were about was rage."

She stared at me, her expression shocked.

"Think about it," I told her. "SDS was formed because the students were enraged by what their elders were doing to the world, and particularly by the war in Asia. The Weatherman bombings: rage because the revolution hadn't come off as they'd hoped. You probably think of the Beatles as an upbeat symbol of the sixties, but have you ever really listened to the lyrics of songs like 'Happiness Is a Warm Gun' or 'Piggies'? Sheer rage at the establishment."

Hank said, "Shar's right. Our generation was raised to expect the good life. And then what did we get? The threat of annihilation by nuclear weapons. The assassinations of the Kennedys and King. An undeclared war whose origins were so complex that most of us had to take a history course to understand them. And it was us who were being drafted to fight it, while our elders feathered their nests with the proceeds of defense contracts. No wonder people were pissed."

Rae frowned, unwilling to give up her illusions. "But what about the Summer of Love? The hippies?"

"They were pissed, too. What better way to get back at the Establishment than by growing your hair down to your ass, dropping acid, and going to live in a commune?"

She was silent, her romantic visions shattered. I felt a little sorry for her.

Apparently Hank did, too, because he said, "You know, I think I have a copy of the Beatles' White Album around here someplace. Let's listen to it one last time. And then let's kiss the sixties good-bye. Frankly, I'm kind of sick of them."

He rooted through a big stack of LPs and put the two-record album on the stereo. It was scratched and tinny-sounding, but nostalgically familiar. For a while time rolled back for me, to the days of Rocky Raccoon, Sexy Sadie, and Bungalow Bill. And to "Helter Skelter," the song that had fueled Charles Manson's twisted imagination. When I finally heard the weirdly atonal strains of "Revolution 9," I thought, *Yes, that's what it was all about—rage.*

I looked up. Hank was watching me, reading my expression. He nodded in agreement, and I knew he was also wondering what that rage might have done to Perry Hilderly.

As soon as the record ended, Rae announced that she and Willie had better be going. He'd fallen asleep with his head on her lap five or six songs before, and she had to shake him awake. They thanked Hank and went down the stairs, Willie leaning heavily on her.

I took my half-full bowl into the kitchen,

dumped its contents down the disposer, and rinsed it before Hank could discover my lack of appreciation. Then I debated staying for another glass of wine, but thought better of the idea. Hank followed me into the hallway, and was just reaching for my coat when the sudden explosive noise came from the street below.

It sounded like a gunshot.

He froze, hand stretched toward the hall tree. Then a woman—Rae?—screamed outside.

I whirled and ran down the stairs. Yanked the door open and looked out.

Willie lay facedown on the sidewalk near the bottom of the steps. His arms were thrown over his head, and he was frighteningly still.

Eight

Rae was running toward Willie from the corner, where her old Rambler American was parked. Under the streetlight her face was white; her breath came in ragged gasps. I scanned the street, saw no one except people peering through the doors and windows of nearby houses. Then I rushed down the steps to where Rae was now bending over Willie.

As I knelt beside her, he groaned and uncovered his head. He wasn't wounded or hurt, I saw with relief. And when he struggled to sit up, I saw that he had been scared sober. Rae said, "Thank God you're all right!" and started to cry.

"Good thing old habits die hard," Willie said shakily. "I heard that bullet whine by and hit the dirt as fast as I ever did in 'Nam."

Footsteps came up behind me. Hank. "Anne-Marie's calling nine eleven," he said. "You okay, Willie?"

He nodded. "Help me up, would you?"

Slowly other residents of the street—some of them clad in nightclothes—had begun to come out of their houses and off their porches. They glanced around fearfully, afraid of more violence. A low murmur started and swelled to a clamor of questions and exclamations. I heard a man's voice say shakily, "Jesus, it must of been another of those random shootings!" As Hank and Rae got Willie to his feet, I asked the people near me what they'd seen. Most had only heard the shot, although one man had been standing at his front window and glimpsed a figure

108

running toward Church Street, where the J-line streetcars operate all night long.

Anne-Marie pushed through the crowd. "Was anybody hurt?"

"Willie's reflexes saved him," Hank said.

"Reflexes, hell! If I hadn't been drunk, I'd be dead right now. First time I ever got any benefit from *that*. I was real unsteady, so Rae went to get her car. Guess I staggered right when he squeezed off the shot. I heard that bullet up close before I hit the dirt; sucker couldn't of gone past more than a couple of inches from my head."

"*Who* fired at you?" I asked. "You get a look at him?"

Willie shook his head, then glanced at Rae and said, "Come on, honey, quit crying."

Rae wiped her eyes on her sleeve and grabbed his arm. He patted her hand absently.

"Did *you* see anyone?" I asked her.

She shook her head. "No, nothing."

"Willie, where was he?"

He gestured vaguely at the other side of the street.

"Can't you pinpoint it more exactly?"

"Christ, McCone, I was dogshit drunk!"

I looked over there, thinking of the random shootings—and of my earlier feeling of being watched. And of Hank's similar feeling at All Souls the previous week.

Anne-Marie suggested we wait for the police in her flat, then led us through the crowd, fishing her keys from her jeans pocket. Sirens were audible in the distance now.

I followed on Willie's heels. "Can you think of anyone who would want to take a shot at you?"

"No. Maybe. I don't know. I suppose somebody might of taken a dislike to one of my commercials." He meant the words humorously, but they came out flat.

"Well, you *are* something of a public figure."

Anne-Marie got the door open and we trooped inside.

"Willie," I said, "will you try to think—"

"McCone, just lay off. My mouth hurts, my head hurts, and now I'm gonna have to talk to the cops. You know how I feel about cops."

"But—"

"Just *lay off!*"

We went into Anne-Marie's living room. Willie collapsed on her pale yellow sofa and stuck his booted feet on the white French

110

Provincial coffee table. She didn't protest. Rae hovered behind the sofa.

I glanced at Willie. He had an odd expression on his face, as if remembering something disturbing. "McCone," he said, "come to think of it, I've had the feeling lately that somebody was following me."

"Did you actually see someone?"

"Nope. It's like I sense somebody's there, but when I look, nobody is."

"When? How often?"

"Couple of weeks now. Maybe six, seven times. Always at night."

"Where?"

"Outside my house, or All Souls when I go see Rae. I—"

There were footsteps on the porch. Hank and two uniformed officers entered. Reluctantly I stepped aside so they could speak with Willie.

By the time they finished getting preliminary information from all of us, the plainclothes team arrived. I wasn't surprised to see Greg Marcus, since he was heading the investigation into the snipings and had told me that morning that he'd been working long hours. He had an inspector named Bridges in tow, and looked as fresh and alert as if he were just beginning his day; Bridges

111

looked sleepy and cross. Although the set of Greg's mouth was grim when he entered the room, his lips twitched in amusement as he surveyed us.

"This is about as wretched as I've ever seen this crew," he said. "Can't you people even stay out of trouble when you're having a dinner party?"

Willie frowned, trying—I thought—to decide whether he ought to take offense at Greg's levity. Rae had no reservations on that score: she glared at him. From their expressions I knew that Anne-Marie and Hank shared my relief; Greg's comment had injected a note of normalcy into a frightening situation.

Quickly he turned to the uniformed men and instructed them to go outside and see if they could locate the bullet. Then he asked Anne-Marie, "Is there someplace where Inspector Bridges can take statements from you folks, while I talk privately with Willie?"

She nodded and motioned for Bridges to follow her. Hank and Rae went out behind him, Rae looking back over her shoulder at Willie as if she were afraid he might vanish in her absence. I lingered near the door.

"You, too," Greg told me.

"Can't I—"

"No."

I folded my arms and set my jaw.

"Don't look at me like that," he said. "You know I hate it when you look at me like that."

I remained where I was.

"Dammit, stay then. But don't interrupt. One interruption and you're out of here."

I nodded and sat down on a spindly chair by the window bay.

Greg sat next to Willie and began to question him about the shooting. Basically he asked what I had asked previously, and received similar replies. But when he came to the subject of people who might have wanted to harm him, Willie retreated into shrugs and near silence. It wasn't, I thought, that he didn't like Greg personally; Greg was also an old friend of Hank's, and that was enough to exempt him from Willie's general distrust of the police. It was more likely that he was embarrassed to mention anything as ephemeral as a feeling of being followed—bad for the macho image he likes to cultivate.

Finally I said, "Willie, tell him what you told me."

Greg glanced my way, eyes narrowing.

"I said I wouldn't interrupt, and I'm

not—neither of you is saying anything. Besides, this is important. Tell him, Willie."

Willie sighed and repeated what he'd said before.

When he finished, Greg looked thoughtful, rolling his ballpoint pen between his fingers. It was a gold Cross pen that I'd given him the first Christmas we'd been together, and the fact that he still used it touched me in an odd way.

Finally he said, "What's interesting here is that it's the first time we know of that the sniper's missed. *If* the person who shot at Willie is the one who did the other killings. I wonder if the four victims felt as if someone was stalking them."

"If someone *was* stalking them," I said, "what does that do to the theory that the killings are random?"

He shrugged. "Could be he just picks his victim and bides his time until he finds a good opportunity."

"But he also might have a motive—however irrational—for picking those particular victims."

"I'd like that better. It would give us more to work with."

Willie scowled. "What if he tries again?"

"We'll put a man on your house right away."

"I can't stay in my house the rest of my life!"

"Willie, we'll do what we can. For now, that's all I can promise you."

Willie nodded—still scowling—and got up. The way he strode out of the room made apparent his displeasure at what he interpreted as a too-casual attitude on Greg's part.

Greg said to me, "Where were you when the shot was fired?"

"Upstairs, in the hall."

"And you were the first person down on the street, I suppose."

"Unless you count Rae. She was at the corner when it happened, getting her car. She didn't see anything, she said."

"Did you?"

"No. But when I arrived around ten, I had the same feeling of being watched as Willie described. And Hank says he's had it, too—last week, at All Souls. And there's a link between Hank and one of the sniper's other victims." I explained about the Hilderly case.

Greg jotted down some notes as I spoke, then said, "I'll talk to Hank about this."

I remained sitting, studying him. Now

115

that the interview was over, he looked tired. He ran a hand over his gray-blond hair, rumpling it, and stretching his long legs out under the coffee table. Oddly enough I found I wasn't thinking about the sniping or its implications; I was thinking about how far Greg and I had come in the years we'd known each other—from adversaries, to lovers, to friends. Of the three, this latter stage suited us best.

I said, "I'm sorry if I kind of bullied you into letting me sit in."

He shrugged. "I'm used to your bullying by now. And as usual, you've done me a favor. Willie wouldn't have talked frankly without your prodding." He rubbed his eyes and added, "Send Hank in here, would you?"

I nodded and stood up.

"And if you remember anything later that you haven't told me, give me a call right away."

I nodded again.

"Or if Willie tells you anything he might not have wanted to mention in front of me."

Once again I nodded—I was beginning to feel like one of those tacky dashboard ornaments with its head on a spring—and backed out of the room.

When I arrived at All Souls at eight the next morning, Ted Smalley sat at his desk, tapping away on his computer keyboard. I checked the chalkboard for messages, then said, "You know, you really could have taken the day off."

Without stopping he replied, "I need to keep busy. Besides, I've got a law co-op to run. What with people being all excited and upset about last night's sniping, I've got my hands full."

Ted is convinced that All Souls would cease to function without his constant attention; half the time I suspect he's right.

I remained by the desk. After a moment Ted lifted his long-fingered hands from the keys and dropped them in his lap. "All right—what?"

"I'm sorry about Harry, and I'm here if you need me."

He nodded and briefly closed his eyes, compressing his lips. Despite his anglicized last name, Ted, a slender man with short black hair and a goatee, is of Russian-Jewish ancestry. His ascetic features make me think of a poet or composer, rather than an efficient and dedicated legal secretary. This morning they were honed fine by pain; his

117

skin had the waxy, translucent quality that comes from lack of sleep.

I went around the desk and gave him what I intended to be a brief hug, but sudden panic engulfed me and I clung tightly to his shoulders. What if Ted contracted AIDS? How could any of us bear that?

He seemed to sense my fear, because he patted my arm—the bereaved comforting the comforter—and said, "Don't worry. I'll be here to get your phone messages garbled when we're both in our dotage."

"At least you'll have a good excuse for it then." I released him and hurried upstairs.

My office is at the front of the second floor—a big room with a fireplace and a bay window that overlooks the flat, characterless sprawl of the Outer Mission district. I dumped my bag and briefcase on the new rose-colored chaise longue that I'd recently bought to replace my ratty old armchair, then took off my jacket and dropped it there, too. My original plan for the chaise had been as a place to lie down and relax while I thought through difficult cases. What I mainly did, however, was pile things on it. At the moment it also held a cardboard file box, a tape recorder, and my camera.

I went to the desk that stood in the window

bay and reached out to dial Hank on the intercom, then realized he'd said he would be in court until noon. "Damn!" I muttered, wishing I could talk to him now.

Before I'd left his flat the night before, I'd asked Hank if he thought the sniping might have been directed at him, as Hilderly's attorney—that Willie might have been mistaken for him in the dark. Perhaps Hilderly's killing *had* had some connection with him changing his will; perhaps the sniper thought Hank possessed more knowledge of Hilderly's doing so than he actually did.

But Hank had been adamant that there was no connection. The sniper striking where he had, he said, was merely a bizarre coincidence. After all, he pointed out, what possible connection could the other victims have with Hilderly?

It was a valid point, but I was unconvinced. And I thought Hank's insistence on sheer coincidence was more of a way of not dealing with a personally frightening aspect of what had begun as a simple probate of an estate. I would have liked to ask him if he still felt so certain in the sane light of morning.

After a moment I stopped brooding about it and removed a handful of files that had appeared in my In box since Friday: background checks on two prospective employees for a small security firm that Larry Koslowski, the health nut, represented; a request for surveillance on a clerk thought to be stealing and reselling merchandise from a liquor-store client; a list of points needing clarification from an interview I'd conducted with a witness to an industrial accident at another client's dry-cleaning plant. I put the surveillance job aside for Rae. She liked getting out into the field, but most of the routine tasks she handled didn't permit that; this would be a chance for her to spread her wings. Then I put in a call to Gene Carver, Hilderly's former employer at Tax Management Corporation, hoping to ask him about the seminar Hilderly had attended in May and later described to his son Kurt as having had a profound effect on his life. Carver, however, was out of town; his secretary said he would call back later in the week.

Finally—in order not to dwell on the events of the night before—I began to work through the other files: telephoning, checking and rechecking facts. When my intercom buzzed for the first time that morning, I was surprised to see it was nearly ten.

"Tracy Miller on line three," Ted said.

"Thanks." Tracy is my friend at the DMV, who—in exchange for lunches, dinners, and an occasional free ticket to a play or a concert—cuts the red tape by running names through her computer for me. I punched the flashing button. "Hi, how you doing?"

"Better than you, I'm sure. That was a hell of a thing you were involved in last night."

The *Chronicle* had been full of news of the city's apparent fifth sniping this morning, and Willie's picture had been prominently featured on the front page. "Sure was. I'll tell you all about it the next time we get together."

"Good. Listen, your assistant's on another line, and since I know this information's for you, I thought I'd pass it on directly. We show no driver's license or vehicle registration for David Arlen Taylor, but I came up with an address on Libby Heikkinen Ross. Post-office box in Inverness over in West Marin, and an address on Pierce Point Road there."

I took them both down and reminded Tracy that I owed her a dinner for various favors done over the past couple of months. She promised to check her calendar and call me back on the weekend. After I replaced the receiver, I swiveled around and stared out the window at the gray-shrouded flatlands.

I knew Inverness, more or less. It was a picturesque country town with a population of no more than a few hundred, nestled between heavily wooded hills and the marshes of Tomales Bay, not far from the Point Reyes National Seashore. One of its chief attractions was a Czechoslovakian restaurant where a former lover and I had taken refuge during a downpour one long-ago October night, warming ourselves by the woodstove and drinking slivovitz with the proprietor. In a place like Inverness, Libby Heikkinen Ross would not be difficult to locate.

I swiveled around again and dialed Rae's extension on the intercom. When she answered, I asked, "How's Willie this morning?"

"I was just talking to him. He's so pleased with his newfound celebrity that he's even forgotten his jaw hurts. KPIX is sending somebody out to interview him for the six o'clock news, and I think he's having visions of stardom."

"God forbid that his head should get any more swelled. Look, I've got an address for

Ross over in West Marin, so I'll probably be gone for most of the day. They didn't have anything on Taylor, but I want you to hold off on checking out-of-county Vital Statistics; there's a chance Ross might know his whereabouts."

"I guess I'll just cover here, then." Rae sounded disappointed at not getting out of the office.

"Only for a while. I need you to finish up a background investigation I've started for one of Larry's clients. But then we've got a surveillance job, starts at noon when the subject comes on shift at Lloyd's Liquors. I'll drop both files by your office on the way out."

"A surveillance job? For *me?*" Now she sounded elated.

I knew how she felt. The prospect of a drive to West Marin had raised my own spirits measurably.

Nine

The western part of Marin County is a world in itself, a spectacularly endowed strip of coast and countryside that has as yet managed to escape the ravages of industrial growth, overpopulation, and tourism. Much of this has to do with the weather, which is often foggy and cold; other factors are the sluggish economy and lack of jobs, coupled with the long, inconvenient commute across the ridge of hills that separates West Marin from the rest of the county. The presence of some sixty large dairy ranches guarantees that a good deal of acreage will be devoted to agricultural use; the Point Reyes National Seashore and Golden Gate National Recreation Area further ensure that much of the land will remain as it was when the Miwok Indians roamed it, before the Spanish incursions of the early nineteenth century.

Up to now my experience with West Marin had been of the ordinary tourist nature: picnics at the Seashore, a tour of the Point Reyes lighthouse, oysters at Nick's Cove, Sunday drives on two-lane roads through the dairylands, and—of course—the Czech restaurant. I'd even once spent the night at the Olema Inn, a former stage stop in a hamlet of less than one hundred people, but by and large my knowledge of the area was gleaned from newspaper features and the California history course that every public-school student is force-fed before graduating. Although I'd heard tales of insularity and occasional hostility toward strangers from east of the hills, I'd had no direct experience with it, nor had I had any real personal contact with the residents.

I drove out that day on a country road that crested White's Hill beyond Fairfax. The topography was softly rolling, with frequent outcroppings of gray rock that rose like cairns from the sun-bleached grass. Gnarled live oak clustered in the gullies or stood lone and wind-bent on the hillsides. At Olema the road crossed Coast Highway One and continued toward Inverness.

The highway skirted the marshland at the southeast end of Tomales Bay. Although it had been sunny and warm in what I thought of as Marin proper, fog hung still and thick above the tule grass; it lurked in the hollows of the heavily forested hills, and I caught the smell of woodsmoke from the fireplaces of homes that were occasionally visible through the foliage. Buckeye trees were in full pink bloom, and wildflowers and white anise grew along the sides of the road. Buildings appeared here and there—a grocery, a pottery studio, the ubiquitous antique stores and real-estate offices. A sign indicated a salt-marsh wildlife refuge; when I looked toward it, I saw a trio of white long-necked cranes standing placidly among the reeds.

After a few miles I reached Inverness itself: a post office that shared a pale blue Victorian building with a pizza parlor; the Czech restaurant and a couple of other small eateries; a few shops that seemed mainly designed to cater to the tourist trade; a Chevron station. I pulled into the station, got out of the MG, and located a man in a heavy plaid jacket who was staring glumly under the hood of a beat-up Toyota. There were cables attached to the car's battery, but the meter on the recharging machine indicated nothing was happening. The man turned away with a discouraged shrug and saw me.

"Help you, ma'am?"

"I hope so." I held out a piece of paper on which I'd written Libby Ross's address. "Can you tell me how to get here?"

He studied it, frowning. "Don't go much by house numbers out there. Who're you looking for?"

"Libby Ross."

He smiled; from the way it touched his eyes, I could tell he liked the woman. "What you want is Moon Ridge Stables. Stay on the main road here, follow it along the water and up the hill past the sign for the Seashore. A

126

ways beyond that the road'll fork; you keep to the right—that's Pierce Point. Libby's place is just this side of Abbotts Lagoon—four, maybe four and a half miles. Big place down in the hollow, with cypress all around it."

"What is it—a riding stable?"

"Sort of. Libby rents horses to tourists, leads pack trips to the Seashore." His expression sharpened with small-town curiosity. "Guess you don't know her personal."

"Not yet. Thanks for the directions." I smiled at him and went back to the MG.

As instructed, I continued along the road. It hugged the shore of the bay, where there were cottages with long docks extending out into the gray, choppy water. I saw a motel, a yacht club, a barbecue restaurant, and a rather bizarre house with turrets that reminded me of a Greek Orthodox church. Then the road began to wind uphill through a conifer forest; I swerved sharply coming around a curve, to avoid a pair of joggers. Shortly after the sign for the Point Reyes National Seashore appeared, the road forked; Pierce Point veered to the right, toward McClure's Beach.

Within a mile the countryside flattened to

dairy graze. Cows stood in clumps or stared stupidly at the road through the fences. Vegetation became sparser—mainly yellow gorse and flowering thistles. The land stretched toward bluffs that overlooked the distant sea and bay, its barrenness broken only by clusters of ranch buildings. Although I encountered a few bicyclists and several other cars, the desolation overwhelmed me, flattening my spirits; I wondered what this place would be like in the dark of a moonless night.

When I'd traveled a little under four miles, I came to a sharp bend in the road and caught my first unobstructed view of the Pacific, breakers crashing onto a sand beach. A backwater extended inland, cut off now at low tide. Its motionless surface mirrored the somber sky. Abbotts Lagoon, I supposed.

I came out of the hairpin turn and pulled into an overlook. Below me the land dropped away steeply, then sloped gently to the lagoon. Tucked into a hollow between two cypress-covered knolls was a collection of buildings—white, and small as toys from this vantage. I drove about twenty yards further before I spotted a weathered sign for the Moon Ridge Stables. A rutted dirt drive-way led away through the pastureland.

I followed it, avoiding the deeper pot-holes. As I neared the first grove of cypress I saw a long, low house tucked under them, its paint mostly scoured off by the elements. The drive continued through more pasture-land, and then I came to a paddock where a half dozen motley-looking horses huddled by an empty feed rack; beyond it was a weath-ered barn and various other outbuildings. Two heavily bundled riders straddled a pair of pintos directly in front of the barn door, and a woman squatted beside one, checking the saddle girth. When she heard my car, she glanced over her shoulder at it, then went on with what she was doing. All I could make out about her was longish curly dark blond hair.

I brought the MG to a stop next to the paddock's rail fence. When I got out, the wind buffeted me, strong and bitterly cold even in this protected place. The woman straightened, wiping her palms on the thighs of her faded jeans. After a few words with her, the riders started off toward a bridle path that snaked under the trees in the di-rection of the lagoon.

The woman turned and came toward me,

moving in a long, athletic stride. She was tall and rangy, with a generous mouth and startling violet eyes. Although she was only in her forties, her skin was as weathered as the paint on the barn, but the lines and furrows gave an odd attractiveness to what otherwise would have been a plain face.

"Hello," she called in a husky voice. "What can I do for you?"

I moved around the MG. "I'm looking for Libby Heikkinen Ross."

The woman slowed, a wariness entering her eyes. "That's me."

"You the owner?" I gestured around us.

"Owner and sole employee, unless you count my worthless stepson and the kid who cleans out the stalls." Her tone was friendly but guarded. She stopped, folding her arms across the front of her blue down jacket.

I went up to her and handed her one of my cards. She studied it, then said flatly, "Is this about Dick?"

"Dick?"

"My stepson, the useless little bastard."

"No." A sudden blast of cold air rushed down from the knoll behind us, whipping my jacket open. "Is there someplace warmer where we can talk?"

She nodded curtly and led me toward the

130

barn. There was a shed attached to one side of it—a tack room. Saddles rested on pegs along three walls, bridles and halters hanging from hooks above them. Each was labeled with an individual horse's name: Chaucer, Shakespeare, Dickens, Molière. Ross obviously had a literary bent.

A bench ran along the wall next to the door, a wooden desk wedged into the corner. Ross scooped a pile of saddle blankets from the bench and motioned for me to sit. A tortoiseshell cat that had been sleeping behind the blankets looked up in mild annoyance.

As I sat, Ross took the desk chair for herself, propping her sneakered feet on the blotter. The tortoiseshell recognized a cat lover and jumped into my lap. It curled into a ball, the purr motor starting immediately. I stroked it, feeling vaguely ill at ease—unwilling to awaken the old feeling of comfort that a cat in the lap engenders.

Ross said, "So what is it?"

"Do you know a man named Perry Hilderly?"

Her reaction was totally unlike Goodhue's or Grant's. Surprise spread across her face, mingled with a bittersweet pleasure. "Yes," she said eagerly. "What about him?"

"He died last month."

The pleased expression faded. ". . . I didn't know that. How?"

"He was killed by a sniper, in San Francisco. Haven't you seen anything about the random shootings in the papers or on TV?"

She shook her head. "I don't have a TV, and I don't take a paper. Suppose that sounds strange in this day and age, but when I came out here I wanted to keep the rest of the world at bay. So far, I've pretty much succeeded."

"Why is that?"

She didn't say anything at first, merely studied her fingernails, which were filed nearly to the quick. Finally she shrugged. "There's nothing but pain in the world. My husband and I built ourselves a safe cocoon here on the ranch. Now that he's gone I value it all the more."

I wondered what had happened to hurt them so badly, but was afraid she would close up if I asked. "I see. Well, the reason I'm here is that shortly before he died, Perry Hilderly made a will leaving you a fourth of his estate—about a quarter of a million dollars."

She looked up, violet eyes widening. "Why?"

132

"I don't know. Can you tell me?"

She shook her head.

"Mrs. Ross, do you know Thomas Y. Grant?"

"Who? No—name's not familiar."

"What about Jess Goodhue?"

"No."

"Jenny Ruhl?"

She took her feet off the desk and grasped the arms of the chair, as if to keep from jumping up. "Jenny . . . Jenny's been dead for years."

"Yes, but her daughter's alive—Jess Goodhue."

"I remember she had a baby, Jessica. Where did she get that last name?"

"It's adoptive. Jess Goodhue is another beneficiary of Hilderly's will, as is Tom Grant. Goodhue thinks Hilderly may have been her father."

A peculiar smile came to Ross's lips— twisted, bitter. "I can assure you he wasn't. He most *certainly* was not."

"Who was?"

She hesitated. "All I can say is that it wasn't Perry."

"But you don't want to say why you're so sure?"

"No."

"What was your relationship to Hilderly and Jenny Ruhl?"

Another long silence. "Jenny and I went to grade school together. Perry and I went back a long way, too. But I haven't heard from him in years, and I'm very surprised that he would leave me money." She looked around the dreary, drafty tack room. "Not that I can't use it. I'm barely holding things together here since Glen died."

"Glen was your husband?"

She nodded. "Maybe you've heard of him—former wide receiver with the Rams?"

I shook my head.

Ross sighed. "Well, it *was* a long time ago. Glen got mixed up in the high life—blew a couple of marriages, a lot of money, his career. Took what was left and came up here, looking for property. I met him while I was working in a real-estate office in Tomales. We made our own world out here, and not a bad one at that."

"Mrs. Ross," I said after a moment, "please tell me about your relationship to Hilderly. It's important—"

"Do I need to, in order to claim the inheritance?"

"No. It's clear that you're the Libby Heikkinen named in his will, and his wishes will be carried out."

"In that case, I don't want to talk about it. It's past history—long past, and much too sad."

I switched to a different tack. "There was a fourth beneficiary whom I've been unable to locate—David Arlen Taylor. Can you tell me where—"

"D. A.?" Again she looked surprised; then the bitter smile returned. "Sure I can tell you. He's where he's been the past fifteen years, where he'll be until he dies—over on the other side of the bay."

"Tomales Bay?"

"Uh-huh. His family owns a restaurant and oyster beds a mile or two up the highway from Nick's Cove."

"Is he a friend of yours?"

She seemed to consider. "We're . . . something like that. I came up here in the first place because I thought I could help D. A. Took me four damn years to realize there wasn't anything that was going to help. Then I married Glen down in San Francisco, where he was waiting for me to make up my mind. For years I've had a life of sorts. But I'm still here for D. A. He knows where to find me, if he needs me."

"What's wrong with him, that he needs help?"

She pulled out the lower drawer of the desk and propped her feet on it, obviously more at ease with the subject of Taylor than Hilderly or Ruhl. "D. A.'s a substance abuser," she said. "He'll use anything that takes the edge off. Generally it's alcohol, grass. Pills or crack when he can get them. Coke or ice when he can afford it."

"Do you know why?"

"I know, but it's not worth talking about. In a way his reasons are the same ones that keep me out here with only the wind and my memories for company. But at least I tried to rejoin the world—for a while. D. A. never did."

"What do you mean—rejoin the world?"

She shrugged. "Just a figure of speech. It's funny with D. A.: he got married about six years ago. Nice wife. A lot younger than him. She's Miwok—so is he, partly. Lots of Indians around here." She paused, studying my face. "Come to think of it, you look like you've got some Indian blood, too."

"Only an eighth. Shoshone. About D. A.?"

"Well, he and his wife have a little boy and girl. Cute kids. You would have thought it'd change things for him, but it didn't. He's still the same old D. A."

"He must be special to you, that you moved here to try to help him."

"Yeah, well, maybe I needed to help myself."

I remained silent, sensing that if I asked what she meant I would just get another shrug. Outside, the wind baffled around the building, setting loose shingles to rattling above our heads. The cat stirred, stood up and arched its back in a stretch, circled, then settled down again.

Finally I asked, "Are you sure you don't know Thomas Y. Grant?"

"Like I said, the name's not familiar. But it's a common one; maybe I've forgotten him. Who is he?"

"A lawyer, in San Francisco. Specializes in divorce work for men only."

"Oh, one of those. Describe him, would you?"

"He's in his early fifties, I'm told, but looks younger. Tall, well built, thick gray hair, handsome, except for a scar on his left cheek that reminds me of something out of *The Student Prince*."

When I mentioned the scar, Ross didn't react as dramatically as she had to Jenny

Ruhl's name, but there was a tightening in the lines around her mouth. "This Grant lives in San Francisco?"

"Yes."

"Where? Is he well off?"

The question puzzled me, but I said, "He must be. He has a house on Lyon Street in Pacific Heights. And the law firm's a big one, with offices in other cities."

"And on top of that he inherits money from Perry. Coals to Newcastle, I'd say."

I watched her, wondering if I'd imagined her reaction to the description of Grant. After a moment she added, "Not that the money's going to do D. A. any good, either. Unless Mia gets her hands on it fast, it'll all go up his nose."

"Mia's his wife?"

"Yeah. You planning to go over there?"

"Right after I leave here."

"Well, try to talk to Mia first, if she's there. No telling what condition D. A.'s in from day to day."

I nodded, but remained sitting, understandably reluctant to rush into what promised to be an unpleasant situation. Besides, I wasn't sure I'd gotten all I could from Ross. Possibly—if I steered clear of the subject of Hilderly or Ruhl—she might open up to me.

I said, "Your land here—is it part of the National Seashore?"

"Yeah. I've got it on long-term lease. The government encourages dairy ranching, for aesthetic and economic reasons."

"Dairy ranching? I thought—"

"The stable doesn't turn a profit; I only keep it going because I love horses. The dairy business I contract out to the neighbor to the east. It keeps a roof over my head and food on the table, but that's about it. Glen loved it here; sometimes I think that's why I stay on." But Ross, in spite of the fact that she must be lonely for company, didn't seem eager for further conversation. She stood, stretching her rangy body much as the cat had stretched its furry one. "When you go see D. A., don't—well, don't take anything he says too seriously."

"What do you think he might say?"

"God knows. The man's off in another world, has been for years. He . . . well, you know what that kind of abuse can do to a person's mind." She reached down and took the cat off my lap, a clear hint.

As we walked toward my car, Ross said, "What do I have to do to claim the money?"

"Nothing. Hilderly's attorney is going to

enter the will into probate, and he'll contact you."

"Good. Like I said, I can damn well use it."

When we reached the MG, however, Ross suddenly seemed unwilling to let me go. She leaned against it, cradling the cat to her down jacket and staring out over the headland toward the lagoon. The two riders who had been here earlier had reached the end of the trail and sat on their mounts beside the glassy water. The pintos' mottled coats were reflected on its surface.

"That lagoon," Ross said, "it's named for a man who ran cattle on this land back in the mid eighteen hundreds—Carlyle Abbott. The story is that Abbott was a heroic type. A ship—the *Sea Nymph*—was wrecked out there off the coast in eighteen sixty-one. Abbot tied himself to some bystanders with lariats and went into the surf after the crew. Saved them all, except for the ship's steward. Steward was the first recorded drowning victim off Point Reyes."

She paused, gaze fixed on the distance. "I'm not much on history, but that story's always stuck with me. Guess I find it symbolic. I came out here to save D. A., but I couldn't. Now *he's* sort of a drowning victim."

Ten

As I retraced my route to Highway One, I went over my interview with Libby Ross. The more I thought about it, the more convinced I became that she had recognized Tom Grant from my description. Perhaps if I played it right with D. A. Taylor he would not only reveal more about the connection among Ross, Hilderly, Ruhl, and himself, but also tell me something about Grant—provided he wasn't too far gone to remember.

At the highway I turned north toward Point Reyes Station, once a stop on the long-defunct North Pacific Coast Railroad that operated between Duncan's Mills and Sausalito from the late 1800s to the Great Depression. Most of the buildings lining its main street are of turn-of-the-century vintage, and the town has a rustic feel that belies the presence of its Pulitzer Prize-winning newspaper, *The Point Reyes Light*. As I passed through it I saw signs of progress since my last visit—spruced-up older build-

141

ings and a number of new ones, including a small shopping center where the *Light* had moved its offices. I couldn't help but wonder how long it would be before the surrounding hills became covered with tracts. The dairy ranches that I passed on the other side of town looked profitable, however; perhaps the demand for their products would outstrip even the greed of real-estate developers and the influx of those seeking escape from urban pressures.

The winding road led me inland, then back to the bay, which was mostly mud flats at this end. Oyster beds began to appear—geometrically arranged rows of stakes poking up from the water, within which the seed mollusks feed and grow, protected from predators. Oystering, I knew, was the only real industry besides dairy ranching in the Tomales Bay area, and I saw signs that it was not a particularly thriving one. I passed an oyster farm that was up for sale; a medium-sized boat yard with fishing craft in dry dock seemed strangely deserted. In the tiny hamlet of Marshall, the oyster restaurant was closed, its broken windows boarded. Cottages—most of them old-fashioned clapboard, but also a few of those oddly angled structures with windows in

142

strange places that people seem compelled to build near the water—stood on the narrow strip of land between the road and the drop-off to the bay. When I passed Nick's Cove, my favorite restaurant for fried oysters, the road began to wind uphill through a thick stand of wind-warped cypress. I consulted my odometer.

In a little less than two miles a faded sign supported by two tall poles appeared: TAYLOR'S OYSTERS. A crushed-shell driveway angled down the slope from the road and ended in a parking lot. I turned the MG and bounced through ruts and potholes.

The parking lot looked like a junkyard: there were dead cars pulled over to one side in a field of straggly anise weed; a couple of rusted trailers with laundry lines strung between them sat next to a mound of oyster shells that spilled down the hillside like tailings from an abandoned mine. Old machinery, truck axles, a corroded automobile engine, and two rotted-out rowboats were strewn about, and among them lay three of the mangiest mongrel dogs I'd ever laid eyes on. The restaurant was straight ahead on the water's edge.

I pulled up in front of the sagging gray-white frame building, between an old red pickup truck that looked like something out of *The Grapes of Wrath* and a newish camper with Oregon plates. The windows of the restaurant were coated with so much grime that it dulled the lighted Coors and Oly signs. I got out of the car, leaning into the crisp wind from offshore, and looked around.

To the left of the restaurant was a path that led past a row of tiny cottages—possibly a defunct tourist court. Their rooflines sagged, their metal chimneys tilted, and many of the windows were covered with plywood or patched with cardboard and tape. More dogs lounged on the path, their matted fur riffling in the breeze. A small boy and smaller girl were playing at the foot of another mound of shells; their voices were borne to me on the wind—cheerful, despite their dismal surroundings.

I went over to the kids and squatted down, smiling. They regarded me solemnly. Both had black hair and dark shoe-button eyes; their clothing, while old and patched, was clean. They couldn't have been more than five and six. I said, "Hi, what're your names?"

The girl stuck her finger into her mouth and merely stared. The boy—who was the older of the two—finally spoke. "That's Mia. I'm Davey."

D. A. Taylor's children, then. People who name their offspring after themselves always make me wonder. Too much ego, or too little? In Taylor's case, I thought I knew.

Remembering Ross's caution that I should try to talk to Mia Taylor before approaching her husband, I asked, "Is your mom around?"

Davey shook his head. Mia Junior took her finger out of her mouth and said, "She went to Petaluma with Aunt Chrissy. Aunt Chrissy's having a baby, maybe right now."

"Well, that's nice," I lied, feeling a flash of sympathy for the newborn who would be brought home to this place. "Is your dad here, then?"

The two exchanged a look. It said, *Daddy. Uh-oh.*

I said, "It's okay. Do you know Mrs. Ross?"

Davey nodded. "Libby."

"I'm a friend of Libby's. She asked me to come see your dad." My job necessitates a fair amount of fabrication, but I'm always vaguely uncomfortable when I have to do so to children.

Mia and Davey exchanged another look.

145

This was the "can we trust this adult?" one. Finally Davey pointed toward the row of cottages. "Ours is at the end."

"Thank you." I got up and started down the path.

I hadn't gone more than a couple of yards when two men materialized from the first cottage. Heavyset men with shaggy black hair, wearing the oilskins of fishermen. They stood together, blocking my way.

"What you want, lady?" the heavier one asked.

"D. A. Taylor. Are either of you him?"

Silently they shook their heads and remained in front of me.

"Look, Libby Ross sent me."

"Sure she did," the man said.

"Call her and ask her if you don't believe me."

"Why would that bitch send somebody?" the other man, who sported a straggly mustache, asked. "She checking up on D. A. again?"

"No. I don't think she's too interested in him these days. She told me where to find him, though."

"What's your business with him?"

"Private."

"D. A.'s family. What's *his* business is ours."

I hesitated, glancing back at Taylor's children. They had not resumed their play, were watching intently. I didn't think the men—their uncles, or whatever—would do anything violent in front of them. Finally I said, "If that's so, why don't you come with me while I talk with him?"

They exchanged a look; it seemed to be the primary mode of communication around here. This one I couldn't read so easily, but it contained an element of relaxation. After a few seconds the heavier man stepped aside. "What the hell—go ahead. Last cottage. You'll probably find him on his dock, staring at his island."

"His island?"

He grinned nastily. "Hog Island. D. A. don't really own it, but he's got it into his head that he does. He's never owned nothing, except in his head. And that's about *all* that's in there anymore."

Some family D. A.'s got, I thought, moving past the men and walking along the crushed-shell path. I heard the two laugh, as if the remark had been terribly witty, but I ignored them. The dogs ignored me as I stepped over and around them.

147

Toward the end of the path the land came to a barren point, a rubble-strewn slope falling away to the wind-whipped gray water. I could see the island from here—rocky, cypress-and eucalyptus-crowned, treetops wreathed in fog. Hog Island—reputedly named for a barge-load of pigs that had briefly been marooned there at some dim point in history—was now owned and maintained in its natural state by the Audubon Society. No one lived there, and the only man-made addition was the ruins of a house built by a German family in the 1800s. I wondered why D. A. Taylor took such a proprietary interest in the iso-lated wildlife preserve.

Taylor's tiny cottage was the shabbiest of the seven I'd passed, with broken and patched windows and virtually no paint, but a tub of pink geraniums stood next to the door. There was an old tricycle parked be-side the flowers. I knocked on the torn screen door, received no answer, and went around the cottage to where a spindly dock leaned over the stakes of the oyster beds.

A man—tall, thin, with black hair that fell to the shoulders of his faded denim jacket—sat at the very end of the dock, look-ing across the bay toward Hog Island. I started out to him, stepping over and around places where the boards were splintered or missing. The dock trembled under my weight. The man turned his head and watched me approach.

At first he appeared perfectly normal, but when I came within a few yards of him I saw his eyes. They were black and dead-looking —pits where the fires no longer burned, containing nothing but ash. When I reached him he didn't speak, merely continued to watch me without a hint of interest or curiosity. I asked, "Are you D. A. Taylor?" and he nodded and looked back at the bay.

The man was in another world, as Ross had said he would be. I didn't know if that particular place was accessible to others, but I had to try to reach him. I sat down on the edge of the dock, drawing my knees up and hugging them with my arms. Taylor didn't even glance my way.

I said, "That's a nice island out there."

No reply.

"Wonder what it would be like to live on it."

Now he turned his strange eyes toward me. I thought I saw a flicker somewhere in their depths, but it could just have been a trick of the light. "Someday I'll know," he said. His voice was mellow, the syllables flowing gently.

"Oh? You planning to move out there?"

Again he looked toward the island. After a long moment he said, "Who are you?"

"My name's Sharon McCone. I've just come from Libby Ross's."

"Libby. Libby of the beautiful violet eyes." He paused, then added, "Libby of the evil tongue."

"The way she tells it, you and she are friends."

"Friends can be cruel when they tell the truth." After my encounter with his relatives, his educated, somewhat formal diction was more of a surprise than his sudden lucidity. I'd known other people like Taylor: substance abusers who seemed perfectly rational at one moment, then could flip over into disconnected raving or protracted silences the next.

"What does Libby tell the truth about?" I asked.

Silence.

I let it spin out a few moments, watching a fishing boat circumnavigate the island. Smells rose from the oyster beds—brackish, fishy—and were borne away on the chill

150

breeze. Finally I said, "What about Perry Hilderly—was he a truth teller, too?"

Taylor turned his head slowly. This time I could see that the flicker in his eyes was real. "Perry believed implicitly in the truth. He had high ideals. He placed the sanctity of life above all else. I looked up to him and loved him like a brother. He was a better man than I. Than any of us."

"And Jenny Ruhl?"

I hadn't thought anything could alter his trancelike state, but at my mention of the name, a wave of pain crossed his face. "Jenny. All these years dead. It was so unnecessary. All of it was so unnecessary."

"All of what?"

He looked down at his fingers, which were splayed against his denim-covered thighs.

"What about Tom Grant?" I asked.

"Who's that?"

"You don't remember him? Thomas Y. Grant?"

"I don't. There's a great deal I don't remember anymore. But it's the wrong things that stay with me. Always the wrong things."

"Bad things?"

"Very bad. No matter what, I can't shake them."

"Tell me about them."

He shook his head violently, long straight locks flaring out, then falling back to his shoulders.

Before he could close up completely, I returned to the subject of Hog Island. "When do you plan to go there?" I asked, gesturing toward it.

His gaze followed my hand. "When it becomes too much here. So far I'm all right. You know I drink?"

"Yes."

"Of course Libby would tell you. She also told you about the drugs. That's all quite true. She despairs of me, but she understands. My wife doesn't understand; her despair is painful to watch. When it becomes too painful, then I'll go."

"And do what there?"

"Be at peace."

It dawned on me that the man wasn't talking about becoming a hermit. Or about *living* on the island at all. He meant to kill himself out there. Despite the fact that I barely knew him, a coldness clutched at me. I pictured his children: their young-old faces, their shared conspiratorial looks. What would his suicide do to them, to the wife I'd yet to meet? To Libby Ross, who pretended to have washed her hands of D. A. Taylor, but in reality cared too much?

I watched him wordlessly for a moment, studied his rugged, hawk-nosed profile, wondered what had made him this way. As if he could hear my unvoiced question, he said, "I've never been a strong man. But I'm not insane, at least in any classical sense. I just slip in and out of touch with reality. Out is better."

"Why, D. A.?"

"Why not?"

I could find no reply to that.

After a moment he said, "I suppose you saw Harley and Jake on your way in."

"The men in the first cottage?"

"My cousins. My self-appointed caretakers. When Mia's gone, it's their duty to watch over old D. A., make sure he doesn't do anything crazy. There has been trouble with the sheriff, you see. Trouble with the customers at the restaurant. Did they try to stop you from coming out here?"

"Yes."

"What did you do to convince them otherwise?"

"Damned if I know."

Taylor actually smiled—a brief upturning of the corners of his mouth. "They probably decided you looked as if you could take care of yourself. And they know I'm not really violent, just bizarre and unpredictable. I insist to Harley and Jake that I actually own Hog Island. They're convinced I believe that. I've always had a perverse streak when it comes to my cousins. Stupidity brings it out."

"Are they stupid?"

"Moderately. My father's side of the family never had too much going for it. Their capacity to choose smart, strong women is all that's allowed them to survive." Again the small smile flickered. "Listen to me. I claim to be so smart, but what have I ever done right but marry Mia? And now I'm destroying her, little bit by little bit."

I decided to let that issue go for now. "You're well educated. Where did you go to school?"

"U.C. Berkeley—in its Golden Age." His wry expression made me think of Hank's when we'd spoken of those days.

"I went there myself, but several years later. Was that where you met Perry Hilderly and Jenny Ruhl?"

He nodded.

"Libby, too?"

"Yes."

"But you still don't remember Tom Grant."

He considered. "No, not even now, and I'm much more clear-headed than when you came out here."

"Let me describe him: he's a tall man, well built. Thick gray hair, but it would probably have been brown back then. Handsome, but he has a scar on his left cheek. I told Libby it looks like something he got in a duel—"

Taylor's face went very pale, then flushed. His eyes came alive, fires rekindling in those previously dead pits. He put his hand on my forearm, grasping it hard enough to create five small epicenters of pain.

He said, "Right man!"

I grabbed his fingers, trying to ease their pressure. "What?"

"Right man!"

"*Who* was the right man?"

"The right man," he said for the third time. He laughed bitterly, the sound harsh, as if his vocal cords had not been used for any kind of laughter in years. "The right man was the wrong man."

"I don't understand."

Abruptly he let go of my arm and slumped

155

forward, staring down at the brackish water of the oyster beds. "Neither do I," he said.

"Who was the right man?" I asked again.

He didn't reply; his breath came fast and ragged.

I touched his arm. "D. A.?"

He remained silent for several minutes, his breathing gradually returning to normal. When he raised his head and looked at me, his eyes were as dead as before.

Formally he said, "Thank you for coming. Please give my regards to Libby." Then he returned his gaze to the distant island.

Eleven

Taylor had withdrawn behind an impenetrable psychic wall, so I left him and made my way back toward the restaurant. Neither his children nor his cousins were in evidence; the dogs still lay on the path, and they still ignored me. The red pickup and the camper with Oregon plates were gone; my car looked to be the only one in the lot that was actually capable of running.

I went up to the restaurant and stepped inside. It was one big room with smeary, salt-caked windows overlooking another sagging dock. Four tables stood by the windows, and more were aligned between them and the door; their oilcloth coverings didn't look any too clean, and a large black cat slept on one. A bar ran along the right-hand wall, and the mustached cousin sat behind it, reading a racing form. A skinny red-haired waitress slumped on one of the barstools, drinking beer from the bottle. Neither appeared to notice me.

I slipped onto the stool in front of the man. He didn't look up, but asked, "You find D. A.?"

"Yes."

"You see why we worry about him?"

"He didn't seem that bad."

He raised his head, frowning. "You don't know. You didn't know him before." He laughed cynically. "Big intellectual, head of his class, college scholarship, when the rest of us didn't even get to finish high school. Now look at him—all fucked up."

"What happened to him?"

"I think we'll keep that a family secret."

"Suit yourself." I took one of my cards from my bag. "Are you Jake or Harley?"

He seemed taken aback that I knew names. "Harley," he said after a moment.

"When's Mia due back?"

"Whenever my wife gets done having her baby."

"Your wife's having a baby, and you're not with her?"

He shrugged. "Chrissy's had three others, she can manage without me."

My earlier sympathy for the newborn, I decided, was fully justified. I pushed the card across the sticky surface of the bar and said, "When Mia gets back, ask her to call me—collect—please."

Harley glanced at it, his eyes narrowing slightly. "What's your business with D. A. and Mia?"

"I told you before, it's private."

"And I told *you* before, they're family."

"If either of them wants you to know, they'll tell you."

He picked up the card and tore it in half. "You don't tell me, Mia don't call you."

I reined in my rising anger, took another card from my bag, and placed it on the bar. "If Mia doesn't call me, you'll never know what I want with them, now will you?"

Harley pushed his jaw out belligerently and glanced indecisively at the card. Then he went back to his racing form, leaving the card untouched where I'd put it.

As I went out, the waitress winked at me

and made a circle with her thumb and fore-finger.

The drive back to the city seemed endless —possibly because the list of questions running through my mind was also endless. Something had happened a long time ago, probably in the sixties at Berkeley, that had welded Hilderly, Ross, Taylor, and Ruhl together—the chains that linked them transcending years, distance, and even death. Something to do with the Free Speech Movement, I supposed. Jess Goodhue had told me her mother had gotten into trouble over something associated with the protests shortly before she killed herself. What? Had it also involved Hilderly, Taylor, or Ross? That didn't seem right; Ruhl had died in 1969, and Hilderly was probably in Vietnam by then. And what had Grant to do with it all—a man whom both Ross and Taylor seemed to recognize but would not own up to knowing? And what was this about the right man? Right man for what?

As I approached the Golden Gate Bridge, the traffic coming from the city slowed to a near standstill. Then the traffic on my side of the freeway slowed, too—due partly to the rush-hour closure of two lanes and partly

159

to a stall just south of the Waldo Tunnel. I left off my reflections and concentrated on not rear-ending anyone. By the time I'd passed through the toll plaza and sped up on Doyle Drive, I was regretting not having a car phone so I could check in for messages. A friend who had one had recently convinced me of their merits, but when I'd broached the subject of getting one to Hank, he'd told me I was fortunate just to have an All Souls telephone credit card.

Traffic was heavy within the city as well, and I fumed all the way crosstown to Bernal Heights. When I arrived at the co-op, it was after five, and Ted was no longer at his desk. I checked the chalkboard for urgent messages, then went up to my office and looked in my In box for the routine ones. Nothing.

I'd hoped for one from Jess Goodhue giving me the name of the investigator who had looked into her mother's background, so I called KSTS-TV. Goodhue came on the line, sounding rushed. No, she said, she hadn't yet had the time to look for the detective's name and wasn't sure when she could get to it.

"I really wish you'd try to find time," I said. "After talking with the two remaining heirs, I think Tom Grant figures in all of this far more prominently than he's letting on."

Goodhue said something that I couldn't catch.

"What?"

"Sorry. I was talking with one of our writers. Why do you think that about Grant?"

"Both of the remaining heirs seemed to recognize his description, even though his name didn't ring a bell. One of them was very startled, said something about Grant being the right man."

"Right man?"

"Yes. What do you suppose—"

"Hang on." There was a clunk, and then I heard papers shuffling. When she came back on the line, she said, "Sharon, I've got to go—urgent conference with my producer. I'll try to call you in the morning, okay?"

I glared at the receiver for a few seconds, slightly miffed by Goodhue's abrupt dismissal of me. Then I replaced it and stood by my desk, feeling deflated and at loose ends. My gaze rested on the new chaise longue, the one I'd bought to relax on, and irritation with myself rose. It was really stupid to buy a nice piece of furniture and then not use it as intended.

I flung off my jacket, stalked over there,

and removed the file box, camera, and tape recorder, depositing them unceremoniously on the floor. Then I lay down and contemplated the ceiling. It was cracked and water-stained, and cobwebs trailed down from the rosette above the fluted light fixture. I refocused on the wall beside the fireplace. That was even worse.

I'd only been working out of the office for a little over a year, and it had taken me six months to really notice the wallpaper. For years previous to that, Hank had lived in the room (because All Souls pays salaries that are lower than the going market rate, it makes a policy of providing cheap living quarters on an as-available basis to employees and partners who request it) and I'd had little occasion to visit it, much less examine the decor. The wallpaper would definitely not have been of either of our choosing: faded rose and gray and cream, with flowers and garlands and cherubs arranged in a repetitious ovate pattern. After moving in, I'd paid it as little attention as I assumed Hank had.

Then one day, in a fit of contemplation, I noticed that it looked uncannily like one of those charts of the female reproductive system usually displayed on the walls of examining rooms in gynecologists' offices. When I mentioned this to Hank, he confessed that he'd noticed it long ago, but had merely been amused. *I* was not amused, however; every time I looked closely at the walls from then on, I was reminded of stirrups and a cold speculum.

I closed my eyes, but the image of the wallpaper remained with me, intruding on my concentration. A car raced its engine in the street below, and downstairs in the parlor that doubles as a waiting room, someone turned up the TV. Shortly afterward there came a thump and a series of scrambling noises from Ted's room next door. Then a second thump and a loud curse.

I sighed, got up, and went out into the hall. When I knocked on his door, Ted's voice called out in harried tones, "Come in, but be quick about it."

I opened the door, and a furry yellow missile hit my shins. Reflexively I reached down and grabbed it, found myself holding a wiggly little cat.

"Shut the door!" Ted shouted.

I did as he told me. He was sitting on his red velvet Victorian sofa, as dejected-looking as I'd ever seen him, and against his chest

163

he cradled an equally wiggly bundle of black and yellow and white fur.

"Good Lord," I said, getting a firmer grip on the creature in my hands. "What is this?"

"Harry's cats." The calico wriggled free from him and bounded to the floor, skidding slightly. Ted rolled his eyes in resignation as it made a beeline for the ladder to his sleeping loft.

"Harry's? These are kittens; they can't be over twelve weeks old."

"Exactly twelve weeks. They were an ill-advised gift from a well-meaning friend who thought they might cheer him up. His land-lady's been keeping them since he went into the hospital, but now she's turned them over to me. I promised Harry I'd find a good home for them."

"Oh." The kitten I held had stopped wiggling and started to purr. It reached out a paw and patted my cheek. Quickly I set it down. "Are you going to keep them?"

"In here? Be serious."

He had a point. Ted's room is really a cubbyhole—the former bathroom for the room that is my office. It's a baroque retreat with red-flocked wallpaper and one of the ugliest lamps this side of Denver, but Ted takes great pride in it. And I have to admit that he's made the most of the least possible space: the sleeping loft, curtained off by red sheers, is suspended above the ornate brass-and-marble sink and toilet; the tub has been removed and replaced by the sofa and an antique armoire; a Japanese screen discreetly separates the two areas. To me, it looks like a tiny room in an 1890s whorehouse, but to Ted it is perfect—minimalist and opulent at the same time.

I sat down beside him on the sofa. Both cats were in the loft now; there was a tearing sound, and Ted winced. "My sheers—again."

"What about Hank?" I asked. "Maybe he'd take them."

"He'd forget to feed them."

"Anne-Marie?"

"She's allergic."

Briefly I considered the other partners and employees of the co-op, but dismissed them all for various reasons. "Do they have to stay together?"

"They're brother and sister, and they get on. It would be a shame to separate them." Now Ted was watching me hopefully. "Shar, maybe you could—"

"No," I said quickly. "I don't want another cat."

He was silent for a moment, then said, "Can I ask you a personal question?"

"Sure."

"Are you kind of . . . closing off since George moved back to Palo Alto?"

"Why would you think that?"

"Oh, I don't know. It's none of my business, really. Forget I asked."

"Ted, the only reason I don't want another cat is that I'm not home very much. I can't care for a cat properly. Wat was different—he was old and very independent. These are kittens; they require a lot of attention."

Another tearing sound. "I know," Ted said morosely.

"Look, I'll ask around for you, see if I can't find somebody who wants them."

"I'd appreciate that."

I got up and went to the door, but before I opened it I asked, "What're their names?"

"Ralph and Alice."

" 'The Honeymooners.' "

He brightened some. "I'm glad you knew that. Half the people I tell don't get it. It makes me feel ancient. Sometimes I think I'm the only one who remembers things like old TV shows."

"I remember," I said, and left the room,

shutting the door quickly against further feline onslaught.

Contemplation no longer seemed possible, so I went downstairs and looked into Rae's office—my former one, a converted closet under the stairs. The light was out and, although there were papers scattered all over the desk, her coat wasn't on the hook where it usually hung. Then I remembered the liquor-store surveillance job; most likely she was still on it.

As I turned to go back upstairs, Hank came through the front door, a sack from a tacqueria down on Mission Street in hand. Seeing it made me realize how inadequate a lunch was the chocolate bar that I'd eaten on the drive to Point Reyes. "Working late?" I asked him.

"Yes. You?"

I shook my head. "I'm going home pretty soon. Did you get a chance to draw up that document for Tom Grant to sign?"

"It'll be on your desk in the morning."

"Good. I want to talk with him again, and that'll give me an excuse." Hank looked eager to go on to his office, but I lingered in the hall, wishing he'd ask me about the Hilderly case so I could put off departing for my empty, lonely house.

167

He noticed my reluctance to leave, plus the way I was eyeing the tacqueria sack, and said, "You want some of this? There's enough for two."

"I don't think I could take Mexican food right now. And I shouldn't keep you from your work."

"Oh, come on to the kitchen with me. Sit a spell, have a glass of wine at least. You can brief me on Hilderly while I eat."

I followed him back there, mildly embarrassed that he'd realized how needy I felt tonight.

For once, however, he didn't feel called upon to dissect my emotional state. While I sipped chablis and outlined what I'd found out about Hilderly *et al.*, he ate two burritos, dripping salsa and grease all over the table, then balled up the wrappings and tossed them at the garbage bag under the sink. They missed and ended up next to it. Hank shrugged and went to get some coffee.

"No wonder Anne-Marie can't live with you," I said.

He grinned, plainly pleased by his own slovenliness. "Speaking of Anne-Marie, did you know the police dug the sniper's bullet out of one of her planter boxes on our porch?"

"No. When did that happen?"

"This morning. I read about it in Brand Ex a couple of hours ago." Brand Ex is the local nickname for the evening paper, the *Examiner*. "Looked like a three-fifty-seven Magnum, and they were rushing the ballistics work on it. Bet it'll match the others."

"You're pretty calm about all this. Are you still convinced the sniping was just a coincidence?"

"I can't imagine any reasonable connection." But his face showed strain as he started for the door to the hallway, carrying his coffee.

"Hey," I said, "you didn't give me any opinion on Hilderly." I'd posed the same questions for him as I'd asked myself on the drive back to the city.

But Hank's thoughts were clearly elsewhere now. He said, "I'm as much at sea as you are. Keep digging." Then he pointed his index finger at me in a parting salute and went down the hall.

I sighed and contemplated my empty wineglass. Even though Hank had more pressing matters on his desk, he could have . . . what? Did I want him to speculate on the case with me, help me try to puzzle it out? Or did I really want him to keep me company, hold my hand? What the hell was wrong with me, anyway? I'd always been self-sufficient, enjoyed my own company, even been something of a loner. Why this recent urge to surround myself with people? I'd never felt it before.

But that was before you knew George Kostakos, my inner voice said. That was before you started to fall in love with him.

"Shut up," I told it, and went to get more wine.

After a while Larry Koslowski came in with Pam Ogata, our newest associate and, like Larry, a specialist in commercial law. We chatted for a while about Pam's difficulties in finding a decent apartment, and pretty soon she and I ransacked the refrigerator and made ourselves sandwiches out of various leftovers—amid much dire warning about potential health hazards from Larry. Then Pam—who was staying with friends who had small kids and thus spent as little time there as possible—remembered they were rerunning *Funeral in Berlin* on Channel 44, and we went to the parlor to watch it. It was after ten when I finally left. Rae hadn't yet returned from the surveillance job, and the light still burned in Hank's office.

The fog was thick again, dimming the

light from the windows of the other houses that clustered around the small triangular park that fronted All Souls' shabby brown Victorian. I paused on the steps, buttoning my jacket and turning up its collar. And as I did, a feeling stole over me—uneasy, strong. The feeling that someone was watching from somewhere in the misted darkness.

Come on, McCone, I thought. More urban paranoia?

But after the events of the previous night, anyone *would* be paranoid.

I stepped back into the doorway, looked around, and listened for a time. The little streets that converged on the side of the hill were relatively quiet. Traffic noises and salsa music drifted up from Mission, and an occasional car drove by. Someone had a stereo turned up too loud, and from behind me I could hear the mutter of the All Souls TV. A man trudged uphill, pulling a handcart of groceries from the nearby twenty-four-hour Safeway. A couple strolled downhill, holding hands. It appeared to be just another Bernal Heights weeknight, the mostly peaceable, law-abiding citizens easing out of their daily routines, getting ready for sleep.

Even so, when I finally left, I hurried down the steps. As I moved toward the corner where the MG was parked, I kept close to the buildings, enveloped in protective shadow.

Twelve

By morning the fog had retreated to sea, leaving behind one of those glorious sunwashed days that make me recall just why it is I've chosen to live in San Francisco. The blue skies and temperate breezes cheered me, and I spent the hours before noon performing routine chores, plus exercising my supervisory skills by listening to Rae's exuberant and oft-repeated account of yesterday's exploits.

It seemed she'd gotten lucky her first day on the job and had delivered photographic evidence of the liquor-store clerk's thieving to the client, who in turn had contacted the police. To hear Rae tell it, her keen wits and talent had been the prime ingredients in this coup (she made no mention of sheer good fortune), and she was at any minute to be inducted into the Detectives' Hall of Fame. Since I was in a good mood and also remembered the thrill of my own first success in the business, I listened patiently and made appropriate congratulatory noises, then ended up treating her to lunch at her favorite bistro on Twenty-fourth Street. It wasn't until we got back to All Souls at one-thirty that I was able to turn my attention to the Hilderly case.

Jess Goodhue hadn't yet arrived at KSTS, and of course the TV station wouldn't give out her home phone number. When I called directory assistance for the number of Taylor's Oysters, I was told it was no longer in service. Finally I phoned Tom Grant's home office and asked Ms. Curtis to schedule an appointment so Grant could sign the document renouncing his share in the Hilderly estate. She put me on hold, and then Grant came on the line. He was booked solid for the day, but said he could see me that evening.

"What time?" I asked.

"I have a dinner with a client and then an appointment for an interview. Make it around nine, and I'll give you a drink and show you my studio."

I hesitated. The invitation held a seductive note that I didn't care for. Then I decided I was behaving too much like a Tennessee Williams heroine, seeing a potential de-

173

baucher behind every tree, and agreed to the appointment.

As I hung up the phone Ted entered the office and placed a pink message slip on my desk. Gene Carver, Hilderly's former boss at Tax Management Corporation, had called over the noon hour. When I called back, Carver was available and agreed to answer a few questions.

"I'm interested in a seminar you required Perry to attend in late May—possibly one with a motivational slant."

"Motivational?" Carver sounded amused. "I don't think so. The only seminar I recall last spring was the one on taxation problems associated with divorce. Big gathering co-sponsored by the bar association and the California CPAs Foundation at the Cathedral Hill Hotel on the last weekend of the month. I went. So did Perry and two of my other accountants."

That was what had promised to change Hilderly's life, as he'd told his son Kurt? An unlikely topic. Unless . . . "Do you recall if a divorce attorney named Thomas Y. Grant participated?"

"Sure. Old friend of Perry's, it turned out. Ran one of the workshops."

"Grant and Perry were friends?"

174

"Apparently they went back a long way. At first they didn't recognize each other; then they both seemed surprised and confused. But Perry spoke with Grant at the morning break, and later I saw them having lunch together at Tommy's Joynt."

"Did Perry say anything about Grant to you?"

"As a matter of fact, he did. Let me see if I can remember it right." Carver paused. "This was when the afternoon session broke. What he said was that Grant was a man who had made a great deal out of an essentially ruined life. That struck me as an odd assessment, seeing how much the man's worth. I asked Perry what he meant, but all he said was that he felt sorry for Grant, because he could see a lot of himself in him."

"And that was all he told you?"

"I didn't pursue it; the session was about to resume. And frankly, until now I'd forgotten about it."

I thanked Carver and jotted a few notes on a scratch pad after I hung up. In no way could I imagine how Hilderly could have considered Grant's life "ruined." Nor could I understand how he could have seen himself in a semi-ethical attorney whose hobby was making things out of dead animal parts. Of course, I hadn't known Hilderly and the way his mind worked; even those who had been part of his life hadn't mastered that.

After a few minutes I got up and wandered downstairs to Hank's office. I stopped in the door and asked, "By any chance did a call from D. A. Taylor's wife get routed to you instead of me?"

He shook his head. "I need to talk with her when she does call, though, so be sure to pass her along to me."

"*If* she calls. That damn Harley probably didn't give her the message. That means I'll have to drive all the way out there again."

"You sound out of sorts. What's wrong?"

I shrugged. "Afternoon malaise, I guess. You know what I just found out? Hilderly and Grant were old friends." I related what Gene Carver had told me.

"So Grant lied," Hank said. "He must want to cover up the association very badly to toss away a quarter of a million dollars."

"Yes—and I intend to ask him why when I take that document for his signature tonight." I paused, glancing at a stack of magazines that threatened to spill off the corner of one of Hank's filing cabinets. "One more question, and then I'll let you get back to work. That magazine that sent Hilderly to Vietnam—what was its name?"

He frowned. "*New* . . . something. Something relatively conservative, for a Movement publication. *New* . . . dammit, I hate it when something's right on the tip of my tongue like this!" He shut his eyes, concentrating fiercely. When he opened them, he said, "Ahah! *New Liberty.*"

"And it was based here in the city?"

"Think so."

"Thanks." I hurried back to my office.

The man on the reference line at the public library had never heard of *New Liberty;* he put me on hold for a few minutes while he looked up information on the magazine. It had enjoyed a long life, as alternative publications go: from 1965 to 1970. While its circulation was never large, at one point it had reached ten thousand. The name of the editor in chief up to 1969 was Luke Widdows. After that there had been a succession of individuals, none of whom had lasted more than a month or two.

"Do you have any idea what Widdows is doing now?" I asked.

"I think I've seen his by-line someplace. He may be a free-lance journalist."

I hung up and called my friend J. D.

Smith at the *Chronicle*. J. D. also said Widdows's name was familiar, and promised to check around and get back to me. I had an appointment to give a deposition in behalf of one of Larry's clients at a downtown law firm at three, so I tidied my desk and left the office. The deposition, as was typical, took far longer than it was supposed to, and by the time I got back to All Souls it was close to five. Ted sat at his desk, the calico kitten—Alice—draped around his shoulders.

"What's that doing there?" I asked.

He started to shrug, but caught himself in time; one really good shrug and the wisp of varicolored fur would have gone flying. "It's the only way I can get her to behave and stop tearing the place apart. For some reason she likes it there."

"Where's the other one?"

He pointed under the desk. I bent down and saw Ralph curled up on his feet. "It's tough being a working father," I said.

He glared at me and went back to the brief he was proofing.

There was a message from J. D. in my box, giving a Berkeley address and phone number for Luke Widdows, as well as a note from Hank saying he'd talked with Mia Taylor and settled matters about the inheritance. I frowned, annoyed to have missed her call; I would have liked to question Mrs. Taylor about her husband's past. Now I'd probably have to revisit West Marin after all.

Again Jess Goodhue hadn't called with the investigator's name. I dialed KSTS-TV, was told the anchorwoman was unavailable. The results of my final call were a bit more positive: Luke Widdows would be glad to talk with me about Hilderly, but was on his way out. Could I come to his place at nine the next morning? I agreed and took down directions.

Now what to do? I thought irritably. I had four empty hours before my appointment with Tom Grant. I didn't particularly want to go home, nor was I enthusiastic about catching up on my paperwork. Finally I went downstairs and lured Rae away from filling out her expense report, and we headed down the hill to the Remedy Lounge on Mission Street.

The Remedy has long been an All Souls hangout. Hank discovered it, I think, only hours after signing the lease on the Victorian, and over the years we've celebrated our triumphs and commiserated over our failures there. Unalterably dark and sleazy, with a frequently broken jukebox and shabby appurtenances, it would seem a good place to stay out of, but its ambience belies mere surface appearances. At times within its four grimy walls I have the sensation that its tolerant—but not intrusively friendly—clientele and I are sailing a stormy sea on a ship, snug and protected from the raging elements. Of course, the ship is a tired old scow and the rocky shoals lie straight ahead, but the temporary sense of security is soothing nonetheless.

Rae and I took one of the rear booths, and within a minute Brian, the bartender, brought her a beer and me a glass of white wine. That was one of the advantages of taking my assistant along: so far as I know, hers is the only table Brian has ever brought a drink to in some thirty years of tending bar. Perhaps she reminds him of some long-lost sweetheart back in Ireland; perhaps he admires her because she naively assumed from the start that such treatment was merely her due as a paying customer. Whatever the reason, Rae rates with Brian—far higher than those of us who have been patronizing the Remedy for years.

She wanted to rerun the liquor-store saga—the realization that she'd have to tes-

tify in court having lent it further drama—
but I cut her short and updated her on the
Hilderly case. We kicked the facts around
for two hours and three drinks plus beer
nuts, but came to very few conclusions.

Rae asked, "Are you going to confront
Grant about his friendship with Hilderly tonight?"

"It's the only way I'll pry the whole story
out of him."

"According to you, the guy is weird. What
if he gets violent?"

"I can handle him. But I doubt he will.
He's not the type and, besides, he's got a
position to protect. He's not about to harm
me when there are people who know I'm
with him. I plan to call All Souls when I get
to his house and make sure he hears me tell
whoever answers exactly where I am."

Rae considered that, then nodded
thoughtfully. I could see she was placing the
technique in her mental file for future use.

I said, "I meant to ask you—have you
heard whether the bullet the police found at
Hank and Anne-Marie's matched the ones
that killed the sniping victims?"

"Yeah. Willie called Greg Marcus this afternoon. It matched."

I'd expected as much, but I supposed on

some level I'd been hoping to hear the bullet didn't match. It would have simplified my investigation if the sniping had turned out to be a copycat shooting perpetrated by, say, someone who had had a diamond ring repossessed by Willie. Rae was watching me as if she expected some insightful comment, but I had none to offer.

When I didn't speak, she said, "What about Hank? Does he still think he's not in any danger?"

"That's what he says. But I'm not convinced of that—and I don't think he really is, either. How's Willie doing?"

"He's housebound and claustrophobic. They've stationed a cop outside, but he's afraid to leave after dark." She looked at her watch. "Come to think of it, I promised to be there right about now."

After she left I finished my wine in solitude and went home. The only message on my answering machine was from Jim, asking plaintively if we couldn't get together and talk things over. No, I decided, we couldn't. I then tried Jess Goodhue again, but the switchboard couldn't locate her. The microwave burned the middle of my frozen lasagna and left icy little lumps on the top. I ate it anyway. Afterward I went to the strongbox where I keep my .38 and took out the pouch I'd found among Hilderly's boxed possessions. The gun weighed heavy in my hand. I fingered the rough place where its serial number had been removed, then replaced it in the pouch, and the pouch in the strongbox, keeping out only the chain with the metal letters *K* and *A* depended from it. After studying it for a moment, I put it into the zipper compartment of my purse.

It was eight-thirty by now, time to leave for my appointment with Tom Grant. I made another quick call to KSTS-TV; this time Goodhue was resting until her eleven o'clock broadcast and couldn't be disturbed. I remembered what she'd said the other day: "Nobody, absolutely nobody, disturbs me in my dressing room." Although I could understand her need for that quiet time, it still irked me that she hadn't phoned as promised, and I fretted about that all the way to Pacific Heights.

The night was clear and unusually warm; the streets of Pacific Heights were hushed, set apart from the rest of the city by that silence that often envelops privileged neighborhoods. Outside the Gate, the foghorns bellowed—a dolorous and faintly menacing

183

reminder that the fog had not left for good, was merely waiting in abeyance at sea. As I crossed the sidewalk from my car to Grant's house I heard other sounds: a cat fight somewhere up the hill; the breeze rustling the leaves of the eucalypti in the vast military reservation behind the homes; the wail of a siren down near Lombard Street.

Then I heard yet another noise: footsteps running and stumbling. As they came closer, they were punctuated by a harsh gasping and sobbing, and I realized the sounds were coming from Grant's property. I hurried up to the gate just as his secretary, Ms. Curtis, burst through it and let forth a wild high-pitched scream that escalated in shrillness until it set a chill skittering across my shoulder blades.

She was dressed much as she had been two days before, but the primness and stiffness were gone. Her face was gray and twisted; her eyes were glassy and jumpy. I grabbed her arm, and they focused briefly on my face, but she didn't seem to recognize me. Then she turned her ankle and the scream cut off as she pitched forward. As I caught and steadied her she said between gasps, "The police! Call the police!"

I glanced around. People were looking

through their windows on the other side of the street, but—as in Hank and Anne-Marie's neighborhood—they weren't about to come outside when someone was screaming. I eased Ms. Curtis through the gate. She stiffened and shook her head. "I can't go back there!"

"Here—sit down." I guided her onto the wall of one of the raised flower beds, then went to shove the gate closed. When I turned, she was hunched over, arms wrapped around her midsection. "Tell me what happened," I said tensely.

She moaned. "Tom. He's in the studio. He . . . I think they've killed him."

I noted her use of the plural, but now wasn't the time to question her. "How do I get to the studio?"

"Path around the house." She motioned to the left and behind her.

"You go inside. Call nine eleven."

She remained hunched where she was.

"Can you do that?"

She nodded.

I hurried across the courtyard and followed a bricked path to the rear of the property, where a second courtyard overshadowed by another acacia tree lay between the house itself and the wall that bordered the Presidio.

It was very dark back there, even though the moon silvered the bricks, but in the far right-hand corner of the lot I saw a small structure faced in the same brown shingle as the house and overgrown with broad-leaved ivy. A faint light shone through its one narrow window.

I moved slowly toward it, aware of the clicking of my heels on the bricks. Around me everything seemed to have stopped moving; even the breeze had died, and the eucalyptus leaves no longer rustled. No sounds came from the small building.

The door was ajar, spilling a fine line of light onto the bricks. Warily I pushed it all the way open. The faint squeak of its hinges made me start.

Before me lay a room with a large central worktable; the wall behind it had drawers at the bottom and tools suspended from a pegboard above them. The other walls were bare, painted white. An odor filled the room: metallic, sickly sweet. The odor I've come to think of as the smell of death.

I stepped inside, moved past the cluttered worktable. Grant lay on the floor behind it. He was on his back, his left arm flung out beside him, his right raised above his head as if to ward off his attacker. Blood covered his face, hands, casual tan clothing. It had spattered over the drawers and pegboard. As I moved closer I saw his forehead was caved in, white bone showing.

I wanted to grip the worktable for support, but I knew better than to disturb the scene; Ms. Curtis had probably done a good bit of damage already. I turned away briefly, breathing shallowly through my mouth. When I felt steady enough, I went over to the body and checked to see if there was any pulse. Of course there wasn't.

Something on the floor a few feet away caught my eye as I straightened. I leaned out, staring at it. It looked to be a partially finished fetish—a heavy gridwork of metal with feathers sticking through the spaces between the rods—and it was covered with drying blood. Grant had been bludgeoned to death with one of his own hideous creations.

Trophies and dead things . . .

The phrase seemed eerily apt here in this workshop-turned-abattoir, where Grant had fashioned his sick fetishes from animal and bird corpses and where, in turn, someone had fashioned his death.

And then I remembered another phrase from the quatrain: *nets to catch the wind.*

Grant had also fashioned such nets, fed his ambition by fanning the greed of his clients and using it against the wives and children they had once loved. And now?

Nothing, I thought as I hurried back to the house. Nothing but empty nets—a life that had produced nothing of value, that would not be long remembered beyond the last obituary.

I found Ms. Curtis sitting in one of the clients' chairs in Grant's office, staring at the telephone on the desk. "Did you call nine eleven?" I asked her.

She looked up as if surprised to see me there. "I . . . couldn't."

"I will." I punched out the three digits, gave the operator the necessary information. Then I sat down on the other chair.

Angela Curtis had been crying. The tears had left a tracery of pale brown mascara on her cheeks. I fished in my bag and handed her a clean tissue. "When did you find him?"

She scrubbed at her face, made a weary gesture. "Just before you arrived. I'd been to a movie on Union Street. Tom told me to go; he had someone coming, and he didn't seem to want me around the house."

When I'd spoken with him on the phone,

Grant had mentioned an interview he had scheduled after his dinner appointment. Perhaps he planned to replace Angela Curtis and was talking with a job applicant; that would explain him not wanting her around. But why send her to a movie? Why not just send her home?

"Why did you come back here?" I asked.

"I live here."

How convenient for him, I thought. A secretary who lived in; no wife to potentially demand her share of the community property. And you could be sure he'd made no promises or statements that would give rise to a palimony suit.

She sensed my thoughts, because she said, "It wasn't like that. It was just . . . easier if I lived on the premises." Then she scrubbed at her face some more, balled up the tissue, and tossed it in the wastebasket. "Oh, God, who do I think I can fool? Of course it was like that. What idiot would believe otherwise?"

I said, "Ms. Curtis, what happened when you came home?"

"I went out to the studio, and Tom was . . ." She shook her head, swallowed.

"Earlier you said 'they' killed Tom. Who did you mean?"

189

She shook her head, distracted. "I said that?"

"Yes. Do you have reason to believe it was more than one person? Suspect someone?"

"I guess I meant his clients. They took and took, and then they weren't satisfied."

"Did Tom ever mention an old friend named Perry Hilderly to you?"

She shook her head.

"There was a seminar Tom participated in at the Cathedral Hill Hotel the last weekend in May. Are you sure Hilderly's name didn't come up in connection with that?"

"I'm positive."

"And you don't suspect any one of his clients in particular?"

"I suspect all of them. Any of them. I'm not blind to what Tom was, Ms. McCone. The reason his clients weren't satisfied was that he'd conditioned them to selfishness and cruelty. Simple stimulus-response. Someone tries to take something from you—even something that's rightfully theirs—and you lash out, take it back, hurt them in the process. Afterward they would turn on Tom; often they didn't even want to pay his fee." She paused, then said as fresh tears welled in her eyes, "I knew exactly what he was, but that didn't stop me from loving him."

Thirteen

And then the police arrived," I said to Hank.

We were sitting at the round oak table in All Souls' kitchen—a place where we'd sat for many an hour over the years, rehashing aspects of his cases or mine, drinking wine or coffee, chatting or talking seriously. Tonight the conversation was of the serious variety. I'd called his flat as soon as I'd left the crime scene, but reached only his answering machine; I'd then called the co-op and found he was working late again. Now that I'd told him all I could about Grant's murder, a lethargy was descending on me. I felt as if I'd been without sleep for days.

He asked, "Who's the investigating officer?"

"Leo McFate. You remember him—the one when I was on that case for Willie—"

"I remember. An asshole. I thought he'd transferred to the Intelligence Division."

"He did, but he's back on Homicide now. Better he had stayed in Intelligence—he's a sneaky bastard, and that's a sneaky detail." The Intelligence Division of the SFPD had

191

come under criticism for spying on environmental, gay, and peace organizations that in no way posed a threat to civil order or the public safety. In the sixties operatives infiltrated meetings of civil-rights workers and antiwar demonstrations; a year ago it had been revealed that—despite a 1975 Police Commission ruling against such activity—during the 1984 Democratic Convention the division had spied on such diverse groups as Solidarity with the People of El Salvador, the National Lawyers Guild, and an independent taxi drivers' association that had threatened to strike just as the delegates began to arrive in the city. To me, it seemed a part of the department that McFate was especially well suited to.

Hank said, "I'm surprised he isn't up in Sacramento by now, doing something 'important.'" McFate was a social climber with political aspirations.

"Yes, and I'm of two minds about whether I'd want him there destroying the state, or down here annoying me."

"I don't suppose he let you stick around Grant's very long."

"He got me out of there as fast as he could. Took a statement, told me to come down to the Hall and sign it first thing tomorrow. He didn't seem particularly interested in Grant's connection with Hilderly, or that Hilderly was one of the sniper's victims. In fact, when I offered to share anything that I might turn up in the course of dealing with the other heirs, he told me that wouldn't be necessary."

"What's his problem, anyway?"

I smiled. "Well, part of it stems from the fact that a while back he came on to me and I rebuffed him. But the real problem is that—even though he's seen around town with some of our most eligible women—underneath he doesn't like or trust any of us."

Hank grunted disapprovingly—whether at the concept of McFate coming on to me or at that of a man who didn't like women, I couldn't tell.

I said, "I'm curious about Hilderly's estate. What happens to Grant's share, since he didn't live to sign that waiver?"

"There was a clause in the original will to the effect that if any of the beneficiaries didn't survive until the final distribution of the assets, his share would be divided among the remaining beneficiaries. Fortunately, Hilderly copied it in the holograph, so Grant's share won't be paid into his own estate."

"Which is probably substantial, anyway. I hope he left something to Angela Curtis. Even though she loved him, it couldn't have been easy putting up with him. She deserves recompense."

"You really disliked him, didn't you?"

"He wasn't at all likable. Those fetishes—" I broke off into a shudder and then a yawn.

Hank looked at his watch. "Almost one-thirty. You want some more wine?"

"Half a glass. I'm still too wired to sleep." I stared out the window at the lights of downtown as Hank went to the fridge and poured from the jug. "Hank, what about these snipings and Grant's murder? Even the sniper striking at your house was too coincidental for my taste, and now one of Hilderly's heirs has been bludgeoned to death."

"That's the problem, though." He returned to the table and set down our glasses. "Ballistics show the snipings were all done with the same gun. And Grant's murder wasn't a shooting. In fact, it sounds like a crime of passion, not at all premeditated."

"I know. I could tell McFate was looking at Angela Curtis for it, but I doubt he'll even try to build a case. There were no traces of blood on her, and if she'd done it, she'd have been covered with it."

194

"You said it looked as if Grant was killed a while before you got there. She could have showered and changed her clothes."

"And then waited for me, since she knew I was due at nine, and faked hysteria." For a moment I reviewed the scene when I'd arrived at Grant's. "No, I don't think so. Her emotional reactions seemed genuine. For her sake, I hope somebody remembers her from the movie theater."

We sipped wine in silence for a few minutes. I was still thinking about the snipings. Something was eluding me there—some connection I should have made. But I couldn't force it. It would come together in its own good time or not at all.

After a bit Hank stirred and took our empty glasses to the sink. "Better get going, huh? It's already well into tomorrow, and I've got a full schedule."

I stood, stretched. "Me, too—I've got to be in Berkeley at nine, which means going to the Hall to sign my statement by seven-thirty, latest."

"What're you doing in Berkeley?"

"Talking with the man who edited the magazine Hilderly worked for. I'm hoping he can give me some insight into Perry's past, his connection with Grant."

"Shar, you've already located the heirs—"

"I thought we agreed that I'd pursue this until we were certain Hilderly wasn't under duress or unduly influenced when he wrote the holograph. Besides, the Hilderly angle is one that McFate seems determined to ignore in investigating Grant's murder."

Hank hesitated, then nodded. "Keep on it a while longer, then." As we went down the hall and I picked up my jacket from where I'd left it on Ted's chair, he added, "You always get so personally involved in your cases."

"And you don't?"

"Good point. Just be careful. Don't tread on any sensitive toes at the Hall. You've got a license to protect, and I'd miss having you around here."

As we started down the front steps I smiled up at Hank. "I will tread as lightly as Ralph and Alice—without leaving half the trail of destruction."

I didn't sleep well or long, due to recurring nightmares in which feathers and bone and blood spatters figured prominently. By seven-twenty I was at the Hall of Justice and had affixed my signature to a typed statement about Grant's murder. Leo McFate was nowhere to be seen; the officer with whom I dealt said he'd been there all night and had gone to the Intelligence Division—his old stomping grounds—only minutes before my arrival. Greg was in his cubicle, however, sifting through a mound of paperwork. I went over there and tapped on the glass. He looked up and motioned for me to enter.

"You're here early," he said as I sank onto his visitor's chair.

"I could say the same for you."

"Been here since six. Pressure's coming down about these snipings. I hear you had quite an evening."

"McFate's already reported on the Grant case?"

He nodded. "And did a fair amount of grumbling about how my former lady friend had managed to foul up one of his crime scenes."

My face became hot with anger. "Damn him!"

"Consider the source." Greg harbored no more goodwill toward McFate than I did.

"I'd rather not." I dug in my bag, where earlier I'd placed the pouch containing the gun I'd found at Hilderly's flat. Greg raised his eyebrows when I set it on his desk blotter.

Quickly I explained how I'd come to have it. "Could you ask the lab to bring out that serial number?"

"Why?"

"Knowing its history might shed some light on why Grant was murdered. Or even why Hilderly was killed."

Greg looked doubtful, but he merely nodded. "Okay, I'll send it down. I can't tell them to place priority on it, though."

"I don't expect you to. Another thing: may I take a second look at those files on the snipings?"

"Again, why?"

"I have a feeling there's something I missed the other day."

His gaze suddenly turned inward, reminiscent. "You remember when we first met, and I accused you in my sexist way of relying on woman's intuition?"

I nodded.

"You were fiddling with a hair ribbon you'd had on, and without noticing what you were doing, you twisted it into a little noose."

"That's right. I'd completely forgotten."

"Well, over the years I've come to realize it's just plain good investigator's instincts you rely on. And I've come to trust them, too. You're welcome to the files."

He picked up the phone receiver and asked that the files be brought in, then made arrangements to have the gun sent to the lab. "You can use my desk again," he added when he hung up. "I'm due in a meeting in fifteen minutes and probably won't be back until afternoon. If there's anything you need to tell me, call me then."

I watched him leave the cubicle, thinking that he looked not all that different from the man who had made me want to hang him in the old days. But underneath he had changed—become more mellow, plus a good bit sadder and more cynical.

Well, hadn't we all? I thought as I moved around the desk and took his chair.

When a clerk brought the files in, I began going over them in a great deal more detail than I had earlier in the week. This time I paid particular attention to the other three sniping victims.

The first victim—the restaurant employee—was Bob Smith. A common name—perhaps false. I noted it on my legal pad, put a question mark beside it. Smith's employment record was spotty: for the nine months prior to his death he'd worked in food preparation at a small pizza restaurant on Market Street; in the fifteen years before that he'd sporadically held various food-service jobs in Seattle, Portland, Salt Lake City, and Phoenix. His only long-term employment— from 1967 to 1973—was with American Consolidated Services of Fort Worth, Texas. I made a note to find out more about the company. Smith had lived alone in a rooming house in the Outer Mission; from police talks with the landlord and other tenants, the picture that emerged of him was of a loner, a drifter, a man without family and friends. Whatever I'd sensed I'd missed in the files did not have to do with him.

The second victim was a nurse, Mary Davis, birth name Johnson. Another common name. Davis had worked at Children's Hospital in Laurel Heights less than two months before she was shot while walking to her car on a quiet side street near the crisis clinic where she'd been on night duty. Before that she'd done psychiatric nursing at Letterman Army Hospital in the Presidio, and S.F. General. There was an eight-year period of unemployment after her 1975 marriage, and in 1983 she'd attended City College for additional training in the psychiatric nursing field. Before her marriage she'd been with the American Red Cross from 1968 to 1974. Davis's family and friends described her as a devoted wife and mother, good neighbor, and active volunteer for an organization providing counseling for AIDS patients.

I noted down several details about Davis, feeling an idea begin to take shape.

The third sniping victim, John Owens, was a veteran living on disability pay in a small home near the beach in the Outer Sunset. His wife and friends described him as the designated neighborhood repairman: he had a shop in his garage and was a genius with balky machinery. The fact that he was confined to a wheelchair due to injuries suffered in shelling near Saigon in 1972 didn't affect his ability to fix practically anything—

Vietnam again.

Hilderly had been there. So had Hank and Willie. And John Owens. All roughly within the same time frame. I checked my notes on Mary Davis: American Red Cross, 1968 to 1973. Had she also been over there? Bob Smith, too, maybe?

Embittered war protester knocking off veterans eighteen or so years after they'd fought their war? No. It sounded too much like the plot of a bad made-for-TV movie.

Besides, Hilderly and Davis hadn't been in the military. And Hank wasn't what you'd call your typical vet. For that matter, neither was Willie.

I wished Greg were there so we could talk it over; he was good at sorting out the possibilities from the improbables. But he wouldn't be back until afternoon, and I had to be in Berkeley in less than an hour.

What I needed was more information. I picked up Greg's phone receiver and called Hank's flat; only the machine answered. The same was true at Willie's house. I got the number of his main store on Market Street from directory assistance. Willie wasn't there, either, but I finally tracked him down at the Daly City store, in conference with its manager.

I asked, "When will you be free?"

"Christ, McCone, I don't know. I've got a full schedule today, going round to the stores."

"Give me a time when you'll be back at Market Street."

"Five? Five-thirty?"

"Good. I'll see you then." I hung up before he could reply and called Ted at All Souls. "What's Hank's schedule today?"

"Let me—dammit, get down!"

"Ted?"

"I was talking to Alice. She just walked across my keyboard and screwed up the computer. Back, you beast!" There was a thump and a tiny, indignant yowl. "Now—what?" he asked. "Hank's schedule?"

"If it won't interrupt your parenting too drastically."

"Don't be sarcastic. You could have taken them off my hands, you know."

"The schedule . . . ?"

"In court this morning. Back around two. Says he's going to clear up a few things and then go home early for a change."

"Okay, will you give him this message, please, and tell him it's urgent? I want him to meet me at Willie's Market Street store between five and five-thirty. Emphasize the urgent."

"Willie's, Market Street, four-thirty. That's so he'll get there on time; Hank, as you know, runs late. Will do, and I'll see that he follows through on it."

There are times when I thank whatever powers-that-be for Ted's calm efficiency. "Great," I said. "One more thing—is Rae in her office yet?"

"I think I heard her stumble in there about five minutes ago. Hold on."

When Rae picked up her extension, she sounded none too cheerful. "I just read about Tom Grant in the paper," she said. "Did you get involved in that?"

"I arrived right after the secretary found his body."

"They didn't mention you."

"Good. I'm notorious enough as is. Listen, I'll fill you in on it later. Do you have time to check into something for me this morning?"

"If it's not too complicated. My brain seems to be on hold. Okay, go ahead."

"I need to know about a Forth Worth, Texas, firm—American Consolidated Services. Specifically, what services they provide, and where. If you can get personnel to cooperate, ask about a Bob Smith who worked for them from nineteen sixty-seven to seventy-three."

"What's my reason for wanting to know about him?"

"Tell them employee background check. No, that won't work—they've been contacted by the police and whoever you talk with might remember he's dead. Well, think of something."

"Sure," she said, a shade glumly.

I scribbled a note to Greg, telling him I

had a possible lead on the sniper and would be in touch later. Then I set off for the town that plays host to my alma mater.

Fourteen

I seldom visited Berkeley anymore—not because I didn't like the town, but because long ago all my old friends had moved away and I had no real reason to go there. As I drove up University Avenue toward campus that morning I found myself experiencing a keen attack of nostalgia. That dark-haired young woman in jeans who moved past me in the crosswalk could easily have been me, walking reluctantly to my nine o'clock soc class and wondering how I could get through it without a third cup of coffee. That sandwich shop on the corner was where I'd often grabbed a hasty lunch, and I was willing to bet their bread was just as stale and dry as ever. When I crossed the Milvia intersection, I felt a swift wrenching; some two blocks away down a little side street was the apartment building where I had enacted the happy, then disillusioned, and finally painful scenes of my one and only long-term live-in relationship. All about me—and inside me,

205

too—things had changed, and yet they hadn't.

It was odd, I reflected, that part of me didn't feel any older than on the day I'd left here with my diploma. Since then I'd entered a profession I'd never given a prior thought to; I'd dealt with people and situations that would have made that graduate's flesh creep; I'd often been in extreme danger, had coped as best I could with violence and death, had even been forced to kill a man. I was more cynical, more judgmental, more prone to anger. But deep inside there was a wistful, yearning part that still felt twenty-three years old.

The changes in Berkeley were contradictory, too. The old landmarks remained, but interspersed among them were new buildings and a fair number of trendy shops and restaurants. The quiet, somewhat funky town of my memory has become chic these days: home of the Gourmet Ghetto, pioneering frontier of the New California Cuisine. The university, while still a major player, is no longer the only game in town. On the streets where you once mainly saw students on bicycles or in beat-up basic-transportation vehicles, you're now just as likely to spot well-heeled executive types in BMWs. Of course, the direction of progress has not been totally upscale: as I reached the edge of campus and went to turn left on Shattuck, I was momentarily taken aback by an enormous McDonald's. Not everyone in Berkeley, apparently, is a gourmet.

Luke Widdows had told me his house was on a section of Walnut Street a block from a shopping complex called Walnut Square. I found it—two-storied, white clapboard, wrapped by a wide porch—and parked in the driveway as directed. His office, he'd said, was in the carriage house out back. I followed a meandering dirt path through a vegetable garden to the smaller structure— shabbier than the main house, with a steeply canting roof. When I knocked on the screen door, Widdows answered immediately.

He was a slender man with curly brown hair and a fluffy beard, dressed in khakis and a blue T-shirt. There was an openness in his manner that I liked, and he seemed so glad to see me that I guessed my arrival had saved him from some distasteful task. He ushered me into a room with a paper-strewn desk and a pair of comfortable old armchairs, offered coffee, and went to fetch it.

"The nice thing about working out here,"

he called from the next room, "is that there's a small kitchen. I don't need to go to the main house if I don't want to. Which is a blessing, because I rent a couple of rooms to students who like loud music. Do you take anything in your coffee?"

"Just black."

"Me, too."

Widdows returned and handed me a large mug, then sank into the opposite armchair, eyeing me with frank interest. "Private detective, huh?" he said. "How'd you get into that line of work?"

"I got a degree in sociology from Cal."

He laughed knowingly. "Mine was in journalism."

"I'd say that's a bit more practical."

"Not much. In journalism, there's no teacher like hands-on experience."

"Well, obviously you've acquired that."

"All of it the hard way." He spoke without bitterness or self-pity; whatever his trials had been, they seemed to amuse him. As he slouched in the chair, one leg thrown over its arm, bare foot dangling, I glanced at the chaotic desk and computer setup—reminders of the work I was probably interrupting.

I said, "I don't want to keep you from anything pressing."

"You are—and I'm delighted. This morning I couldn't get any of the Jumble—that word scramble in the paper—so I know this is going to be one of those days when I won't be able to string the parts of a sentence together. You wanted to know about Perry Hilderly?"

"Yes. I understand he worked for you at *New Liberty*."

"If you could say that any of us really worked. Perry was a reporter. Investigative, I guess you could loosely term it. He couldn't write worth a lick—I had to rewrite most of what he turned in—but he was a Movement figure, had contacts with people who might not otherwise have talked with reporters."

"How long was he at the magazine?"

"He started in sixty-eight, after he left Berkeley."

"And he lived in San Francisco then?"

"Somewhere in the lower Fillmore district, I think. A lot of Movement people did back then—it was cheap, and they could get in touch with the 'real people,' as we were fond of calling minorities."

"And he went to Vietnam in sixty-nine?"

"Spring, it was. He came to me, said he

was burned out and disillusioned with the Movement. He wanted to see firsthand what the war was all about. We didn't have the funds to pay him, but we struck a deal that if he paid his way, we'd supply press credentials. So off he went."

"And what did he report on?"

"He hadn't so much as delivered a line of copy by the time the magazine folded." Momentarily Widdows looked regretful. "That was my fault, I'm afraid. My draft board was after me—this happened about a month after Perry left for 'Nam—so I took what I thought was the easy way out and split for Vancouver. The magazine never had strong management after I left."

Now I eyed him with interest. Strangely enough, I'd never met anyone who had moved to Canada to avoid the draft. "From the way you phrase it, I take it the 'easy way out' wasn't?"

"Not really. Draft resisters weren't all that welcome up there. There were simply too many of us, and not enough jobs. Not enough commitment to the country for the Canadians to accept us. And a lot of us got homesick—I know *I* did. I came back here under the amnesty program. Wrote a book about my experiences that did well enough that I could buy this house. I'm pretty apolitical these days; mainly what I write is gardening books and articles. You saw my vegetables?"

I nodded, thinking that Luke Widdows was as much of a victim of the turmoil of the war days as those who had gone to Asia and fought.

"Where did you first meet Perry?" I asked.

"Here in Berkeley. I interviewed him for a couple of articles in the *Daily Cal.*"

"Can you tell me something about the people he was close to?"

"You mean like the other leaders of the FSM?"

"Let me give you some names, see if they were friends of his. Thomas Y. Grant?"

"Where have I—isn't he the attorney who was murdered in the city last night?"

"Yes."

Widdows's eyes widened. "You're working on that?"

"A related matter."

"I see." He seemed intrigued by my reticence. "Well, as near as I recall, the first time I ever heard of Grant was when I unfolded the paper this morning."

"What about David Arlen Taylor—D. A. Taylor?"

"Oh, sure. He was a close friend of Perry's, probably his closest."

"And Libby Heikkinen?"

"Taylor's girlfriend."

"What about Jenny Ruhl?"

"Ruhl. Ruhl. Yes, I remember her. Tiny girl, long black hair."

"And chance she was romantically linked with Perry?"

"Oh, I don't think so. Perry liked women, but he was basically shy around them. He wouldn't have taken up with someone like Jenny."

"Why not?"

"How can I put this without—Jenny liked men, in quantity. For a while, around sixty-four or -five, she was living with a guy, a real sleazebag hanger-on. One of those guys who was just in Berkeley for the sex and drugs and rock and roll, as they used to put it. Then he disappeared from the scene about the time she turned up pregnant. She had the baby, and I guess she put it up for adoption. After that she just drifted from guy to guy, never staying with anyone very long."

"What was her connection to Hilderly, then?"

"Just as one of a group that hung out together. Very involved with the protests."

"This . . . sleazebag Ruhl was living with—what was his name?"

"I don't think I ever knew."

"Can you describe him?"

"Other than as a typical drifter, no. You remember the type—long unkempt beard, the same with the hair, generally grimy-looking, a little older than most students."

"Nothing at all memorable about him?"

"Not that I remember. Those people were all of a kind, and not too many of us trusted them. Their motives weren't pure, you see." Widdows laughed—both amused and self-mocking. "We had a long list of people who weren't to be trusted. Anyone over thirty, of course. The university administration and most of the faculty. Politicians, if they were of a major party. The military-industrial complex, including scared second lieutenants in the National Guard. There were spies lurking behind every tree: the Berkeley cops, narcs, the FBI, the campus police, and—when bombing became the thing—the ATF, Alcohol, Tobacco and Firearms."

"A hotbed of paranoia?"

"Right. And not totally drug-induced. But one thing about the spies: not too many

213

of them worked out, no matter what agency they were from. Button-down collars and cordovan shoes did *not* go down too well at SDS meetings. And the ones who did manage to worm their way into the counterculture usually went over to the other side—got hung up on drugs or women. The FBI, I've heard, had to periodically call them in from the field for a sort of deprogramming. It was a bizarre time, all right."

"What happened to Perry's group of friends, do you know?"

"Either got kicked out or dropped out of school. I think he told me that a bunch of them had moved to the city, set up as a commune. Political action shifted around sixty-eight or -nine—to S.F. State. Perry was in contact with them, that much I know. Once he said they might make a good story for us, but nothing came of it."

"What kind of story?"

"Who knows? Perry was very independent-minded; I never knew what he was going to turn in until it was on my desk. But by then communes were a dime a dozen, and when he thought it over, he probably decided it was a story whose time had gone."

I was silent, reviewing what Widdows had told me. Finally he asked, "Have I helped?"

"Yes, you have. I didn't come to Berkeley until years later, and you've given me a feel for those times. And now I won't keep you from your work any longer."

"I'm not sure you're doing me a kindness."

Widdows walked me to my car, pointing out the prize tomato plant of his vegetable garden. I confessed to having a black thumb even when it came to houseplants, and he smiled and suggested that it helped if one watered them. After I got into the MG, he leaned on its doorframe, looking down at me through the open window.

"Would you like to go out sometime?" he asked.

I hesitated, thinking I preferred men who lived more in the real world than he seemed to. Then I thought, what the hell. "Yes, I would."

"Great. I'll call you soon, or you call me. We could see a play or take in a concert. Go on a picnic, whatever. Or," he added, "I could always pay a house call on your plants."

Fifteen

When I left Berkeley, I didn't feel like going back to the office; only routine chores awaited me there, and I was primed for more active pursuits. So I decided to drive over the Richmond Bridge to Marin County and pay a call on Mia Taylor.

The fog had remained in abeyance, and although the wind still gusted across the West Marin headlands, the sky's clear blue was reflected brilliantly on the rippling water of Tomales Bay. The sun made the cypress and eucalyptus groves a deeper green, the summer-burnt hills a warmer shade of tan. As I drove I made absent note of the natural beauty—not without appreciation, but with only a small part of my attention. My mind was on the past, and the possible ramifications of its events on the present.

When I arrived at Taylor's Oysters, there were a couple more operational-looking vehicles in the parking lot than on my past visit, but the restaurant was again devoid of customers. A slender, blue-jeans-clad young woman with waist-length black hair was scrubbing with a rag at one of the oilcloth-covered tables. She turned when she heard the door close behind me, her hair swaying. Her face was bronze, with prominent handsome features.

I asked, "Are you Mia Taylor?"

She nodded, studying me and frowning slightly. For a moment the intensity of her gaze puzzled me; then I realized she was probably trying to place me on some remote branch of the family tree. As I'd told Libby Ross the other day, I only have one-eighth Shoshone blood, but it shows in my hair color and high cheekbones. I seldom think of myself in terms of either my Indian heritage or the Scotch-Irish blood that makes up the remainder of my genetic composition. My attitude is a symptom of what's happened to ethnic groups in America, and I suppose in some ways the blurring of differences is a good thing. But on the other hand, there's an inherent sadness in the loss of consciousness of our roots, the loss of touch with the history and traditions that make us who we are.

To spare Mrs. Taylor further confusion, I said, "I'm Sharon McCone, the investigator with All Souls Legal Cooperative. Is your husband available—"

"No," she said quickly. "D. A.'s sick."

Her nostrils flared in disgust. "Passed out, if you really want to know." She went behind the bar, flung the rag into the sink. Her body was rigid with tension; she grasped the edge of the counter, fighting for control. After a moment she spoke in less harsh tones. "Look, you want some coffee?"

"That sounds good. Thank you."

She shrugged and poured two cups from a pot on a warmer. "Black?"

"Please."

She carried the coffee over to the table she'd been cleaning and motioned for me to take a chair. When she sat across from me, her face was impassive, all emotion reined in.

I asked, "D. A.'s been drinking heavily?"

"Yeah. He's been awful upset for a couple of days now. Yesterday he took Jake's truck"—she motioned out the window at the antiquated red pickup I'd seen on my previous visit—"and went running off to see Libby Ross. When he came back he got into the beer. It always starts with beer. Jake took the truck keys away from him, but he must of had another set made sometime, because next thing we knew he was gone again."

"Where?"

"Joyriding, like always. Barhopping. By

the time we caught up with him, it was after one in the morning, and he was in Wiley's Tavern out Two Rock way. Shit-faced. He'd been in a bar fight, had lost his jacket, was acting meaner than a snake. Took the three of us to drag him home."

"Does he do that often?"

"Often enough. He's not supposed to be driving. Hasn't had a license in years. There's been a lot of trouble with the sheriff. I'm scared to death that someday some deputy's gonna take a shot at him, and that'll be the end of D. A." Her fingers clutched her coffee cup, their nails going white.

"Isn't there something you can do for him?"

"You're thinking maybe of a psychiatrist or a drug rehab clinic?"

"Those are possibilities."

She laughed bitterly. "And how am I gonna pay for that? Look at this place." She gestured around the room. "You see any customers? We don't even have a phone anymore. They took it out last month because we couldn't pay the bill."

"But after D. A. gets his inheritance—"

"Jake and Harley've got plans for that money, and none of them have got anything to do with D. A.'s welfare." Her voice had

219

risen. She glanced over her shoulder toward the door and modulated it. "Besides, ain't nothing can help D. A. Something inside that man is broken. Happened when he was in prison. You know about him being in prison?"

I hadn't, of course, but in a way the revelation didn't surprise me. Prison does terrible things to most people—but particularly to those who are neither strong nor insensitive. By his own admission, Taylor was not a strong man; from my observations I knew he was not shallow or calloused. Rather than answer Mia's question directly, I said, "I'm not clear on what he did that got him sent there."

"Me neither. It happened back practically before I was born. D. A. don't talk about it—leastways anything that makes sense. Jake and Harley *won't* talk about it. All I know was it was mixed up with Vietnam, and D. A. and his friends being against the war. The whole thing was stupid, if you ask me. D. A. had a chance to go to college and better himself, and instead he ruined his life." She paused. "Don't suppose it matters anymore what happened. What matters is that he's my husband and my babies' daddy, and I got to take care of D. A."

I was silent for a moment, thinking of the people in this world who somehow always manage to be taken care of. While many of them are genuinely helpless, others are extremely clever in shifting responsibility for themselves to friends' and loved ones' shoulders. In D. A. Taylor I sensed a curious combination of the types, and I wondered if his young wife was aware of it. It was not, however, my place to point it out.

I said, "Mrs. Taylor—"

"Mia. I don't like that 'Mrs.' stuff. Makes me feel *old*."

"Mia, has D. A. ever mentioned anyone named Tom Grant to you?"

". . . Not that I recall."

"What about Jenny Ruhl?"

"Who's she?" The response was quick and reflexive, tinged with suspicion. I supposed she was the jealous type and that her husband might give her reason to be.

"She died a long time ago."

"Oh. No, I've never heard the name."

I reached into the zipper compartment of my bag and removed the medallion I'd found in the pouch with Hilderly's gun. "Does this look familiar?"

Her face tightened. "D. A.'s got something like that. Different letters, though."

221

"May I see it?"

". . . I guess that would be okay." She shivered, drawing her arms across her breasts. "It's creepy—he hasn't worn it, not ever so far as I know, but sometimes I catch him taking it out of the dresser drawer and looking at it like it's some kind of . . . I don't know, charm, maybe. Like it's got power over him. I think it's got something to do with . . . all that."

"All that?"

"The stuff, you know, that happened before." She stood abruptly and moved toward the door. "I'll get it. You best wait here."

While she was gone I went to the window and peered through the salt-caked glass at the bay. Hog Island was visible in sharp relief today, rocky prominences standing out among the thick trees. I thought of the allure the island had for D. A. as he sat at the end of his dock day after day; I remembered his stated intention of going there when things became too much here on the shore, and my uneasy certainty that he meant to take his own life. A life that he'd long ago ruined for what his young wife claimed was a silly cause.

I didn't agree with Mia on that. For one thing, the antiwar movement had not been silly; it had saved lives, gotten our troops out of a place where they had no business being, given us—for a time, at least—hope for the future. For another thing, D. A.'s ruination had its roots not in his antiwar activism so much as in his own internal weaknesses. He could just as easily have fallen prey to those weaknesses had he completed his education and gone on to achieve the full professorship or the partnership in the prestigious law firm or the place in the boardroom of a Fortune 500 company.

To me, D. A. Taylor was both a pathetic and heroic figure. Pathetic because of his drug abuse and inability to let go of the past, but heroic because of what that past had been. At least the man had once cared passionately about something besides himself, had stood up for what he believed in. Perhaps I was allowing my view of him to be colored by the negative feelings I harbor toward much of what is currently going on in America: the lack of compassion, the fear of taking risks, the failure to embrace and hold tight to unselfish ideals. But Taylor was a man who had tried to make a difference— at whatever the personal cost.

After a while a motorized skiff piloted by Harley pulled up to the ramshackle dock behind the restaurant. The mangy dogs that had been sleeping in the sun—there seemed to be virtually dozens of them—jumped up and ran to meet him as he disembarked. In the kitchen that opened off the bar something made a pinging noise. A motor—the refrigerator's?—whirred, ground, and stopped. I turned away from the window and surveyed the empty, cheerless restaurant.

No amount of money, not even what Hilderly had willed to D. A., could reclaim this moldering place. No amount of renovation and financial acumen—which I doubted any of the family possessed—could make a go of the moribund business. Recalling what Mia had said about Harley and Jake having plans for D. A.'s inheritance, I made a mental note to speak with Hank and encourage him to convince Mia that the money should be placed in trust for D. A., her, and their children.

The sound of the door opening broke into my musings. Mia entered, her face drawn and mouth pursed tight, as if to restrain tears. "Is something wrong?" I asked.

"Something's always wrong. D. A.'s woke up and wandered off again. I don't know where—none of the trucks or cars is gone. And you know what? Maybe I don't care. Maybe if he stumbles out onto the high-way and a car picks him off, or if he falls in the bay and passes out and drowns, maybe that would be the best thing for me and my babies." Her eyes flashed with anger now. She tossed her head defiantly.

I sensed that anger was how she got through—that, and a devotion to her family that made me forgive her not understanding D. A.'s similar, although long-dead, devotion to the wrongness of the Vietnam war. I said, "You know you don't mean that."

She shrugged and sat at the table again. I reclaimed my chair.

"You're right," she said after a moment. "I don't mean it. But I get so damn tired. Look at me: how old do you think I am?"

"I can't tell. I'm not a very good judge of age."

"You're just trying to be nice. I'm twenty years old." She smiled bitterly. "Twenty. Not even old enough to serve drinks here, though I do, when we get a customer who wants one. I was fourteen when D. A. knocked me up. My mother had to sign so we could get married. The way it was, I was working in a market down in Point Reyes after school, and he'd keep coming in and talking to me. I was so young and dumb I didn't realize how fucked up he was. And then there was Davey, and I couldn't let my baby go without a daddy, could I?"

"I suppose not."

"Jake and Harley came around after I told D. A. about the baby. They tried to talk me into getting an abortion. Said they'd pay. Maybe I was stupid not to take them up on it. You think I was stupid?"

"Do *you* think you were?"

"I don't know. I love my kids. They're mine; at least I have *something*. No way of knowing if my life'd been any better if they'd never come along. But sometimes I wonder—could I have made something of myself if I'd of at least had a chance?"

Age-old question, never to be answered. "Did Jake and Harley tell you why they were making such an offer?"

"Oh, sure. They went on and on about D. A. being weirded out. But like I said, I was young and dumb and didn't want to believe them. Fourteen. Jesus. I thought I could help him." She laughed mirthlessly. "You hear that? Help him! I can't even help myself."

"Mia, the money will make a difference."

"Not if Jake and Harley have their way."

"Hank Zahn can get around them—I promise."

Her eyes stared intently into mine for a few seconds. I thought I caught a glimmer of hope, but then she shrugged—as if to say she knew all about promises and that everything she knew was bad.

"Anyway," she said after a moment, "here's that necklace thing you wanted." She pushed a handful of gray metal across the table at me.

I picked up the chain, which was the same type as the one I'd found at Hilderly's, and let the letters dangle from it. They were an *A* and an *M;* the *A* was bracketed with the same kind of curved edging as the one on the other chain; there was also a clip-like protrusion on the back of the *M*. I took the other chain from my bag and lay the two beside one another on the table, beginning to visualize the whole. It would have been an oval, perhaps two inches across and three high. I wondered how many pieces it had been broken into.

"May I borrow this?" I asked, pointing at the one that belonged to her husband.

She hesitated, then shrugged. "If you bring it back soon. D. A.'s gonna be too out of it for a while to notice it's gone."

"Thanks." I put both chains in my pocket.

Mia asked, "Do you know what those are?"

"I think so."

"Some devil-thing, maybe?"

"No, nothing like that."

"But then why does that one have this . . . power over D. A.? What does it mean?"

"Nothing much now. But it's not bad. You shouldn't worry. It's . . ." I paused, searching for the right words. "It's nothing but a symbol of things that are over and done with."

Sixteen

When I stopped the MG next to the paddock fence at Moon Ridge Stables, Libby Ross was emerging from the tack room. She again wore faded jeans and a down jacket, and in her hand she carried a plastic bucket full of brushes and currycombs. She saw the car and shaded her eyes with one arm as she peered toward it.

I got out and called hello. She acknowledged me with a wave and went to a rail where one of the pintos stood, the lead rope of its halter looped around it. As I approached she selected a rubber currycomb from the bucket, fitted it to her hand, and began brushing the horse's coat in a circular motion.

"Didn't expect to see you here again," she said over her shoulder. "I talked with your boss; he said everything's in order about my inheritance."

"Yes, it is. Actually, I stopped by to check up on you, make sure you're all right."

She glanced at me, the lines around her eyes crinkling. "Why wouldn't I be?"

I recalled that Ross neither owned a TV nor took a paper. "You haven't heard, then."

"Heard what?"

"One of the other beneficiaries of Hilderly's will, Tom Grant, was murdered last night."

She turned slowly, her wide mouth pulling down. "Murdered? By who?"

"I don't know. The killer got away unseen."

"Last night, you say?"

"Yes."

"How?"

"He was beaten to death, in a studio behind his house."

229

She shook her head. "What is it—you think this has something to do with him being named in Perry's will?"

"It might. And then again, it might not."

An odd expression came across her face —part fear and part comprehension. For a moment she seemed to be lost in thought. "So what you're thinking is that if it did, the rest of us might also be in danger."

"It's a definite possibility."

Ross looked around—at the cypress-covered knoll, the paddock, the barren stretch of land between the ranch buildings and Abbotts Lagoon. I knew what she was thinking: this was an isolated place, where a solitary person would be easy prey for a killer.

I asked, "Are you alone here?"

"The kid who cleans the stalls is here right now." She motioned at the barn. "But most of the time, yes. My stepson Dick comes and goes, but even when he's around, he's pretty useless."

"Is there someone you could get to stay with you for a while? A friend or a relative?"

"No, no one." She continued to contemplate the lagoon for a bit, then shrugged and went back to grooming the pinto. "Don't worry about me," she said. "I've got a rifle and a couple of twenty-twos in the house, and I'm a damned good shot when I have to be."

I went over and leaned against the rail, watching her brush the horse. The wind blew her dark blond curls across her face, so I couldn't see her expression. I said, "I was just talking with Mia Taylor. She told me about D. A. having been in prison."

Her hand slowed in its circular motion, then picked up the rhythm again. "So? It's not exactly a secret."

"What did he do?"

For a moment I thought she wasn't going to answer. Then she said, "Tried to bomb the Port Chicago Naval Weapons Station out at Antioch."

"When?"

"August of sixty-nine."

"Who else was at Port Chicago?"

"Why do you ask?"

"Bombing a federal military installation isn't something one undertakes alone."

"The collective—"

"What collective?"

Silence.

"What collective, Libby?"

Abruptly she tossed the currycomb back

into the bucket and turned as if to go to the barn.

I stepped in front of her, reaching into my pocket for the two medallions and holding them up at eye level. "Do you remember these?"

Her violet eyes widened. Then she looked away, trying to sidestep me. "You're not making a whole lot of sense today. First you tell me I might be murdered. Then you dangle some cheap jewelry in front of me—"

"Drop the pretense, Libby. A man's been killed."

She was silent, biting down on her lower lip. It was dry and chapped; when her teeth came away from it, blood welled from a fine crack.

I continued to hold the medallions up. Their gray pot metal gleamed dully in the sun. Ross stubbornly refused to look at them.

I asked, "What did the whole thing look like, Libby?"

No response.

I glanced around, saw a stick on the ground, and picked it up. Then I squatted in the dirt in front of her, drawing with the stick's sharp point. "It was an oval. Like so.

On this side, the letters *A* and *M*. And on this side, *K* and *A*."

I looked up at her. Her gaze had been drawn to the stick, and she was watching its motion intently.

"I'd guess there were more letters in between those," I went on. "Like these—*E,R,* and *I*. Am I right, Libby?"

She made a gesture with her hand, as if to erase the letters I'd just drawn.

When she didn't speak, I said, "Amerika. The way people in the Movement spelled it—taken from the Kafka novel, and used to say that the United States was an imperialist, fascist, racist, militaristic country."

Ross sank to the ground, staring at my drawing. Then she took the stick and added a peace symbol, the branches of the inverted *Y* converging at the *R* of "Amerika."

She said, "I haven't thought of those medallions in years. I don't even know what happened to mine. Our talisman." She laughed ruefully. "From this vantage point, it seems like just one of those silly things that kids do—like sitting around in a clubhouse in a vacant lot and cutting your fingers so you can exchange blood oaths. But at the time it was a big deal: we'd each have a piece of this thing that stood for what we believed in and be connected forever."

"In a way, I guess you are."

"Yes. Yes, I guess so." She sighed, then took them from me, examining them as they lay on the palm of her hand. "Where did you get these?"

"One from Perry Hilderly's flat. The other was given me by Mia Taylor."

"D. A. actually kept his?"

"Mia says he takes it out occasionally and looks at it. She thinks it has power over him, like an evil charm."

I thought Ross might scoff at that, but she merely said, "Maybe it does."

I said, "I take it this . . . talisman, as you call it, was something you shared with the other people who were involved in the Port Chicago bombing attempt."

"You think you know a lot about us. But not everyone in the collective was in on the Port Chicago thing."

"The collective again. What was it?"

She sank into a full sitting position, arms wrapped around her knees. "We were a political collective, loosely affiliated with the Weathermen. The Weather Bureau—the top leadership—was supposed to control policy, but there was a lot of ideological

234

struggle, and the Weather Machine was informally structured to begin with."

"When was this?"

"Sixty-eight, sixty-nine. Things were bad: the Movement as originally conceived was losing momentum, and the cops were really cracking down on us. Everybody was dropping out, preparing for direct, violent action. On campus, the scene had shifted from Berkeley to S.F. State. So a bunch of us split for the city."

"And?"

"Like I said, the Weathermen were pretty loosely structured. We just did our own thing."

"Which was?"

She shrugged. "Debated ideology. Engaged in political education. Refined skills that we'd need in the struggle."

"Skills?"

". . . Well, self-defense, propaganda, marksmanship, weaponry."

"Bombmaking?"

She nodded. "But mostly what we did was talk—endless, intense talk. We were so self-consciously political. And romantic. We thought it was so damned romantic to live in a crummy flat in the Fillmore and share everything—clothes, food, money,

235

drugs, sexual partners. God, when I think of how naive we were! We were going to change the world, but we knew no more of it than . . . than old Chaucer over there." She gestured at the pinto.

"The individual Weather collectives were quite small, weren't they?"

"Well, yes, they had to be, in order to create trust among the members and prevent infiltration."

"How many in yours?"

". . . People came and went, but there were never more than six or seven of us at a time."

"You and D. A. and Jenny Ruhl?"

She nodded.

"What about Perry?"

"He was . . . part of it. He had this job on a magazine and was supposed to get our propaganda across to the people through his stories. But he was *not* in on the bombing. He went to Vietnam as a reporter when that was still in the planning stages."

Hilderly apparently hadn't told his comrades that he was so fed up with the Movement that he was willing to pay his own way to Southeast Asia. Nor that he'd thought about writing a story on the collective. "Who else?"

236

"No one."

"You said up to seven."

"People came and went."

"Who else was at Port Chicago with D. A.?"

She got to her feet, brushing dirt from the seat of her jeans.

"You, Libby? Jenny Ruhl?"

She turned and started for the tack room. I followed. "What about Tom Grant?"

At the door she faced me. "How many times do I have to tell you that I don't know Tom Grant?"

There was something in her voice—a tone oddly close to relief—that gave me pause. I watched as she entered the room, dumped the medallions that she still held on the desk, and collected a bridle and saddle. As she brushed past me and went back outside I said, "What about the right man?"

She stopped halfway to where the horse stood. "Are you talking about Andy?"

I covered my own surprise, asked, "Was he there at Port Chicago?"

"Are you kidding?" She continued over to the rail, set the saddle on it, and began to bridle the pinto.

"Why wasn't he?"

"Because by then Andy Wrightman was

long gone. It was . . . as if he'd never existed." Her fingers moved clumsily with the bridle, her hands shaking slightly; she had difficulty getting the tongue of the buckle through the hole.

"He was Jenny Ruhl's lover back in Berkeley, wasn't he?"

"One of them."

"Was he Jessica's father?"

"God knows. For a while there Jenny was fucking a lot of guys. But yes, he probably was. The timing was right."

"Did Andy Wrightman run off when Jenny became pregnant?"

"Yeah."

"What do you know about him?"

Ross hoisted the saddle onto the pinto, positioned it, and squatted to buckle the girth. Her voice was muffled when she said, "Virtually nothing. He was a . . . nobody."

"Any idea where he was from?"

"No."

"It's my guess that he was from somewhere in the Southwest, and that he came back to Jenny—at least for a while, and as late as sixty-nine."

Ross straightened, her face red—whether from exertion or anger, I couldn't tell. "For God's sake, where do you *get* these ideas?"

"Jenny's daughter tells me that her father came to see her with her mother once, when she was four years old. That would have been in sixty-nine. The man wore a string tie, as many people from the Southwest do."

Ross seemed to find that amusing. She chuckled and said, "All sorts of people wear string ties—including tourists who buy them on vacation. And as for Jenny's daughter, I don't know anything about her other than that she existed."

"And you know nothing about Andy Wrightman?"

"I told you, he was a nobody, a nothing."

"It's funny: when I went to see D. A. the other day, I described Tom Grant to him, same as I did to you. You know what he said?"

"Where D. A. is concerned, I have no idea."

"He got very excited, said, 'Wrightman!'"

Again Ross bit her lip, then gave me a long, measured look. "I have to ride over to see the neighbor who runs cattle on my land. I want you gone by the time I get back. And don't come again."

"I need to ask—"

"No more questions. I told you before:

it's an old, sad story, and I don't want to talk about it. I've said far too much already."

"D. A. came to see you yesterday afternoon. What was that about?"

Her eyes narrowed as she mounted the pinto. "I suppose Mia told you that?"

"Yes."

"She would. Mia's young and insecure. She can't understand what D. A. and I have . . . had. So she puts the easiest interpretation on it and is jealous. Every time he takes off, she thinks he's coming here. But he doesn't. I haven't seen him in a good long time, and I don't expect him in the foreseeable future."

Abruptly she turned her horse and urged him into a trot. I watched as she took the trail under the trees—not toward the ranch of the neighbor who contracted to run the cattle, but toward Abbotts Lagoon and the seacoast.

When she was a fair distance away, I went over to the barn. Inside I could hear sounds of activity—the kid she'd mentioned who cleaned the stalls. Ross had neglected to lock the tack room; I went in there and retrieved the medallions from where she'd tossed them on the desk. Then I began looking around.

There was a calendar blotter on the desk,

with notations in its squares of upcoming pack trips and rentals. Next to it was a phone and a neat stack of periodicals such as *Horse & Rider*. The center desk drawer held the usual assortment of pens, pencils, and paper clips; the deep bottom drawer contained files. In the one above it were blank checks, envelopes, a ledger, and a box of business cards. But toward its back, in a separate compartment, a framed photograph lay face-down.

I took the photo out and found it was a color shot of Ross, Hilderly, Taylor, and a woman whom I first mistook for Jess Good-hue. They were grouped on the wide stone steps of some building—I thought it might be Sproul Hall at Berkeley. While Ross, Hilderly, and the other woman were seated, D. A. stood behind them, one arm raised in a clenched-fist salute. Ross didn't look much different than she did today; Hilderly I recognized easily from the old photos I'd seen in his albums. But Taylor was another man entirely: his stance was aggressive and proud, his eyes burned fiercely. Seeing all that intensity, however poorly preserved on film, made me understand how D. A.'s internal fires could have flared out of control and burned themselves out in the bitter aftermath of failure and imprisonment.

The other woman was such a mirror image of Jess Goodhue that I knew she had to be Jenny Ruhl. She'd passed on her elfin facial features to her daughter, and her hair—while long and straight—had the same dark sheen. Next to Hilderly's and Ross's lankiness, she was tiny and compact, also like Goodhue. But while she smiled brashly at the camera, her eyes held none of the uncompromising quality of Jess's. While her daughter's photos impressed the viewer as direct, Ruhl merely looked tough and defiant. I suspected the difference was in their upbringings: Ruhl was from a wealthy family and probably had had everything handed to her; Goodhue had had to rely on her natural strength to survive.

I stared at the photograph a while longer, wondering whose eye had been behind the camera's lens. Wondering why Ross had framed it and kept it all these years. And wondering about the disparate reactions of these four people to the cataclysmic events of the late sixties.

According to Luke Widdows, Hilderly had become so deeply disillusioned with the cause the others were fighting for that he set off on a trip halfway around the world in search of the truth—and then retreated into an emotional void for the rest of his life. Ross's silence about Port Chicago led me to suspect she'd been in on the bombing attempt and served time in prison herself. But after that she'd made a life for herself—albeit one that she'd hinted was at best only a life "of sorts." Taylor had been broken by prison—turned into something far less than a functional human being. And Ruhl? She'd shot herself.

What fundamental flaw had caused the crack-ups of Ruhl and Taylor? What made Ross and Hilderly survivors—however wounded? Taylor claimed he'd never been a strong man, but I suspected the crucial difference had less to do with strength than with flexibility. The eucalyptus trees that formed the windbreaks on this headland looked strong, but in a bad storm they were easily torn apart or uprooted. Conversely, the relatively delicate-looking cypresses could bend to the ground and live on, bowed and warped as they might become.

Finally I replaced the photo in the drawer and left the tack room. The air had grown chill; high wisps of fog drifted in from the coastline. I looked toward the sea, along the path that Ross had taken. And saw them, on the edge of the lagoon.

Ross sat on the pinto, and a denim-clad man with long black hair who surely was D. A. Taylor stood beside it. Ross leaned down toward him; Taylor had one hand on her shoulder. For a moment they spoke, their faces close, and then Taylor raised his other hand and pulled her head even closer. In spite of the distance, I could tell there was no resistance on Ross's part when their lips met.

Seventeen

I bought a sandwich and a bottle of Calistoga water at a deli in Inverness, then drove down the road and parked by the salt-marsh wildlife refuge to eat a late lunch and think. The white cranes were there again—half a dozen this time—and the sight of them standing placid among the reeds soothed my anger at Ross's deception and put me in a cooler frame of mind.

Actually I wasn't so much angry at Ross as I was at myself. In the course of my work people frequently lie to me—sometimes for no better reason than that they think they *should* lie to a detective. I should have been more on my guard with Ross, pressed harder about what now appeared to be her ongoing relationship with D. A. Taylor. But the interview had been valuable nonetheless: I now knew about the Port Chicago bombing attempt—a crime that would doubtless be well reported in back issues of area newspapers. And I also had a few ideas about the man called Andy Wrightman.

When I arrived at KSTS-TV at about four-thirty, I spotted Goodhue driving into the parking lot in a little yellow Datsun. I beeped the MG's horn and followed her, pulling up behind her rear bumper. She got out of the car and waved at me.

"I know what you want," she called, "but I don't have it for you. I had a late night, then an early breakfast with some people from a charity benefit we're cosponsoring, and *then* a luncheon speech for Women in Communications. I'm an hour late and running ragged and hoping I can make it through until it's time to rest between broadcasts."

She did look tired—not totally exhausted, but red around the eyes and hollow in the face. Her staccato chatter made me wonder if she'd been taking uppers to keep going. I said, "Jess, I wouldn't bother you if this wasn't important."

Her mouth tightened, and I caught a hint of the testiness that she'd displayed with her coworkers Monday afternoon. "We all have our priorities," she said, "and mine is to make it through the day without screwing up our newscasts."

"I thought you wanted to find out about your father, about Perry Hilderly's reason for naming you in his will."

She shrugged and began walking toward the rear entrance to the studio. "Frankly, I've decided it's not all that important. I was right when I burned that detective's report; the past is dead, and I ought to be getting on with my future."

"Does that mean you won't look for the investigator's name?"

"Jesus!" She turned toward me, her irritation plain now. "I said I would look for it when I have the time. I *do not* have the time today. Besides, there probably wasn't anything valuable in his report; he was just some big Italian guy with a crummy two-man office on the edge of the Tenderloin. For all I know, he was incompetent."

Unwittingly she'd given me something to

go on. Except for the "incompetent," the man she described sounded suspiciously like an investigator friend I call Wolf. But it was strange that a newscaster wouldn't have remembered his name right off; Wolf—a nickname I'd long ago derived from the press claims that he was "the last of the lone-wolf detectives"—has had more than his share of publicity, and fairly recently.

It was for that reason—plus the fact that I'd been lied to by one of the other heirs earlier that afternoon—that I concealed my satisfaction with Goodhue's revelation and merely said, "I'll call you later."

Willie Whelan's flagship jewelry store was situated on the south side of Market Street between Seventh and Eighth—an iffy location at best, and one that had reaped little benefit from what city planners are fond of calling "the Renaissance of Market Street." All the rebirth is going on further downtown, where high-rises have mushroomed and cautious shoppers now venture into what used to be a minefield in the war between the haves and the have-nots. Willie's block remained largely unchanged: street people pushed grocery carts loaded with all their belongings; winos sprawled on the benches that were part of the beautification project; merchants hawked cut-rate wares from sidewalk bins; private security guards were stationed at most of the doorways.

When I entered the store at a few minutes after five, Willie was already there, extolling the merits of a ring with the world's tiniest diamond to a young Asian couple. He'd point to it and then gesture expansively; the couple would look at one another and nod dubiously. Then he'd enthuse some more and they'd nod again, a little more firmly. When both nodded decisively, Willie flashed his most sincere smile of congratulation and whipped out a credit application from under the counter. As the couple began filling it out, he gave me a victory sign.

"Is Hank here yet?" I asked, casting a sympathetic glance at the latest victims of Willie's salesmanship.

"He called, said he'd be a few minutes late."

"Just as well. I need to make a couple of calls of my own."

"Use my office—you know where it is."

"Thanks." I skirted the central counter where he stood and went through an opening in a smaller counter that bordered the showroom on three sides. Numerous customers

—none of them terribly solvent-looking—leaned over its displays of watches and charm bracelets and pendants and birthstone rings. On the other side of the counter was a door; beyond it lay the stockroom and Willie's office.

My first call was to Wolf, but I reached only his machine. That was no surprise; he and his partner spent more time in the field than at the office. I left a brief message. Next I called All Souls and caught Rae just as she was on her way out.

"Oh, good," she said. "I've got the information you wanted on American Consolidated Services. They're a government contractor that operates restaurants and cafeterias for the military on bases all over the world."

"I thought it might be something like that. Were you able to find out anything about Bob Smith?"

"Unfortunately, no. Personnel knew he was dead, and the person I talked to became suspicious when I asked."

"Doesn't matter. I know enough now, and if the police want to make an official inquiry, it'll only confirm what I suspect."

"Shar, what's this about?"

"I'll tell you later."

"You keep saying that, but I never get fully caught up."

"Have patience. Got to go now." As I replaced the receiver, the door to the office opened and Willie and Hank entered.

Hank looked around the cramped cubicle, then sat on a folding chair under the window. Willie perched on the edge of the desk, swinging one cowboy-booted foot. He said, "This'd better be important, McCone. I had to cut short my visit to my Oakland store to get back here on time."

"It is." I opened my briefcase and took out the legal pad I'd made notes on while at the SFPD that morning.

"Well, aren't you going to enlighten us?" Hank asked. "*I* was planning to go home early, but your message kept me at All Souls just long enough for a client to call with an emergency, and now I've got to work through the evening again."

I was trying to save their lives, and they were complaining about me wasting their time! I said, "Did I ever tell either of you what a pain in the ass you can be?" The words and their tone were unusually harsh for me; both Hank and Willie looked taken aback. They exchanged quick looks, but neither spoke.

I said, "First I need to ask you some questions about Vietnam in nineteen seventy. Both of you were in Cam Ranh Bay at the same time as Perry Hilderly?"

Hank nodded.

"And Hilderly hung out with a bunch of you from the base?"

"Yes, at an off-base bar . . . What was it called, Willie?"

"Something French."

"Moulin Rouge? Rouge et Noir?"

"Rouge et Noir," Willie said.

"Good memory."

I asked, "Who usually hung out with you?"

Hank looked blank, then glanced at Willie. Willie shrugged. Hank said, "Well, people came and went a lot. In a place like Cam Ranh, the personnel fluctuated daily."

"A big base, was it?"

"Cam Ranh itself was a port—built from the ground up by the U.S. in case Saigon fell. There was the army supply depot, where Willie and I were stationed, plus navy and air force bases, an airfield serving the area, a hospital. About twenty thousand military stationed there, and God knows how many civilians." He paused, smiling ironically. "Government sunk billions of the taxpayers' dollars into Cam Ranh; then after the pullout it became a virtual ghost town. Now it's a port of call for Soviet ships."

"So what you're saying is that it would be difficult to remember specific individuals whom you hung out with?"

"Some I probably could, people who stayed around for a long time. But like I said, they came and went."

I leaned back in the desk chair, considering what I knew about the military. It was a fair amount; my father had been a chief petty officer in the navy, a thirty-year man. I said, "For a minute, let's talk about the people who we know *were* there. You"—I motioned at Hank—"were politicized by the war, went over there a liberal and came back a radical. Hilderly was a war protester, a reporter, and a civilian. And you"—I looked at Willie—"would by no means have been your ideal enlisted man. In addition, Hank was an officer. It's fairly unusual for officers and enlisted men to socialize."

"Well," Hank said, "in a combat zone it's a little looser. But what you're getting at is correct: we were a bunch of liberal misfits."

"Then I assume your group caused comment, might have been resented by the more hawkish element?"

252

"Christ, yes," Willie said. "Was like everybody in our corner of the bar had leprosy, except for when some asshole decided to pick a fight." To Hank he added, "You remember that night I almost got into it with that fascist lieutenant? For sure I'd of ended up court-martialed if you hadn't stepped in."

I sat up straighter. "Do you remember the lieutenant's name?"

". . . I can't remember. Hank?"

Hank shook his head.

"Do you recall anything about him?"

"Nothing except the attitude."

"Besides him," I said, "do you remember anyone else who tried to pick fights or otherwise antagonize you?"

"There were plenty of them, but after all this time the names and faces aren't clear."

"Hank?"

He shook his head. "Frankly, I've repressed a lot of things about those days."

"Try to think back to Rouge et Noir. Picture it, and yourselves there in your corner. Who else is with you?"

Both of them closed their eyes. After a moment Willie said, "That radio operator, got killed in the patrol plane crash."

"Sorry. I should have told you I'm only

interested in people who so far as you know are still living."

More silence. Then Hank said to Willie, "The guy from Atlanta—the one who'd met Martin Luther King."

"Bernie—nah, he bought it at Da Nang."

"Mike, the one who always had the terrific grass?"

"Dead, too."

"What about Chris, from Philadelphia?"

"Helicopter crash."

If I let them go on, it would begin to sound like a reading of the names from the Vietnam War Memorial. I said, "What about John Owens?"

"Owens," Hank said.

Willie frowned, then snapped his fingers. "Johnny Owens. I should of remembered him. Was a crazy man, actually wanted to kill the fascist lieutenant. Probably would of, too, if he hadn't transferred out and got sent up to Saigon. Wonder whatever happened to the crazy son of a bitch?"

"He was the sniper's third victim."

Willie's mouth dropped open. Hank's face went taut and still—the way I've seen it when something unexpected happens to him in court.

I asked, "Were there any women in your group?"

Hank said, "A few. Mostly nurses."

"What about a Red Cross nurse named Mary Johnson?"

". . . It's such a common name."

"I remember her," Willie said. "She wasn't there long. A blonde with a fiancé in the marines. I lusted after her, but she wasn't having any."

Hank looked at me. "Mary, too?"

"The second victim."

"Why didn't I realize it when I saw the story in the paper? And the one about Johnny?"

"Mary Johnson had married and was going by the surname Davis. And even if her name had been the same, or Owens's more distinctive, there would have been no reason for you to connect them with people you'd known casually in a bar in Vietnam. That was a long time ago."

They were silent for a moment. Willie finally asked, "What about the sniper's first victim?"

"He's the one who originally didn't fit the pattern. Bob Smith. A drifter, worked in restaurants mainly. But I have an idea about him. Military food services are usually provided by civilian contractors. What was the name of the one at your base?"

Hank shook his head. Willie said, "Damned if I can remember. Ought to, for all the bitching about the food that I did. What was it we nicknamed them?"

Hank smiled faintly. "American Constipated."

"American Consolidated Services," I said. "Right!"

"Then there's your link. You may not remember Bob Smith, but he worked for American Consolidated during that period, and I'm willing to bet he hung out with you at the Rouge et Noir, too."

"Okay," Hank said, "I see where this is leading. Someone who didn't like our political orientation and disregard for protocol is now—after close to twenty years—tracking down people from the group and killing them. But why, after all that time? And how does he find us?"

"In Willie's case, it's obvious—the TV commercials. And you don't keep all that low a profile. The others he could have stumbled over by chance, or by less circumstantial means."

Willie shook his head. "McCone, this is fuckin' crazy. The *guy* must be crazy."

"When did you hear of a sane person stalking others with a gun?"

They were silent again. I was busy formulating an idea that I wanted to run past Greg. After a while I said, "The important thing right now is for both of you to stay safe. You're going to have to be extra cautious, even during daylight. He's missed once, and that might have made him impatient."

"Don't you worry about me none," Willie replied. "I'm going home and locking myself in until this is all over."

"And you," I said to Hank, "are going back to All Souls?"

"I have to. As I said, an emergency came up."

"Why don't you stay there tonight?"

"Where? On the couch? I tried that last winter when Anne-Marie and I were broken up, and hardly slept for nights. The case I'm trying is winding up tomorrow; I have to get a decent rest."

"Okay—go to All Souls, then. But don't leave until I get there."

"And then what do you intend to do?"

"Act as your bodyguard on your way home."

"Shar, that'll make me feel like an old man

being helped across the street by a Girl Scout."

"Like it or not, that's the way it's going to be."

Hank merely nodded, once again cowed by my obvious irritation.

I stood up and stuffed the legal pad into my briefcase. "There's one other thing I want both of you to do: keep thinking about the hawkish element in that bar. Try to recall confrontations, threats. Try to remember names. I'll check with you later about it."

As I started for the door Hank asked, "Where're you going now?"

"To talk with Greg Marcus. I have an idea that may help him identify the sniper."

Eighteen

Greg said, "Damn, you may have something there."

I reached for the cup of coffee I'd set on the edge of his desk and waited for him to go on.

After a moment he added, "The motive might sound farfetched, but I've encountered stranger ones. Let's hear your theory on who's responsible."

258

I replaced the cup and began enumerating items on my fingers. "First, I assume we're in agreement that we're dealing with a seriously disturbed individual."

He nodded.

"Second, given the length of time that's elapsed, there has to have been some event that triggered the shooting spree."

"I'm not sure that's a given. Sometimes people brood for years—decades, even— and then just tip over the edge."

"But usually with a nudge from some event or situation—however minor."

"I'll agree with that if you stress the minor."

"All right." I got up and began to pace about the cubicle, allowing the regular motion to lend order to my thoughts. "Let's assume the person is a man. He's disturbed. He's probably a Vietnam vet."

"Not necessarily; two of his victims weren't, but they were still in Cam Ranh at the same time he was."

"For the sake of this particular argument, let's assume he is. Suppose he's been receiving psychiatric treatment as an outpatient. Where in this area would he go?"

"Letterman."

"Where Mary Johnson Davis worked in

259

psychiatric counseling before she went to Children's Hospital. And where John Owens probably received medical care for his disability."

Greg nodded. "So our perp is at Letterman and he runs into Davis. Maybe she's even the counselor assigned to his case. Whatever the circumstances, that's the nudge."

"And he also spots Owens. Now he knows they're both living in San Francisco. From then on it's easy to stalk them, learn their habits, wait for the right moment."

"That's fine. And I can see why he would have been able to locate Hank and Willie— but what about Hilderly?"

"Hilderly was Hank's friend. They met for drinks fairly frequently."

"And Bob Smith?"

I sat down again. "Smith's the one who didn't seem to fit the pattern originally, and at first glance he doesn't fit this one too well, either. But that pizza restaurant where he worked when he died is only a couple of blocks from Willie's store, and I looked in there on the way over here. It's the kind where the kitchen is only separated from the dining area by a counter; you can watch the people preparing the food. Our man's coming across Smith could have been circumstantial. If it happened after he saw Davis and Owens at Letterman, he might have been on the alert for familiar faces."

"But why go after Smith before the others, in that case?"

I shrugged. "Opportunity. Smith was a loner, easier to stalk."

"Okay." Greg leaned back in his chair, rubbing his chin, eyes trained on a point above my head. Once again I waited.

Finally he said, "The time lapse bothers me. I know we've said Davis or Owens, or the combination thereof, pushed him over the edge, but surely in twenty years there would have been other nudges. Why didn't he go after his victims long ago?"

"I've thought about that. There's an additional factor—and fortunately, it's one that may speed an identification. I think he might have been in a mental institution most of that time. Perhaps he'd only recently been released."

"Good point." Greg's gaze remained focused on the distance as he considered. "What we've got here," he said, "is a lot of conjecture, if you want to know the truth. But it's better than any lead I've developed. And obviously the place to start investigating is at Letterman. As it happens, I've an acquaintance in the CID at the Presidio who will expedite requests for information." He reached for his Rolodex and thumbed through it.

I asked, "Do you still have a man on Willie's house?"

"No. We're so damned understaffed. But I'll try to get one back on, plus another on Hank."

"I don't think you need to worry too much about Willie; he told me he was going home and not coming out until it was all over. And I'll take care of Hank, at least for tonight."

"You sure you want the responsibility?"

"I don't mind. It's a calculated risk. The sniper's pattern has been to fire when the victim's alone. Even when he shot at Willie, Rae was way down by the corner."

"Well, be careful. I don't want to lose either of you."

"You won't."

Greg picked up the phone receiver and punched out a number. "Busy, dammit."

I stood and shrugged into my jacket. "I'd better get over to All Souls."

"I'll phone you there when I have something." Greg came around the desk and walked me to the door of the cubicle. Then he paused, his hand on the knob. "And Sharon—thanks for your cooperation. The chief's been on my case since Willie was shot at, as the mayor's office has been on his. This comes at a time when nailing the sniper could make my career—and failing could break it."

I looked up at his face, somber in the neon light that glared down from the ceiling fixtures. "How so?"

"A captaincy is opening up—Narcotics. I'm the major contender for it."

"Greg! Congratulations!"

His answering smile was wistful, and I knew why. The captaincy was a desk job, one in which he would juggle paper, policy, and politics. There would be no actual field investigations, no more satisfaction of personally piecing together a solid case against a perpetrator. And yet, it was time . . .

"You *want* the promotion, don't you?"

He sighed. "Yes and no. But I know it's the only logical step. And I'm tired, Sharon. I'm tired of being called out in the middle of the night to crime scenes. I'm sick and tired of violent death. And I'm sick of dealing with scum, of being reminded at every turn of how vile people can be."

"You think you won't be in Narcotics?"

"Maybe I just need another brand of vileness." He paused, his lips quirking up mischievously. "Besides, my appointment will really piss off McFate. He was recently passed over for lieutenant."

"In that case, I hope it comes through fast. And speaking of McFate . . . ?"

"Probably over at the Intelligence Division again. He seems to prefer his cronies on the old detail to those on Homicide." Greg glanced through the door. "Well, what a surprise. Maybe now I'll actually get a report on the Grant case out of him." He motioned to a desk on the far side of the squad room. A pearl-gray suit jacket was draped precisely over a silly-looking brass garment rack that was more appropriate to a bedroom, and I could see the back of McFate's head.

"You know," I said, "even though I need to talk with him, I was kind of hoping he wouldn't be here."

"I know how you feel. Good luck."

I crossed the noisy, cluttered room, avoiding boxes of files, misplaced chairs, and even someone's bowling bag. When I stopped next to McFate's desk, he kept his eyes on the report in front of him. Moments later, he looked up, expression going glacial when he saw me.

"Ms. McCone," he said, "what may I do for you?"

McFate didn't ask me to sit down, so I remained where I was. His gaze moved up and down my body, taking in my jeans, sweater, and suede jacket in a manner that stopped just short of being contemptuous. A slender needle of irritation pricked at me, but I adopted a businesslike tone.

"I have some information pertaining to the Grant case."

He smoothed his luxuriant brown mustache—surely it wasn't real; could one purchase a fake, like a toupee?—with his index finger. "Yes?"

"I've found evidence that Grant's real name may have been Andy Wrightman."

"Evidence."

"One of Perry Hilderly's heirs mentioned the name when I described Grant to him."

"Oh, I see—*hard* evidence."

With an effort I kept my voice level. "It's something you may want to look into. Wrightman was associated with Hilderly in the late sixties; he was a campus hanger-on at Cal, something of a hippie and a drifter—"

Now McFate smiled superiorly. "I can assure you that Thomas Grant was never a hippie or a drifter—quite the opposite. Frankly, I think you're becoming obsessed with this Hilderly business."

"And frankly, I think it's logical that there might be a tie-in."

"Ms. McCone, my background check on the victim was very thorough."

"Would you care to share what you turned up?"

"No, I would not. I am not, as you put it, in the habit of sharing the details of my investigations with civilians. Nor do I care for any further input from you."

I glared at him. McFate remained impassive. I said, "Do you plan to share the details of your investigation with Lieutenant Marcus? He mentioned to me a few minutes ago that he was hoping you'd brief him."

McFate's cleft chin jutted out. "I intend to speak with him momentarily." His impatient glance toward his superior's office indicated that only my annoying presence was preventing him from doing so. He picked up a file, stood, and motioned at the way out of the squad room.

I remained in front of him, blocking his path. "You know, Leo," I said, "it strikes me that the past of a man who practiced law

266

the way Grant did can't have been any too savory."

McFate smiled thinly. "And that, Ms. McCone, shows exactly how much you know." He brushed past me and moved toward Greg's cubicle. Greg still stood in its doorway; apparently he'd been watching the entire exchange. As McFate entered and took a seat, Greg smiled at me and shrugged sympathetically.

Irresistible impulse overcame me: I made a single-fingered gesture at the back of McFate's well-barbered head. Snickers erupted from the desks around me. Greg rolled his eyes and went back into his office.

I left the squad room, oddly elated by my display of temper. I'd always been the good kid on the private investigators' block: cooperative, professional, rarely antagonistic. But even good kids have their limits. I figured I was entitled to throw an occasional fit.

As I punched the Down button at the elevators, I wondered why I'd allowed Leo McFate to enrage me. The man was petty and mean-spirited; why couldn't I just ignore him?

Because, I told myself as I brutalized the button some more, the man's an asshole.

267

When you're dealing with someone who suffers from that altogether-too-prevalent malady, it's very often catching.

I made two detours on my way to All Souls: first to pick up a pizza, so I wouldn't have to sponge off the folks who lived there (and probably have to eat some god-awful health food), and then to my house to pick up my gun.

The strongbox where I keep my .38 is actually an ammunition box that my father pilfered from the navy years ago. The box sits on the floor of the linen closet in my bathroom, hardly an original hiding place, and one that it wouldn't take a competent thief two minutes to find. However, its lock is a good one, and when I had the closet built while I was renovating the cottage, my clever contractor put a bolt straight through the bottom of the box and into the floor joist. Any thief who wants to make off with it will have to take part of the cottage along, too.

I went into the bathroom, pushed aside a jumble of cleaning supplies, and flattened myself on the floor so I could work the lock. I hadn't had the .38 out in so long that it lay beneath the velvet pouch containing my grandmother's garnet earrings that I'd last worn on New Year's Eve. The sight of them gave me a flash of bittersweet nostalgia. I'd met George Kostakos on December 30; he'd called me for the first time at a few minutes after midnight on New Year's.

So much had happened since then: we'd come so close, only to move apart. George had said he cared deeply for me, that when his estranged wife's mental condition stabilized he'd come back and see if I'd still have him. But months had passed, and I'd heard nothing; now I wasn't even sure I wanted to. Maybe it was better to go through life alone, protected from its hurts and disappointments. Maybe people who only indulged in casual, short-term relationships were the ones with the greatest chance at happiness.

But casual, short-term relationships had never worked for me. And I wasn't sure that happiness was a reasonable goal, anyway. At times it seemed a myth—something an advertising agency had dreamed up to sell more toothpaste.

"Enough!" I said aloud. "You've got things to do." I took out the gun, locked the box, and got up off the floor.

That was another thing: I found that I talked to myself more lately. People always talk to themselves, particularly those who live alone, but with me it was as if the sensible, self-sufficient side of my personality was trying to tell the other, vulnerable side to shape up. And I suspected that the sensible McCone was losing the debate.

Before I left the house I checked my answering machine in case Wolf had tried to reach me at home. The first message was from Jim Addison, sounding angry because I hadn't returned his call. I fast-forwarded through it, unwilling to allow my uneasiness about his potential for violence to compound my tension about the sniper. The only other message was from my mother, complaining because I hadn't called her last week. I should have, but I'd let it go because I really didn't have anything to say. And now I couldn't, because Ma is very sensitive to undertones in my voice and would catch on quickly to the fact that things weren't right. Then she would worm it out of me about the sniper and about my friends being in danger, and finally, because she was way down in San Diego and couldn't have done anything to help even if she were right here, she'd worry. When Ma worries about one of her children, she calls the other four and tells them all about it, and soon she has a big

McCone worryfest going. The only family member who doesn't feed into it is my father; Pa just stays out in his garage workshop, playing the guitar and singing dirty folk songs in a voice loud enough—because he's getting deaf—to scandalize the neighbors.

No, I decided, I can't call Ma back until this whole thing is over.

At quarter past eleven Rae and I sat cross-legged on her brass bed playing what seemed like our thousandth game of gin rummy; we'd been at it since nine. Initially we'd discussed the snipings and the Hilderly case, but then we'd fallen silent. Now the only sounds were the slap of the cards, the distant bellow of foghorns, and small moans and sighs of contentment from the trunk under the dormer window, where Ralph and Alice curled together in luxurious sleep. Rae was baby-sitting them tonight, since Ted had gone to a memorial service for their former owner.

I had to admit how tranquilizing the presence of a sleeping cat could be. And Rae's room—which she'd created herself at the rear of the Victorian's unfinished attic, after she'd lived in her office for months and none of the regular rooms had become available —was lovely. A snug aerie full of plants and white wicker furniture and splashed with yellows and golds and greens, it revealed her heretofore unknown flair for interior decorating on a small budget.

I picked up a king and discarded a trey. "Gin."

She glared at me. "I've been waiting for one card since the deal."

"Them's the breaks." I didn't even bother to write down the score, just let my hand gravitate toward a stainless-steel bowl containing the dregs of a batch of popcorn. Comfort food is what I call things like popcorn and macaroni-and-cheese and milkshakes and butterscotch pudding—food that is reminiscent of childhood and reduces the world to simple terms when it becomes too complicated to bear.

Rae said, "What's the matter—you feeling gruffly?"

I smiled at the word, one of those that I've come to consider Rae-isms. "Yes. I'm sick of gin rummy, even if I am winning. Is Hank *ever* going to go home?"

"He's turning into a workaholic. I guess it keeps his mind off the possibility of being shot at." Rae gathered up the cards and score pad and set them on the nightstand. She wore an old gray-and-red-plaid flannel bathrobe and had conditioner on her hair; it stuck up in greasy-looking points. As she flopped back against the pillows, I noticed she seemed tense and faintly depressed.

"You look kind of gruffly, too," I said.

She shrugged.

"Worried about Willie?"

"Not really. He was settled in for the night when I left there. Had an adult western—the sexy kind, you know?—and a twelve-pack of Bud. That'll hold him."

"Things not going well with you two?"

"They're fine. The relationship's not complex enough for us to have problems. No, what it is, I need to talk to you about my job."

Uh-oh, I thought. "Go ahead." I leaned back and whacked my head on one of the bed's brass posts. Rae saw my predicament and tossed me a pillow.

"Okay," she said. "I'm not complaining, you understand. You're a great boss. It's just that . . . the other day when I was out in the field? It really felt good. And it made me realize that I'm not sticking to my original game plan. Shar, I'd like to take on more work, build up my hours to the point where

I can get my own license. And I want to get firearms-qualified. I think it's time."

I felt a wrenching: chick leaving the nest. In Rae's case getting the license would surely motivate a departure. For one thing, she was too bright and talented to remain at All Souls doing my scut work; for another, that was the game plan she'd referred to. I couldn't blame her for wanting more than a relatively small salary, a pile of debts, a room that wasn't really a room, and a bathroom one flight down that she shared with numerous other people. And I certainly wouldn't stand in her way.

"I think you're right," I said. "I haven't really been giving you as much responsibility as you're capable of handling. Tomorrow we'll look over what we have on tap, and I'll assign more to you."

She smiled, pleased and relieved. Then she studied me over her bent knees. "You don't look too happy about this."

"I'm glad that you've progressed so far in such a short time. In a way, it's a compliment to me. But I'll miss you. I've come to rely on you. Besides, who am I going to play gin rummy or take long lunch hours with?"

"Miss me? I'm not going anywhere."

"I thought you'd want to go to a better firm."

"Shar, that was *before*, when I had Doug dependent on me for everything. I don't need as much money anymore. And I love All Souls as much as you do. In a way, it's like the family I never had." Rae had been brought up by her grandmother after the early deaths of her parents, and the grandmother, by her own admission, hadn't relished the responsibility.

I said, "Do you realize that's one of the first times I've heard you refer to your ex without 'the asshole' appended to his name?"

"Yeah, well, maybe I'm growing up." There was a knock at the door. She called, "Come on in."

Hank entered, looking drawn and weary. He glanced at Rae's hair and said, "Jesus, you look like you're wearing a greasy fright wig."

"Perhaps, but tomorrow I will have sleek auburn tresses. And you will still look like you're wearing a used Brillo pad."

That coaxed a smile out of him. *"Touché."* To me he added, "I'm ready to go home now, if my secret-service woman will deign

275

to accompany me." In spite of the light words, his tone was tense.

I grabbed the popcorn bowl and stood. "Let's go."

Rae got up, too, and removed the bowl from my hands. "I'll take that. I want to check and see if there're any good late movies on the tube."

Together we trooped down two flights of stairs. Ralph and Alice followed, taking an occasional tumble, refreshed for another attempt at ripping the place to shreds. In the hallway Rae said good night and herded them toward the kitchen.

Hank already had his coat on. I collected my bag and jacket from Rae's office. When I came out, he was standing by the door. I said, "Wait a minute," and took out the .38.

Hank's eyes moved to it, and he swallowed. The possibility that the sniper might wait outside was tangible to him now. I asked, "Are you sure you wouldn't rather just stay here tonight?"

". . . Can't. This case I'm trying is important. I've got to get some sleep."

"All right, then. Stay put while I take a look around."

I opened the door and went out onto the front steps, gun ready. The fog was dense and still. Through it I could barely make out hazy lights in the houses on the other side of the little park; its few shade trees and trash dumpster were deep in mist-laden darkness. I stood for over a minute, watching and listening. Nothing moved, and the only sounds that came to my ears were those of a normal late evening in a quiet neighborhood.

Finally I stepped back inside and said to Hank, "It looks okay out there, but what we're going to do is make it obvious that there are two of us. My car's in the driveway, and the passenger door is unlocked. Don't hesitate or look around, just get in and slouch down. We'll drive to your place and pull right into the garage."

"What about my car?"

"We'll just leave it here. I'll pick you up in the morning so you can get it before you have to be in court. Hopefully this'll be cleared up by tomorrow night." I opened the door again and stepped back onto the porch.

Hank hesitated a few beats before he joined me. Behind him I saw Rae watching us, backlit against the kitchen door.

Outside, everything was as still as before. I scrutinized the park once more. Hank closed the door behind us. I started down the steps, putting my body in front of his. But for some reason he moved to my left. "Hey!—"

And then the branches of a tree at the edge of the park moved. Rippled, even though there was no breeze. I moved back in front of Hank, yelling at him to get down.

There was a whine. The pillar next to me splintered. A wood fragment grazed my cheek as I heard the gunshot.

Hank froze.

I hit him with the full weight of my body. Knocked him against the far railing.

Another whine. Another report. Hank grunted and tumbled down the steps.

I slid after him. Flattened my body on the pavement. No more shots. Nothing.

I moved my hand toward Hank. Touched something warm and wet. Brought my fingers up in front of my eyes. Blood.

I raised my head to stare at him. He lay very still, and the pavement around us was already staining red.

Nineteen

Frantically I felt Hank's neck for a pulse. It was there—weak and erratic.

Someone at the top of the steps shouted something about calling 911. Then Rae was kneeling beside me, grasping my arm. "Oh, Jesus—is he alive?"

"Yes—barely." I shook off her hand and stood, scanning the park. A figure was running uphill from its apex, barely visible in the thick mist.

The bastard had waited to make sure he'd hit Hank!

Rage welled up in me—cold, controlled, purposeful. I glanced at Hank, saw Jack and Larry were with him now. Doing more for him than I could. Doing more than I had. I felt as if I were viewing the scene through a polished pane of glass—one I wanted to smash into jagged, glittering shards.

I gripped my gun so hard my fingers hurt. Then I began running uphill, too, just as the sniper disappeared into the mist.

The sidewalk was uneven and steeply canted. I stumbled and banged into a car that was parked across it. A couple who were cautiously descending toward the commotion at All Souls saw my face, then my gun, and gave me a wide berth. I ran to the top of the grassy triangle, where I'd last spotted the fleeing figure.

Higher up, the fog was even thicker. It

dimmed what lights were on in the surrounding houses, made the familiar terrain alien, confusing. I stopped to get my bearings.

Several narrow streets converged at the top of the park, then fanned off in different directions. He could have strolled down any of them like an ordinary pedestrian, perhaps intending to return as a bystander to the chaotic scene below. The thought heightened my rage, which was already burning dangerously high—directed outward at the sniper, but also inward at myself for failing to protect Hank. I hesitated, damping it down, peering through the shifting grayness.

Diagonally from where I stood was one of those little wooded areas that dot Bernal Heights—a mere strip of land covered with fir trees. I studied it, then moved slowly across the intersection, gun raised.

A tall figure darted from the trees' dark shelter. I shouted for him to stop. Would have fired, but then he vanished again. Lights flashed on in a nearby house; their rays showed him fleeing uphill, on the steepest section of Coso Avenue. I went after him.

The man—he ran like one—took the steps that were cut into the sloping sidewalk three at a time. I raced along on the pavement beside them. I could hear his gasping, wheezing breath now. His feet slapped the concrete in counterpoint to mine. From behind me came excited voices and distant sirens.

He overshot the intersection with Prospect Avenue and kept climbing. Beyond the iron railing bordering the steps were houses; across Coso was a long lot enclosed in a high wooden fence and then a cliff face—some fifty or sixty feet of sheer rock. He kept on climbing the steps, but then two figures appeared at the top of the hill, their outlines blurred by the fog. Their voices carried—young, strong, male. I yelled for them to stop the running man.

He whirled. Hesitated for only an instant, then darted across the street. Looked from side to side, then disappeared into a two- or three-foot gap between the high fence and the cliff face. The young men whirled, too —and vanished over the hill.

Cowards!

I sprinted across Coso. Stopped and flattened my body against the fence next to the opening. My breath came hard; blood roared in my ears. I tried to listen, but could hear nothing from the gap behind the fence.

A trap? Was he aiming his gun at the opening?

After a moment I inched along and peered down there. The fog was trapped in the narrow pocket—waist-high and thick as smoke from a brush fire. It moved sinuously away from me and trailed off into the darkness.

I still could hear nothing, not even a telltale pant or wheeze. Finally I slipped around the corner, staying flat against the fence. The ground was rocky and uneven; I tested it carefully with my foot before I took each step. Ahead was total blackness. It was as if I were entering a tunnel that had no end.

And then I heard something: the snap of a branch. I moved along more quickly, and my foot banged into a heavy object. It rolled and thumped into the fence.

More branches snapped and cracked. Then there were thrashing noises, stumbling footsteps.

I felt along the cliff face with my left hand, moving quickly toward the source of the noise. Now I could make out a stand of brush whose uppermost branches were outlined against the sky. It appeared to completely block the narrow passageway. When I neared it, I smelled the sharp odor of anise.

The thrashing noises were more distant

now. I took my hand off the cliff face and parted some branches. The brush was dense, impossible to see through. On the other side of it footsteps slapped on cleared ground. Running again.

I plunged into the brush, batting aside branches, fighting through tall weeds. Vines caught at my legs and ankles; blackberry thorns scratched at my bare hands. I tripped over a rock, caught myself on the limb of a fir tree, my fingers coming away sticky with sap. Then I burst free of the wild vegetation and came out on a cement path.

There was a concrete retaining wall to my right now—perhaps four feet high. Roofs peaked on the other side of it. Several houses away, the cliff jutted out and formed a dead end. The man was scaling the wall down there.

I couldn't see him clearly enough to risk a shot. As I raced along the path he disappeared over the wall. Then there was a loud clanging of metal.

I jammed my gun into my belt, grasped the top of the wall with both hands, and boosted myself up. For a few seconds I teetered on top; then I jumped, landing on the balls of my feet. Pain from the impact shot upward. I staggered, banged into the garbage can he'd upset.

Lights were flaring up in the windows of the houses ahead of me; they illuminated an alley between them. The man was fumbling at the latch of a picket fence that blocked it at the street end. I shouted for him to halt. He got the gate open and disappeared onto the sidewalk.

Gun in hand again, I went after him. A window opened above me and a man yelled something unintelligible. I kept going. When I reached the gate, it was still swinging violently and caught me hard across my lower body; I shoved it open and ran out onto what must have been Prospect Avenue, looking frantically from left to right.

He was going uphill again, to the left, feet pounding. Dogs barked and more people shouted, marking his passage.

On the other side of Prospect was another small wooded area. The sniper sprinted toward it. The porch light of the house next to it shone on him; briefly I made out jeans, a dark windbreaker, and a baseball cap. Then he disappeared into the misty shadows.

I put on speed, throat aching with each breath, pain stabbing at my right side. When I reached the little grove, the odors of eucalypti and conifers clogged my nostrils. I skirted the trees, following the sound of his footsteps.

Beyond the grove lay a bricked parking area full of cars, then one of the little ladder streets that scale Bernal Heights—a wide set of steps, bisected by a waist-high iron railing, that descended to Coleridge Street. The sniper was running down it, his baseball cap flying off and longish gray hair blowing free. If I lost him here, he would be only a block from crowded Mission Street, where buses ran at all hours.

I started down the steps, yelling hoarsely at him, threatening to fire. He looked over his shoulder. Turned and raised his gun.

I squeezed off a shot. It went wild, but the man stumbled, smacked into the iron railing. Dropped his gun. It clattered on the steps, bounced into the bordering vegetation. He righted himself, glanced over there, turned and fled.

I shouted again. He kept going, leaped over the last few steps, and thumped onto the sidewalk. The impact jarred him; he went down on one knee.

I stopped, bracing myself. Brought my gun up in both hands and fired again.

The shot knocked him the rest of the way

to the pavement. He landed facedown, then tried to crawl forward. I jumped off the steps and grabbed one of his arms. Pinned it behind his back. Sat on him.

All up and down the street dogs barked and people peered from their windows or front porches. Voices babbled. I glanced along the block, panting, and realized we'd made a rough circle, were on the other side of the park that fronted All Souls. I couldn't see the house clearly through the trees, but they were backlit by the red and blue pulsars of the police cars. The mutter and squawk of their radios was plainly audible.

Beneath me, the man struggled. I yanked upward on his arm and he lay still. A woman was staring at us from the yard of the nearest house; she seemed incapable of speech.

I shouted at her, "Go down to Coso, tell the cops I've got the sniper!"

Without a word, she took off at a run.

The man under me struggled again. I brought my gun up, jammed it into the soft spot at the base of his skull. "Lie still, damn you!"

He went limp, acquiescent.

My rage was spent now. I felt only a letdown, as if I had run a hard race and then found that the other contestants had never left the starting line. That, and a dull curiosity . . .

I jammed the gun harder against the man's skull. Took my other hand off his arms and grasped his longish, thinning hair. Yanked his head up so I could see his face.

It was ordinary, as faces go. Fine-boned, with regular features and a bushy, untrimmed mustache. His blue eyes rolled in panic as they met mine; his mouth writhed in an unspoken plea. After staring at him for a moment I let go of his hair, and his forehead smacked onto the pavement. Shudders of pain and terror racked his body.

Then I noticed the people who had gathered around me. They were silent, watching me guardedly; in the eyes of some I saw accusation. It was as if I, not the sniper, were the person to be feared.

I turned my gaze toward the end of the street, where the pulsars of the squad cars stained the night red and blue. Let the people think what they might; I simply didn't care.

All that mattered to me now was whether or not Hank was still alive.

Twenty

Anne-Marie and I sat in the fluorescent glare of the nearly empty waiting room at San Francisco General's trauma center. Her face was pale and tense; her fingers twitched convulsively as they clutched at my hand. Hank was in surgery, had been for quite some time. The bullet had entered the right side of his chest; the doctor had told us there was no way of assessing the internal damage until they did an exploratory.

Greg had driven me here from All Souls, taking my statement on tape in the car. Ostensibly his purpose in coming was to interview the sniper, John Weldon—upon whom I had inflicted only a shoulder wound—but I knew that his major concern was for Hank. Reporters had arrived at the same time we did; Greg had given them a brief statement, but I'd refused to talk with them at all. Now they were gone, and Greg and Hank were both somewhere beyond a pair of swinging doors that gave admittance to the hospital proper. Anne-Marie and I waited alone.

By now I felt mostly numb. My guilt at failing to protect Hank had dulled; nobody

—not the folks at All Souls, Greg, Anne-Marie herself—blamed me. Even my dread at what the outcome of his surgery might be was curiously deadened. In spite of the people around us and the occasional arrival of other victims of crime or accident, it was as if we were trapped in an emotional vacuum, deprived of all but the slightest of sensory stimuli.

At around three-fifteen Greg came through the swinging doors. He didn't look much better than Anne-Marie; his impassive cop's facade had cracked, leaving his face ashen, his eyes worried. He sat down next to me and took the hand Anne-Marie wasn't holding, then put his arm around me so he could pat her on the shoulder.

"Any word?"

I shook my head.

"Chest wounds—sometimes they look worse than they are."

"He's been in there a long time."

Anne-Marie's fingers tightened again, and I realized what I'd said wasn't helping her any. "I'm sure he's going to be okay, though," I added. "It's just that there was so much blood, and Hank—well, unconscious isn't a state you associate with him."

Oh, God, I was only making it worse! *Shut up!* I told myself.

Anne-Marie said, "Stop worrying about me, Shar. I know it's bad, but I can handle it. You've got every right to be shaken up. You love Hank, too."

We fell silent then. Behind us a baby began to cry. Its screams rose to a crescendo that made me want to scream, too. Finally the mother took it outside.

I realized Greg hadn't mentioned the sniper. "Were you able to talk to him?"

He didn't have to ask who I meant. "Briefly. He was conscious and lucid; you shot him high up in the shoulder, no serious damage done. From what he admitted to me, it was pretty much as you theorized, and what he wouldn't tell me I'd already gotten from Letterman." Greg had received the information on John Weldon only minutes before he'd caught the call about Hank's shooting.

Odd that I felt so little curiosity about the man I'd pursued and wounded. It took an effort to say, "Tell me about him."

"He's a superpatriot. Was an army CID officer in 'Nam. Apparently he developed a James Bond complex, spied on people he considered subversive or disloyal. From

290

what he admitted to me, he became obsessed—'justifiably concerned' is how he put it—with the 'peacenik' group that hung out at the Rouge et Noir. Followed them, documented what he considered their transgressions."

"But he wasn't doing that officially?"

"No. When he tried to pass the information along to his superior officers, he was told to stick to his job. That only made him more fanatical, and eventually they decided to transfer him stateside. He was discharged in seventy-two, and shortly afterward he suffered the first of several breakdowns. Since then he's spent most of his life in V.A. hospitals, but six months ago he seemed to be cured, and was released on the condition that he continue with outpatient counseling at Letterman. From there it happened just about the way you thought it might have."

For a while I didn't speak, staring down at the checkerboard pattern of the linoleum. Anne-Marie's hand was limp; for all I knew she might not have been listening to Greg's description of the man who had shot her husband.

Finally I said, "We're only now beginning to fully realize what that war did to us. It destroyed a lot more people than those who

died in Asia. And it didn't discriminate—
dove, hawk, civilian, military, American,
Vietnamese. All of us were wounded one way
or another—"

Suddenly Anne-Marie's fingers clenched
mine. I looked at her and saw she was staring
at a surgeon in blood-spattered scrubs who
had come through the doors and was con-
ferring with the nurse at the desk. She motioned toward us, and he started over, but
Anne-Marie stood and hurried to him. They
spoke briefly, then she turned to Greg and
me, her face, if anything, more drawn.

"He's out of surgery," she said. "They're
going to let me see him."

I asked, "Will he be—"

"They don't know yet. It could be hours.
Why don't you and Greg go home, get some
rest."

"No, we'll—"

"Please, Shar. After I see him, I think I
want to be alone for a while."

I nodded, feeling unreasonably shut out
and rejected. Anne-Marie followed the surgeon out of the waiting room.

She does blame me, I thought.

After a bit Greg asked, "You okay?"

I made a motion with my hand that was

292

meant to indicate yes. What it said was "only marginally."

"Come on." He stood, tugging at my other hand. "I'll drive you home."

"No, to All Souls. My car's still there."

He pulled me from the chair, put both hands on my shoulders, and looked into my eyes for a long moment. Whatever he saw there seemed to satisfy him, because he nodded and led me out to his unmarked car.

Whenever I am very upset, I head for water. In fact, the one and only time I ran away from home, I packed a small wicker basket with my stuffed kangaroo, some Uncle Scrooge comic books, and three peanut-butter sandwiches and took the bus—transferring twice—to a beach my family frequented. My father found me there hours later and drove me home.

So at four-thirty that morning—driven by depression and a fear of finding reporters camped on my doorstep—I went to Point Lobos and sat in the foggy pre-dawn on the edge of the ruins of the old Sutro Baths, staring to sea at the hazy outlines of the Seal Rocks.

The area out there between Land's End and Ocean Beach is normally infested with tour buses and RVs—which in my opinion take up far more than their fair share of God's earth—but at that hour on a foggy, drizzly morning it was deserted except for a few early joggers, dog walkers, and me. I could smell the sea odors, hear the sea lions; foghorns up by the Gate answered their cries. Sitting on the wet foundations of what was once an aquatic playground on the edge of the Pacific, unheedful of the chill and dampness of the seat of my pants, I gave some thought to the way that things should be, and the way that they are.

People *should* lead productive lives, pursuing—if never catching—the myth of happiness. They should not be made to feel so powerless and victimized that in turn they attempt to become the powerful, the victimizers. They should not die senselessly—either on the battlefield or the city streets. And they should not be driven so insane that they either become an attacker or self-destruct.

Of course I knew that the way things *are* is an entirely different matter. All of those should-nots happen, over and over again. As a people we profess to hold lofty ideals—equality, peace, stop the killing, save the whales—but given what I'd seen in my career, I'd begun to wonder how many of us truly believe them. Or believe in their feasibility, the human animal being what it is . . .

The sky was lighter now, but the fog showed no signs of lifting. I could make out the rocks where the sea lions raised their heads and bellowed, but not the line of the horizon. Although it promised to be a gray Friday, I kept sitting there, waiting for some hopeful sign. After a while, when none was forthcoming, I got up and took myself home for a couple hours of sleep.

My sleep was restless and when I woke around nine, I felt even more depressed—a victim both of the persistent fog and the dreadful events of the night before. Unlike last Saturday morning, the dream I'd had before waking came back immediately, with disturbing clarity.

I'd been seated among a crowd in a large auditorium, and on the stage a distinguished man in scholar's robes was giving out diplomas. Perry Hilderly stepped up to the podium, dressed not in the traditional cap and gown, but in a glittering suit of gilt armor. The man presented his piece of parchment, praising Perry's intelligence. Then Perry faced the crowd and held the diploma aloft;

the parchment was tattered around its edges. Instantly I knew it had been gnawed by rats.

As I recalled the dream, my flesh rippled unpleasantly, and I drew my quilts higher against the chill in the room and within myself. I ought to check my paperback on dreams to figure out what this one was all about. But did I really want to know?

Fortunately I had little time to dwell on dreams this morning. It was already late, and I wanted to call the hospital to check on Hank. Then I needed to go to the Hall of Justice and sign the statement I'd given Greg in the car the night before; he'd said it would be ready by ten. And after that I wanted to track down my private investigator friend, to see if he had indeed been the one who looked into Jenny Ruhl's background for Jess Goodhue.

So many places to go, so many things to do. So many ways to keep my mind off worrying about Hank.

Twenty-One

Patient Information told me that Hank was still in intensive care, his condition critical but stable. That covered too wide a range of possibilities to offer me any reassurance, so I tried unsuccessfully to reach Anne-Marie. No one at All Souls knew any more than I did. In the end I set off for the Hall of Justice in an apprehensive frame of mind, with a headache from too little sleep and a case of the shakes from too much coffee.

McFate was not in the squad room, even though his suit coat—a blue pinstripe today—hung on the foolish little rack beside his desk. That, I thought, could be considered the first positive circumstance of the day. I had nothing to say to the inspector, but I was sure he would have had plenty to say to me—most of it barbs about my abilities as a bodyguard, and none of it praise for apprehending the sniper.

As promised, Greg had my statement on his desk. I read through it slowly, made a couple of changes, initialed them, and added my signature.

I said, "There it is, all wrapped up. I kept thinking it had some connection with Hilderly and his will, but it didn't."

Greg was shuffling papers, his brow creased in annoyance, and didn't reply. I got up to leave.

"Wait a minute," he said, motioning for me to shut the door.

I did so, then sat down again.

"How're you coming on the Hilderly matter?" he asked.

"I located all the heirs, and then one was killed—but you know that."

"Grant."

"Right. I told McFate I thought there might be a connection between his death and Hilderly's will. Didn't he mention that to you?"

"Only to say he'd found it wasn't relevant. Apparently he's seriously looking at a couple of Grant's clients." Greg paused, his frown turning to a scowl. "Brief me on what you've found out about the heirs' connection to Hilderly."

I did, trying not to omit any details, however tenuous. Greg made a few notes as I talked, then studied them before speaking.

"Interesting thing," he finally said. "That gun you brought in for identification—the lab called about it yesterday evening. Technician who owes me a favor processed it on overtime. I initiated a check on the serial number, and the information's come back."

"And?"

"Gun's one of a half dozen that were stolen from a shop in the Outer Mission in February of sixty-nine. Four of them were found on the persons of a radical group that attempted to bomb the weapons station at Port Chicago the next August: Taylor, Ruhl, and Heikkinen. A fifth was used in the suicide of Ruhl several months later."

I drew in my breath, let it out in a long sigh. "And Hilderly had the sixth. I wonder if they actually stole them?"

"Our data's not complete enough to tell."

"Doesn't really matter. What I'd like to know more about is that bombing attempt and the trial. FBI made the arrests?"

Greg nodded.

"And it would have been a federal prosecution. Probably it would be easier and quicker if I did some library research than if I persuaded you to request information through channels."

"That's really out of the scope of your investigation for All Souls, isn't it?"

I shrugged. "It'll keep my mind off worrying about Hank."

"Well, as long as you're determined to research it, keep me posted. McFate's probably right about Grant being killed by a disgruntled client, but I still don't like him not following up on all lines of inquiry."

"And if he's wrong about it being irrelevant, you'll use it as ammunition against him."

"Something like that."

"Well, I'd better let you get back to work." I stood up and Greg walked me out the door. "By the way," I added, "how did McFate take my collaring the sniper?"

"Not too well. Huffed about civilians treading on departmental territory—as if it mattered *who* collared him. Actually he seemed relieved that the Hilderly slaying was solved; maybe he didn't completely believe in the lack of relevancy of that will to Grant's death. And right after that he took off." Greg glanced across the squad room, where McFate's suit coat still hung on the brass rack. "Frankly, I'm getting annoyed at the way he keeps disappearing."

"Where do you suppose he is?"

"Not far away. Usually he puts on his jacket just to go to the can."

"Well, I think I'll get out of here before he comes back."

Greg grinned and went back into his office. I rode the elevator down to the lobby and joined the line in front of the bank of pay phones.

The lobby was crowded and noisy, the sounds of footfalls and voices reverberating off the marble walls. Cops in uniform passed by, going to the elevators or the Southern police station, housed just beyond the security station at the entrance. Attorneys in sober suits and carrying briefcases strode toward the municipal courtrooms on the building's eastern side. A poorly dressed man on the uncertain edge of sobriety was eating a sandwich on one of the marble benches. The roles of the other participants in the unfolding drama of justice were less easy to define: Was the sharply dressed black man over by the concession stand a pusher, pimp, or parole officer? Was the woman in the smart black business suit a prosecution witness or a defendant facing charges of prostitution? I spotted another woman with punked-up purple hair wearing tattered jeans and a dirty T-shirt, and recognized her as a nark Greg had once introduced me to.

As I waited for a phone booth to free up, I shifted from foot to foot, listening to snatches of conversation.

". . . Hon, I *tole* you we gonna get the bail money . . ."

". . . case has been continued until next Thursday, so you'll have to shift my calendar around . . ."

". . . Babe, it's me. If you get home before

I do, stick that roast in the microwave so it'll defrost . . ."

". . . Can we still make the early edition . . . ?"

When the man with the frozen roast relinquished his phone, I stepped into the booth and dialed Patient Information at S.F. General. No change in Hank's condition. Then I called All Souls for my messages; there were three from media people—none of whom was Goodhue. In light of the fact that she knew me personally, I found it odd that the anchorwoman hadn't tried to contact me for an exclusive story for one of KSTS's reporters on collaring the sniper. Perhaps her resistance to turning the investigator's name over to me had its roots in more than being too busy to look for it? But I couldn't imagine what.

A fourth message, however, was one I'd been hoping for—from Wolf. I dropped two more dimes into the slot and punched out his office number. He answered on the first ring.

"Well, Sharon," he said when I identified myself. "What's up?"

"Do you recall a client named Jess Goodhue? The TV news anchorwoman? The job would have been a background check on her mother, Jenny Ruhl, a few years ago—"

"Sure I remember. What about her?"

"She's peripherally involved in a case I'm working, and I need to take a look at your report on the investigation. It's okay with Goodhue," I added, since I didn't really know that it wasn't, "but she's been too busy to contact you, so I thought I'd go ahead and request it myself."

"Funny."

"How so?"

"She called Tuesday morning and asked for a copy of the report. Picked it up that afternoon."

So Goodhue, like Ross, had been lying to me. But why didn't she want me to know she already had the report? I said, "And now I'm unable to reach her. I know that technically you shouldn't give me a copy without her permission, but what are my chances of getting a look at it?"

"Depends. Why do you need it?"

I explained about the Hilderly case, stressing our need to know that Perry had not been under duress or undue influence at the time he made his holograph will.

Wolf said, "Well, I don't see any reason why you shouldn't have a copy, since you say Jess Goodhue has already agreed to that. I can't get to it until this afternoon, though. If you want I'll drop it off at All Souls around four."

His mention of All Souls made me realize that Wolf—who makes a point of avoiding the often depressing contents of the morning paper—probably knew nothing about what had gone on there the night before. By the time I'd finished telling him that story, my rage at the sniper had been rekindled, and when Wolf expressed his regrets about Hank being shot, I could hear some of the same anger in his voice.

Before I hung up, I thought to ask one last question. "I don't suppose you recall what you found out about Goodhue's mother?"

"Sorry, I don't. My memory isn't what it used to be."

I thanked him and hung up the receiver. The phone booth was quickly claimed by a young woman with reddened eyes and runny mascara. Someone had once commented to me that more tears must be shed in the Hall of Justice than any other building in San Francisco—public or private, and not excepting the funeral homes. I had never doubted the truth of that statement.

By eleven-thirty I was seated at a machine in a quiet corner of the microfilm room at the main branch of the public library. Ghostly images flickered before me as I fastforwarded through the reels I'd requested, stopping at articles on the Port Chicago bombing attempt and trial. When I'd checked the various periodical indexes, I'd found that coverage had been extensive; one of the national newsmagazines had even run a long piece on the case: "Revolutionaries' Plot Runs Afoul of Government's Tough New Stance on Violence."

What I gleaned from the article jolted me. Taylor and Heikkinen had been sole defendants in the trial; the government had asked for stiff sentences in order to make examples of them for other would-be saboteurs, and each had received five years in federal prison—Taylor at McNeil Island in Washington State, and Heikkinen at a facility in Alderson, West Virginia. The crime of conspiracy to bomb a military installation had held more serious undertones than I'd originally assumed: had they been successful in planting and detonating the bombs, their blast would have taken several lives.

But what surprised me the most was the

identity of the prosecution's chief witness. Jenny Ruhl had been the one to offer the particularly damning testimony that the collective had "deemed the sacrifice of life acceptable and even desirable, given the cause for which they were fighting."

Libby Ross had told me that what the collective mainly did was engage in endless intense talk; now it seemed that the rhetoric had gotten seriously out of hand. Even though—as the accounts of the trial pointed out—there were significant reasons to doubt parts of Ruhl's testimony, it made me look at the affair in a new light. If the members of the collective had been comfortable with the concept of killing innocent strangers, what other crimes might they have contemplated—or committed? If I kept digging, what else might I turn up? And was that really necessary at this late date? There were people who could be badly hurt: Jess Goodhue, D. A. Taylor's wife and young children. Perhaps it would be kinder to let the past die, as most of those involved in the case had.

But even as I thought about it, I knew I wouldn't stop. Tom Grant had been murdered, and my gut-level feelings told me that the forces leading up to his killing had been set in motion by something in that past. True, Grant had been a poor excuse for a human being, but when it comes to murder, an investigator doesn't establish an A List and a B List. I would keep going simply because it was a valid line of inquiry that McFate seemed unwilling to pursue.

My pages of notes quickly piled up: a chronology of events, key phrases from the trial testimony, addresses, names. Hilderly was only mentioned once, in a list of people suspected of being former members of the collective; the names Andy Wrightman and Thomas Y. Grant appeared nowhere at all.

After I finished with the first batch of films, I went out to the reference room and rechecked the indexes for articles in radical and alternative publications. Then I returned to the microfilm room and checked out a few reels containing the coverage in the *Berkeley Barb*—an acerbic, muckraking paper that had achieved national prominence in the sixties. While the establishment press had not attached any particular significance to the fact that four guns had been seized from three people at Port Chicago—Taylor had been carrying two at the time of his arrest—the *Barb* viewed this with suspicion. One reporter wrote of rumors (possibly created by himself) that there had been a "mysterious fourth person" at the weapons station, who had handed Taylor his or her gun and walked away from the scene when the federal agents appeared. "A Setup!" the *Barb*'s headlines proclaimed. "An informant in the midst of our courageous brothers and sisters," an editorial insisted.

"Jenny Ruhl, Traitor" was the title of the profile that appeared immediately after she'd testified at the trial. Ruhl was described as "the pampered daughter of rich Orange County pigs, who was too soft to stand with her brother and sister during their persecution." Another reporter, less kind, said she was "seriously fucked up, had probably fed information to the enemy all along." By contrast, Ruhl's obituary some weeks after the trial categorized her as "a martyr to the Movement" and a "victim of bourgeois values." It was also posited that she had been "murdered by the pigs." At that point I decided that the *Barb* hadn't been able to make up its mind about Ruhl any more than I could.

My library researches done, I turned in the microfilms and went out to delve further into the past. But first I found a phone and called the hospital for a report on Hank's condition. Again there had been no change. After some calling around I reached the nursing station at intensive care; Anne-Marie was there, and I convinced the woman on the desk to let me talk to her. She sounded tired and distant, and when I offered to come over and keep her company later, she said she'd rather I didn't.

"His lung was collapsed, and there was other internal damage as well. They may have to operate again, and if they do, it'll take every bit of control I have not to fall apart. Seeing a face that's more than professionally sympathetic would about do me in. Besides," she added, "his parents are here. And you know how they can be."

"By that I take it you mean they blame me for him getting shot."

"Well, it's a long list. I think perhaps God has been absolved, but I wouldn't even count on that."

It was more or less the reaction I would have predicted. The Zahns had spent too many years insulated by their affluence and social position to know how to cope with real adversity. Since their only son had been shot, it was necessary that blame be affixed; accusations and recriminations were excellent weapons against fear and powerlessness, and they both wielded them like pros. I'd often wondered how two such closed and insecure people could have produced someone as open and confident as Hank.

"Well, hang in there," I said, talking to myself as much as to Anne-Marie. "I'll check back with you later on."

Often when I'm working a case I find myself drawn to the places where its key events have occurred, even if it's a long time after the fact. The urge to view these physical settings is more or less instinctive on my part; half the time I'm not even aware of why I'm going there until I arrive. But unscientific and illogical as such behavior might seem, I've come to trust the impulses that prompt it. And while I rarely stumble upon some overlooked clue or receive a blinding flash of insight, just being there gives me a better sense of the individuals involved and their possible motivations. So, in lieu of any better way to pass the time until I could pick up Wolf's case file at All Souls, I decided to see what remained of the landscape of twenty years ago.

There was no point in driving all the way out to Port Chicago; I wouldn't be permitted inside the weapons station and, besides, the scene of the arrest didn't seem relevant. Nor did I need to return to Berkeley; I knew that territory, and it wasn't where the story really centered. The Federal Building, where the trial had been held, was only two blocks from the library, but I knew what courtrooms looked like and could easily imagine the dry proceedings.

The government's case, according to the newspaper accounts I'd just read, had been impressive: physical evidence, including the guns, pipe bombs, detonating devices, maps of the military installation, and diagrams of where the bombs were to be placed; eye-witness testimony of the arresting agents; and the apparently unshakable testimony of Jenny Ruhl. The chief government witness, according to one reporter, "never once looked at her former comrades. While on the stand she betrayed neither guilt nor nervousness, speaking in a flat, uninflected voice. When she left the courtroom, she did not look back." And in the face of her testimony, what little case the defense had built crumbled.

I could understand what had probably driven Ruhl to testify against her former friends. Like many of the would-be revolutionaries of the sixties, her involvement with the collective had been a rebellion against a conservative upbringing, but once arrested, the specter of years in a federal penitentiary had most likely been more than she could bear. In addition, she had a daughter dependent upon her—one whom she might not see for a long time if convicted. The federal prosecutors would have realized Ruhl was the weakest of the three and plied her with offers of a deal.

Yes, I could easily understand why Ruhl had testified for the prosecution. But what puzzled me was her suicide, some weeks after the trial. If Jessica had been one of the reasons for sacrificing her loyalty and twisted code of honor, why had she then left her daughter motherless, with no means of support?

No answer for that—not now, maybe not ever.

The lower Fillmore district—just the other side of Van Ness Avenue from the Civic Center—is one of the city's neighborhoods in transition. Gone are the pig farms of the late 1800s, the jazz clubs of the World War II era, the blighted ghetto of more recent years. Gone too is Winterland—the former ice-skating rink that became a mecca for stoned, music-loving hippies in the sixties. What you have now is an uneasy mixture of urban cultures: luxury condominium complexes next to shabby three-story Victorian houses; trendy restaurants across the street from greasy spoons; a wine shop on one corner, a cut-rate liquor store on the other.

The house on Hayes Street where the members of the collective had lived immediately after their move to San Francisco was no longer there; that block had been cleared to make way for a high rise. But down the street I spotted Jude's Liquors, where D. A. Taylor had taken on odd jobs from time to time. I parked the MG and followed a plywood-covered walkway around the construction site to the store. There were bars over its plate-glass windows, and the neon signs and faded posters displayed there advertised at least two kinds of beer that were no longer brewed. When I entered, I spotted a young Asian man taking bottles of vodka from a carton and setting them on a shelf behind the counter. I showed him my license, said I'd like to ask him a few questions.

How long had he worked here? He was the owner, had had the store three years now, since the former owner died. No, he didn't know anything about the people who used to live in the neighborhood, didn't know much about those who lived there now. He commuted from the Richmond. This wasn't a good place to raise kids.

I went back to the MG and drove a few blocks to Page Street. The collective had had some kind of dispute with the landlord of the building on Hayes, and after only a few months had found another place not too many blocks away. That building still stood: three-storied, with a pink concrete-block facade and a sagging front stoop. Again I parked and crossed the street, studying the building. Climbed the steps and examined the mailboxes. There were no names on any of them; one of their doors hung open on broken hinges; a bell push dangled on exposed wires; the steps were littered with newspapers and advertising circulars. The building gave me no sense of the past. I could feel no connection between it and the violent plans that had been formulated within its confines.

I went back down the steps, looked toward the eastern corner of the street. A dry cleaner where Libby Heikkinen had occasionally picked up extra cash by clerking had turned into a too-cutely-named bakery— You Knead It. A young white woman

314

emerged, pushing an infant in a stroller, a baguette protruding from her net shopping bag. But on the opposite corner was the grocery store whose owner had allowed the members of the collective to scrounge through the dumpsters for salvageable food—Rhonda's Superette. Rhonda Wilson had testified as a character witness for the defense. I hurried down there.

The grocery was the same as corner stores the city over: full of dusty boxed and canned goods that had been too long on the shelves, with narrow aisles, cracked linoleum, and antiquated, wheezing refrigerator cases. A middle-aged black woman sat behind the counter, going over some invoices.

No, she wasn't Rhonda Wilson. She and her husband had bought the store from her back in the mid-seventies. Rhonda had moved to Nevada, but she wasn't sure she was still there. No, she didn't recall anything about the people up the street who'd been arrested by the FBI—she'd still been living in Texas then and had never even heard about the case. Anyone in the neighborhood who might remember? Well, there was old Cal. Cal had gotten busted up in an accident at the shipyards back in the early sixties. On good days he sat out on the sidewalk in his wheelchair and passed the time of day with whoever came by; on foggy days like this you could usually find him in the family Dodge that his wife kept parked at the curb.

"Cal's a do-gooder," the woman added. "Writes letters, takes up things that're wrong in the neighborhood with the folks at city hall. People like him; even the junkies and the cops on the beat like him. That car? It hasn't been moved in years, that I know of. But it just sits there and the street cleaners go right around it and nobody ever gives it a ticket."

When I heard things like that, it restored my faith in a city that often struck me as increasingly cold and indifferent. I thanked the woman, bought a Hershey bar—the emergency chocolate supply in my purse was probably running low—and went out to see what Cal could tell me.

Twenty-Two

The faded maroon-and-white Dodge with swooping tailfins was parked three or four doors from the collective's last address. A pair of old men stood next to it, their arms propped on its roof, talking with someone inside. Both men were bundled in overcoats against the chill fog; one even wore a knitted cap with earflaps. I walked down there and loitered on the sidewalk behind them, waiting for them to conclude their conversation. It was about the possibility of the new downtown stadium to replace Candlestick Park. The men on the sidewalk were all for it; the man in the car—whom I couldn't as yet see—wasn't opposed to the idea, but he considered it evidence of the prevailing "two-faced attitude" at city hall.

"They tell you one thing during the campaign," he said in a gravelly voice, "and after you vote 'em in, you got something else entirely."

The man with the knitted cap said, "Well, why don't you just write a letter, Cal, let the mayor know what you think?"

"I might at that."

I was about to interrupt during the brief lull in the conversation, but the other man on the sidewalk stepped back a little, and the car's occupant saw me. "Move aside, boys," he said. "Here's a young lady come to see me. I got better things to do than shoot the breeze with a couple of old farts."

"You just too popular, Cal." The man in the knitted cap motioned for me to step up to the Dodge, and he and his companion turned away. "Catch you later," he added.

Old Cal was perhaps in his mid-sixties, with white hair and the kind of dark skin that has an almost purple tinge. His upper body was powerful, with heavily muscled shoulders and biceps; in contrast, his crippled legs, covered by a green plaid blanket and extending from the car so his feet rested on the curb, looked deflated. One glance into his lively eyes told me that the ability to walk was the only faculty this man was lacking.

He smiled in welcome and jerked his head toward the departing men. "That's what happens when a man retires," he said. "Ain't got no resources, neither a them. They'll sure as hell end up down to the Two A.M. Club and be shit-faced by a normal man's quitting time. Now, me—I ain't been able to work a day since sixty-three, but you can always find me here listenin' to what people got to say. Nighttimes, like as not I'm at my typewriter writin' letters, seein' things get done around here. Keeps a man going." He paused, shook his head. "Makes him talkative, too. Cal Hurley's the name. I take it you looking for me."

I shook his extended hand. "The lady at

Rhonda's Superette told me where to find you."

He took the business card I held out and examined it with interest. "I like what I hear about you folks at All Souls. You don't put up with shit from city hall any more than I do. How's that fellow got shot last night? He gonna be okay?"

". . . I don't know. He's in bad shape."

"Shame. You the lady collared the sniper. Picture of you in the *Chron*. Didn't do you justice, though."

I knew which picture he meant. Why the paper persisted in keeping that particular one on file . . .

I must have looked fairly depressed, because the lines around Cal Hurley's eyes crinkled in sympathy. He said, "Whyn't you get in the backseat there? You look like you could use to sit. Cold on the sidewalk."

I opened the rear door of the Dodge and climbed in behind him. The plush maroon upholstery smelled of cigar smoke.

Cal Hurley twisted slightly so he could look at me. "This about that business last night?"

"No, although it's related in a way." Briefly I filled him in on the background to my case. "That pink house four doors

319

down"—I motioned at it—"was where the people lived when they were arrested. I wonder if you remember anything about them."

He didn't need to look to see which house I meant. "Funny thing, that was. I took note of those kids right off, on account of them not fitting in here."

"You mean because they were white?"

He nodded. "All except for the Indian. You Indian, too?"

"Some."

"Thought so. That offend you—me saying 'Indian' instead of 'Native American'?"

I shrugged. "They're just labels, and I'm not much of a labeler."

He smiled his approval. "You know, seems like only a little while ago I was a Negro. Then I was black. Not real descriptive, since we mainly brown, but what the hell. Next thing I know, black's out and African-American's in. What a mouthful! Then the other day my grandson—he goes to college, knows about that stuff—he tells me *that's* out, now we're 'people of color.'

"So I says to him, 'What *is* that? Back when I was your age we were colored people. The way things goin', pretty soon we gonna get to be niggers again.' The young man, he didn't find that funny."

I did, however, and I could tell my laughter pleased Cal Hurley. He'd probably been saving that story for a suitable audience. After a moment I turned serious, though. "About the kids in the pink house . . . ?"

"I getting to that. Don't think I'm one of these old men that rambles. Just wanted to cheer you up some; you looked down in the mouth for a minute there. The thing about those kids not fitting in didn't so much have to do with being white as it did with coming from money. Kids, they can put on old clothes, hang out in a poor neighborhood, scrounge for garbage—and to me that's a filthy habit no matter how down-and-out you are—but they can't get rid of the look. Maybe their people weren't rich, but none a them except the Indian ever gone without in their lives. But they were quiet kids, didn't bother nobody, so folks around here let them alone."

"What did they do while they were living here?"

"Came and went. The fellow with the blond curly hair seemed to have some sort of real job; I had the feeling he didn't really live there, just hung out. A couple a others worked part-time. But mostly they stayed

321

inside the flat. Doing what, I couldn't guess at the time."

"How many of them were there?"

"Hard to say. You'd see people for a while, then you wouldn't. But mainly it was the Indian, the blond girl, the blond boy, the little dark-haired girl, and the fellow with the scar."

Excitement pricked at me. This was the first time anyone had placed Tom Grant in the company of members of the collective. Cautiously I said, "Would you describe the one with the scar, please?"

"Handsome kid, except for this ragged red gouge on his left cheek. Dark hair. Tall. Older than the others by a few years, I'd say. You'd see him alone or with the little dark-haired girl. There was something about him . . . well, like he wasn't really part of things. Like the girl was his connection to the rest. When they'd walk down the street with the others, they'd stay apart. But when it was just the girl, she'd walk with her friends."

Interesting, that dynamic, I thought. "Was the man with the scar there at the time the three were arrested?"

"Yeah. Afterward, too."

"What about the blond-haired boy?"

"Oh, he was gone by then. Months before."

"But the man with the scar stayed on after the arrests?"

"Well, not exactly. They raided the place, you know. The feds, they came in there and took all sorts of stuff away. And the man with the scar was with them."

"What? Was he handcuffed?"

"Not that I could see. If they arrested him, they must of let him go later. That flat was sealed up all through the trial, but when they took the seal off, he was living there again. And after she got done testifying against her friends, the little dark-haired girl stayed with him for a while. Then *she* was gone, and the next thing I knew, end of the month a family moved in."

"So when was the last time you actually saw the man with the scar?"

He considered. "Well, a day or two after the little dark-haired girl left."

I leaned back against the cigar-musty upholstery, revising quite a few of my preconceptions. And putting together some things that hadn't made sense or hadn't seemed important before. But I didn't want to jump to conclusions; I needed proof.

I asked, "If I brought you pictures of those people, could you identify them?"

"Think so. The older I get, the sharper I am on things that happened a long time ago. Damn, I wish I could say the same for what's going on day to day."

"I don't think you're doing so badly. I'll see if I can get hold of some pictures, and as soon as I do, I'll check back with you. Meantime, if you think of anything else, call me, please."

After I got out of the car, Cal Hurley smiled at me and extended his hand. "I'll do that," he said. "And you stop back anytime. I'll be here, that's one thing you can count on."

All Souls was as quiet and deserted as if it were a sleepy Sunday afternoon. No clients or media people waited in the parlor; Ted's desk was vacant. I went past it and stuck my head into Rae's office. Empty. I frowned, checked my watch. Four thirty-seven, too early for everyone to have gone home. Then I heard a murmur of voices in the kitchen. I hurried back there, feeling what I told myself was an unreasonable foreboding.

The scene in the kitchen reminded me of wakes I'd attended. Rae, Ted, and Jack sat

324

around the table, faces somber, drinks in hand. Ted clasped Ralph the cat as if he were a security blanket. Alice, subdued for once, perched on the windowsill. I set my bag and briefcase on the counter and leaned against it, braced for bad news.

"There you are," Jack said, a little too heartily. For once he didn't cast a lustful glance at my legs or cleavage. Jack was recovering from a divorce and for some reason had made me the object of his yearnings. If he wasn't ogling me, something terrible must have happened.

"What's going on here?" I asked, my voice matching his for false cheer. "You guys starting the Friday happy hour early?"

"Something like that." Ted stood and handed Ralph to me. "You look like you could use a drink." He went toward the cupboard where the glasses were kept.

I took the last empty chair, setting the cat on my lap. He tucked his tail around his front paws and stared solemnly at me. I turned him around so I wouldn't have to undergo his yellow-eyed scrutiny. "What's going on?" I repeated in a more urgent tone.

Ted returned with a glass of white wine and handed it to me. "Hank had additional surgery this afternoon. He started bleeding internally again, so they had to go in and tie off some blood vessels. None of us could work, so we decided to knock off early."

I froze, glass halfway to my lips. "Will he be—"

Rae said, "Anne-Marie called a little while ago. He's in recovery, holding his own."

I set the glass down on the table and pressed my hands against Ralph's round sides, so hard he grunted. "What does that mean—holding his own?"

It was a stupid question; no one bothered to answer me.

Did I imagine it, or was there a tension in the room that hadn't been there when I entered? I looked around the table, saw in the others' guarded expressions that they didn't know quite how to deal with me. To them I was not the same person they thought they'd known before last night. Rae had seen my face just before I'd started up the hill after the sniper; Jack and Ted had arrived with the police and found me straddling his supine body, gun pressed to his skull. I doubted any of them would ever fully reconcile their prior conceptions of me with the near-murderous stranger they'd seen. And while time would somewhat dull the memory, it would always be there, always set me a little apart from them.

The realization filled me with sadness. I squeezed Ralph harder, and this time he let out a tiny *mowl* of protest. "Sorry," I whispered, and handed him back to Ted. Suddenly I needed to be out of there, to be alone. I got up, grabbed my bag and briefcase, and fled into the hall. Behind me Rae said, "Let her go. She'll be okay."

But footsteps followed me. I turned and saw Ted, still clutching the cat. "Shar—"

"What now?"

He blinked, recoiling from the harshness in my voice. "I only wanted to tell you there's an envelope for you on my desk."

"Oh. Oh, thanks, Ted."

Without a word he went back into the kitchen.

The sadness came on more strongly. As I went down the hall my sight blurred from tears. Angrily I brushed them away, got the manila envelope from Ted's desk, and took it up to my office. It contained the copy of the report Wolf had promised me. I sat down at the desk and began to read.

Wolf appeared to have consulted the same published resources as I had, plus interviewed a number of people who had known

327

Jenny Ruhl. The most fruitful of these talks was with a woman who was Ruhl's roommate during their freshman year at Berkeley. Although their lives took off in very different directions after those first semesters, the two remained close. The woman confirmed that Andy Wrightman was the father of Ruhl's child. He was, she said, a campus hanger-on who was auditing the course Ruhl was taking on the origins of the Vietnam war when they met; they lived together a year or so before Ruhl became pregnant. When she told him about the expected child, Wrightman disappeared from Berkeley. But he returned to Jenny before she moved from the East Bay to San Francisco, and after the trial, when Ruhl's friend contacted her to see if there was any way she could help out, Ruhl and Wrightman were living in the flat on Page Street.

I read the report twice, the second time trying to guess what Jess Goodhue's reaction to it had been. Then I reviewed my contacts with the anchorwoman, eventually focusing on the telephone conversation we'd had late on the afternoon that she'd picked up the report. I'd told her that I thought Tom Grant figured in my case more than he would admit; said one of the other heirs had been startled by my description of Grant; said he'd said something about Grant being the "right man."

But by then Goodhue had known it was a name—Wrightman. The name of her father. And Grant was someone she'd met, had interviewed and found "charming."

Then I thought of the conversation I'd had with Grant the next morning. We'd set our meeting for nine that evening because he'd scheduled a client dinner and then an appointment for "an interview." When Angela Curtis had told me he'd sent her out to the movies because he didn't want her around the house, I'd assumed the interview was with a prospective employee, possibly a replacement for Curtis. But media people also scheduled interviews. And when I'd tried to call Goodhue before I'd left for Grant's, she'd supposedly been in her dressing room, where no one ever bothered her.

It was time, I thought, to have a frank talk with Jess Goodhue.

Twenty-Three

Goodhue was already on the air by the time I reached KSTS. I didn't want to risk miss-

329

ing her in case she planned to leave the studio between broadcasts, so I told the receptionist I'd wait. There was a grouping of chairs to one side of the lobby, and an assortment of magazines on the low table they surrounded; I selected *Metropolitan Home* and leafed through it, glancing at the ads but barely seeing them. My thoughts were preoccupied by the upcoming confrontation with the anchorwoman—and the unpleasant truths that might emerge during our talk.

The hands of my watch moved slowly toward seven o'clock. The lobby was deserted and the building seemed hushed, as if everyone were holding his breath until the newscast was successfully completed. The impression, I knew, was deceptive: frantic activity would be going on behind the locked door by the reception desk; stories would continue to break up until the eleven o'clock report; other stories would constantly be updated. And Goodhue could very well use that activity as an excuse for avoiding me.

So far no one had entered the studio from the street. It occurred to me that there was a door from the parking lot. If Goodhue wanted to duck me, she could slip out that way when the receptionist told her I was here. I glanced at him; he was reading a current best-seller, totally absorbed. When I got up and meandered around the lobby, pretending to study the blowups of KSTS personalities, he paid me no attention. I moved closer to the locked door, staring at the face of Les Gates, Goodhue's co-anchor.

At five minutes to seven, a tall, curly-haired man strode into the lobby, announcing that he had to see someone named Rick—was he in the building, and if so, where?

"Studio D," the receptionist said, his hand moving automatically to the buzzer.

The man hurried over to the door, opened it as soon as the buzzer sounded, and went inside. I caught it before it closed and slipped through. The man was already at the other end of the corridor and didn't notice me.

The pace in the newsroom was even more hectic than it had been on Monday afternoon: phones rang; people rushed about; the sound was turned up on the monitors, and the competition's newscasts blended into an unintelligible babble. I entered as if I had business there and went straight to Goodhue's empty cubicle.

The anchorwoman's desk was covered with papers: scripts, memos, correspondence, a copy of the *Examiner*, sheets from

331

yellow pads. As I was about to sit down, one of the latter caught my eye; it was covered with doodles that looked like crude representations of Tom Grant's fetishes. At the top of the sheet was a name and a phone number—Harry Sullivan. Sullivan was one of the city's top criminal attorneys; it looked as though Goodhue planned to consult him.

Quickly I flipped through the appointments calendar on the desk. Notations were scrawled all over it, but there was no indication of any meeting with Sullivan—not in the past couple of days nor in the near future. Goodhue must have been debating calling him. Ironic what she'd doodled while thinking it over.

Voices rose louder in the newsroom. I recognized Goodhue's. Footsteps approached the cubicle. I turned as she and Les Gates entered.

Gates looked mildly surprised to see a stranger there. Goodhue blanched and exclaimed, "You!" Her eyes moved from me to the yellow sheet on the desk; when they met mine again, they were flooded with fear. Her mouth twisted as if she suddenly felt sick.

I said, "Jess, we have to talk."

She took a step backward. "No."

Gates was frowning. "Jess, what's wrong? You want me to call security?"

"No!" She turned quickly, bumping into a woman who was passing.

"Wait," I said.

Goodhue ran for the door of the newsroom.

Gates put a restraining hand on my arm. "What's going on? Wait a minute—aren't you the investigator who collared that sniper? How come you're here—"

Typical newsman, all questions. I wrenched free, went after Goodhue. The door to the lobby was just closing. I ran down there, yanked it open, saw her pushing through the street door. As I ran across the lobby, the receptionist shouted, "Hey, what were *you* doing back there?"

Outside, the Embarcadero was gray with mist. Heavy traffic moved swiftly in both directions; from above came the hum of cars on the Bay Bridge. Goodhue was running awkwardly across the railroad tracks that fronted the building. She caught the toe of her high-heeled shoe on one of the rails, stumbled, righted herself, and kept going.

I yelled for her to stop, but she didn't even pause at the curb, dodging cars and trucks on her way across the Embarcadero. A sports

333

car screeched to a stop, barely missing her. Horns blared. Goodhue ran for the piers on the other side, seemingly oblivious to the commotion.

I started after her, was almost mowed down by a van whose driver screamed obscenities at me. Goodhue had reached the sidewalk and was angling to the left, past the SFFD's fireboat station. I stepped into the crosswalk, holding up my hand to stop an oncoming car like a traffic cop. It braked, and the cars traveling in the opposite direction halted, too. I spotted a look of astonishment on one driver's face as I sprinted in front of him and down the sidewalk.

It was cold, and the wind blew strongly off the bay, redolent of creosote and salt water. Ahead, a gust threw Goodhue off stride as she reached the wide strip of promenade. I passed the fireboat station, gaining on her.

Goodhue stumbled, looked over her shoulder, and saw me. She glanced at the traffic whizzing by, then at the chest-high seawall to her right. For a moment I thought she might climb it and fling herself into the bay. Then she kicked off her shoes and ran faster.

Ahead was a concrete shelter topped by a

flagpole—part of some waterfront design plan that didn't appear to have come off properly. The promenade widened at that point, jutting out into the bay. Goodhue made a sharp right turn and suddenly disappeared from sight. I sped up, reached the corner of the seawall, and rounded it.

On the other side was an area between the wall and an arm of the promenade that looked like a large boat slip. Steps led down to it and vanished under the lapping waves. Goodhue was descending them. I shouted for her to stop. When she reached the bottom step, she didn't hesitate a beat, just waded into the water.

Two concrete landing piers rose a couple of feet above the water in the middle of the slip—another part of the design plan that hadn't been thought through, since there was no way of reaching them without getting soaked. Goodhue was slogging toward the closer of them, in up to her knees now. I ran down the steps and waded in after her; the water felt icy through my athletic shoes.

Goodhue reached the pier and clung to it, arms outstretched above her head. Waves lapped at her waist and sprayed the back of her tan suit jacket. I moved toward her, fighting a strong current. She was crying, clawing at the concrete with her fingernails. When I came up behind her and grasped her by the shoulders, she flinched.

"Come on, Jess," I said. "Out of the water. We'll both catch pneumonia."

She sobbed and rolled her head from side to side, face pressed against the rough surface of the pier.

"Jess!" I shook her.

She muttered something I couldn't understand.

"What?"

"Don't care."

"Stop it!" I yanked on her shoulders, dragged her upright. She sagged against me. I slipped my right arm around her, extending the other for balance, and began guiding her back toward the steps. My feet were numb now. Halfway to the steps, she stumbled, and we both nearly went down.

"Walk, dammit!" I said.

She walked. But when we got to the steps, she sagged again and sat down.

"Jess," I said, "get up!"

She shook her head and doubled over, arms wrapped around her bare knees. Her pale skirt was molded to her thighs, water streaming off it. In spite of her soaking she didn't seem to feel the wet or the chill. Finally I took off my jacket and draped it around her shoulders, then sat a little way down, avoiding the puddles forming around her. I couldn't single-handedly wrestle her to warmth and shelter. It was obvious she wouldn't help me, and nobody else had been drawn to the vicinity by the sight of two wet, struggling women. At least not yet.

I fumbled in my damp shoulder bag and came up with a couple of reasonably clean tissues. Pressed them into her hand. She took them, scrubbed at her face, and blew her nose.

"What was all that about?" I asked her.

She didn't reply, merely hunched over, clasping her knees again.

"Well, I think I know," I added. "But maybe it's not that bad. Let's talk about it, see what can be done."

"There's nothing that can be done. I want to die."

I doubted her wading into the bay had been a suicide attempt; more likely she'd been running in blind panic—both from having to face me and having to deal with what had happened. I said, "You don't want to die, and you don't know there's no solution. Come on, we'll go back to the studio and talk this through."

This time she let me help her to her feet. When we reached the promenade, we encountered Les Gates and the bald man from the assignment desk, who had come out looking for us. Together the two men and I got Goodhue back to her dressing room. Gates and the other man didn't want to leave us, but Goodhue dismissed them—a bit imperiously, I thought, for someone who had recently been wallowing and crying in the bay. While she changed into dry things, I went to my car and carried in the overnight bag I keep in the trunk in case an investigation unexpectedly takes me out of town. Finally we sat down to talk, me clad in a fresh sweater and jeans, Goodhue wrapped in a warm robe.

I said, "Jess, there are extenuating circumstances in Grant's death. I noticed you'd written down Harry Sullivan's number. A good lawyer like him—"

"Can get me off," she finished. "But my life's wrecked, anyway. My career. And how can I live with what I did? I keep seeing him . . ."

"Tom Grant—your father."

After a moment she nodded, bending her head so I couldn't see her face.

"You picked up the report on the background investigation of your mother Tuesday afternoon—"

Now she looked up. "How did you—"

"Doesn't matter now. You read in the report that a man named Andy Wrightman was your father. Later that afternoon I called and mentioned that one of the other heirs had said something about the 'right man' when I'd described Tom Grant to him. So you decided to go see Grant, but you didn't tell him the real reason why you were making the appointment. Did you claim you wanted to interview him for another story?"

". . . Yes."

"And what happened when you went to his house?"

She sighed deeply. "Why go into it? The end result is the same."

"You're going to have to talk about it sooner or later. There's no way I can withhold this kind of information from the police."

Goodhue stared off into the shadows, her face reflected murkily in the unlit mirror above her dressing table. For some reason I was reminded of D. A. Taylor staring at Hog Island, and I knew Goodhue's thoughts were as bleak as those Taylor entertained. In spite of what I'd said earlier about her not really

339

wanting to die, I was afraid for Jess. I wanted to yank her back to the present, reintegrate this new, fragile personality with the strong, confident woman she had been until two days before. But I doubted my ability to do so.

Finally she turned her gaze to me. "Why do you need to know these things?"

"I want to help you, if I can. And as I told you on Monday, the truth is important to me."

After a moment she said, "All right, then—the truth. I went to his house right after the early-evening broadcast. No one saw me leave the studio; they just assumed I was resting in my dressing room. I'd got myself all prettied up." Her lips twisted in bitter self-mockery. "Daddy's little girl, wanting to make a good impression. But there was something about his manner . . . I couldn't ask him right off. We had a drink in his office. I was trying to think of a way to get into it. I asked him about those horrible . . . what did he call them?"

"Fetishes."

She closed her eyes, swallowed. "Disgusting things. And the way he talked about them . . . it was very calculated, for shock effect. He took me out in the backyard to his workshop, showed me the . . . stuff he made them from, the one that he had in progress. And then . . . oh, Jesus!"

"What, Jess?"

"The bastard came on to me. His own daughter. And that's when I just blurted it out."

"What was his reaction?"

"At first he was very surprised—more, I think, because I knew. I suspected he'd known all along. He didn't bother to deny he'd known my mother, or that his real name was Andy Wrightman. Then he became defensive, nervous. Said I was mistaken, he couldn't be my father, because he'd left Berkeley before I was born. I'd brought the detective's report along, and I showed it to him. He read it and laughed—forced laughter. He said of course Jenny would have told her conservative friend that she knew who my father was, but in reality she was a tramp who fucked everybody. There was no way, he said, that she could have figured out whose child I was."

"Did you believe him?"

"No. When you've interviewed as many people as I have, you get so you can sense when someone's lying. Well, I guess you would know that, too."

"Did you ask him if he was the man who came to see you at Ben and Nilla's?"

She bent forward, resting her face against her open palms. When she spoke, her voice was muffled. "He admitted he was. Said my mother needed someone to drive her there, so he went along. He told me I'd been a cute little thing, the way I'd sat on his lap and played with the ends of the string tie his peace medallion was clipped to."

So that was the medallion the collective had broken up to make "talismans." I thought of the small metal protrusions on the backs of the two pieces I had in my purse, which would have held the string.

Goodhue added, "And then it all came back to me so clearly: the big gray metal clip, and above it his face—the way he looked back then. And I also very clearly saw my mother kneeling beside us, looking prettier than I'd ever seen her, saying, 'Honey, this is your father.'" She was silent a moment, crying quietly. Then she raised her tear-wet face.

"The way he spoke, I thought he might be softening toward me. But when I told him what I remembered my mother saying, he started to attack her character again. Said that in addition to being a roundheels, she was mentally unstable, that she'd been breaking down long before the thing at Port Chicago, which was why she testified against the others. Afterward, when just the two of them were living at the flat in the Fillmore, she kept talking about suicide, and finally she took the gun they had left and . . . you know."

But something was wrong with that. Cal Hurley had told me the federal agents had raided the flat, taken evidence away. If the gun had been there, they would have found it. "Did Grant tell you why he wasn't in on the Port Chicago bombing attempt?"

"He said he was, that he'd done a cowardly thing. When he saw the FBI men, he gave another man his gun and then faded into the background. A Weather collective in Oakland hid him until after the trial, when he and my mother got back together."

A second contradiction to what Cal Hurley had told me. According to the old man, Grant had been at the flat on Page Street when the agents conducted their search. Of the two, I tended to believe Hurley, who had no reason to lie.

Goodhue added, "Grant said he hung out in the Weather Underground for a long time, then bought false documentation, set up a new identity, and went to law school. But he claimed that what had happened had ruined his life, anyway—because of his shame at his cowardice and his fear that one day someone would recognize him and destroy everything he'd built up. He became quite maudlin about it, practically cried, but I sensed he was working on my sympathy. Unfortunately for him, after what he'd said about my mother, I couldn't feel much."

Ruined his life. It was the same as what Hilderly had said of Grant to his employer the day he'd encountered Grant at the taxation seminar. Had Grant also become maudlin when he'd told Perry a similar story over lunch at Tommy's Joynt? Perhaps added the heart-wrenching detail that he lived in such fear that he was unable to acknowledge his own daughter?

It struck me that Grant, who had been interviewed by Goodhue, could not have helped but notice the newswoman's striking resemblance to Jenny Ruhl. And the name Goodhue must have rung a bell with him, since he had visited at Ben and Nilla's home in the Portola district. I would not have been at all surprised if Grant had a background check run on Jess to ascertain that she was indeed his offspring.

On the other hand, Hilderly had lived in the past and probably seldom watched TV newscasts. In all likelihood he had not known the whereabouts of Ruhl's daughter until Grant told him, and this finishing touch to Grant's tale of woe would have been sure to deeply affect a man who was more or less estranged from his own sons. The bond that he imagined between himself and his former friend—evidenced by his telling Gene Carver that he saw a lot of himself in Grant—could only have been reinforced by it.

But there was a great deal wrong with Grant's story . . .

I asked, "Then what happened?"

"He threatened me, in a subtle way. Said it would be dangerous for me to go up against someone in his position, that sort of thing. It didn't frighten me. It only made me sad. I started to cry. He put his arms around me and told me to cheer up. He said that just because he wasn't my father, it didn't mean we couldn't be *very good* friends. And then I realized he was coming on to me again— this man who really *was* my father, who knew that, no matter what he said." She covered her face with her hands; tears welled through her spread fingers.

"I'd finally found my father," she added, "and he was a pervert."

I doubted that. My guess was that Grant had been trying to put her off so that she would leave him alone in the future. There was something in his past that he didn't want to come out—but it wasn't the story he had handed her.

After a bit Goodhue went to get some tissues and wiped her face. She sat on the stool by the counter, her gaze turned inward, on the hopelessly bleak memory of Wednesday night.

I said gently, "Tell me the rest of it."

"The rest is just . . . ugliness."

"Don't bottle it up."

A long silence. Then the words came out in a rush; she was eager to get the telling over with. "I was outraged. Shoved him away, hard. He stumbled and reached out for me. I shoved him again. He fell, and his head slammed into the iron leg of the worktable. And he just lay there, bleeding."

"And then?"

"I got out of there. Ran. I was halfway down the path by the house when I remembered I'd left my coat in his office. I went in, got it. There were the glasses we'd drunk from. I put them back in the cabinet under

346

the wet bar. Then the phone rang. I panicked, rushed out of the house, right through the front door."

I frowned. There was a gaping hole in her story. Had she blacked out, repressed the memory of how savage her attack on Grant had been?

"Jess," I said, "think back to the studio, after Grant fell. Did you touch anything?"

"Like what?"

"Well, the fetish he had in progress?"

"No."

"What about his body? Did you touch it? Check to see if he was actually dead, or—"

"I *couldn't* touch him. Afterward I hoped maybe he'd just been knocked unconscious. But back at the studio, when the reports started to come over the police-band radio in the newsroom—I knew I couldn't go before the cameras and report a murder I had committed. So I went home, and one of the co-anchors from the weekend news filled in for me. I didn't have to fake being sick—I *was.*"

"Did you watch the news that night? Read any of the accounts in the papers the next day?"

"Just the story in the *Chronicle.* I wanted to see if they suspected . . . and they didn't."

The newspaper article had merely said Grant had died of blows to the head; the police had held back the brutality of the attack and the nature of the murder weapon. In her panicked state, Goodhue could easily have ignored the plural, or thought the reporter was mistaken. I wasn't yet willing to fully credit her story, though; I asked her to go over it again. She did, with enough backtracking and minor inconsistencies to give it the ring of truth.

I asked one final question. "Did you see anyone on the street when you ran out? Did anyone see you?"

". . . There was a truck, one of those ancient pickups. It was weaving down Lyon Street, and I ran in front of it."

"What color was it?"

"I don't know. Orange, maybe. What does this matter, anyway? Like you said before, you'll have to tell the police—"

"I can be selective about what I tell them, though."

"I don't understand."

"There's a lot of this that need never come out. You didn't kill Tom Grant, Jess. A person who arrived after you left did."

Twenty-Four

Goodhue was so relieved and elated at what I explained to her that she wanted to contact the police and set things straight immediately. I cautioned her against doing so until she consulted an attorney.

"The inspector in charge of the case is a real . . . well, asshole. He'd see charging someone as well known as you with obstruction as a major coup. Talk with Harry Sullivan. And in the meantime, I'll keep at it, try to wrap the investigation up quickly."

"You think you can do that?"

"Yes."

"Do you know who killed my . . . Tom Grant?"

"No," I lied, in the interests of saving time, "not yet. But I think I will soon."

Goodhue turned on the lights around the mirror and began repairing her makeup. I was impatient to make some calls, so I went downstairs to the newsroom and used the same phone as I had Monday afternoon. As then, I put in a credit-card call to the Fleming residence in Blackhawk.

Judy Fleming answered. I identified myself, asked for Kurt. She said she'd call him to the phone. Then she asked, "Does this have to do with why Perry changed his will?"

"Yes. I'm still working on it."

That seemed to satisfy her. She went away, and half a minute later Kurt came on the line.

I said, "I need to double-check a few things about your discussion with Perry the last time you saw him."

"Sure. Go ahead."

"When he talked about making decisions, what did he say about them coming back to haunt you?"

Pause. "That even if the decision was the right one, it could do that."

"And he said you shouldn't take it out on yourself because you can't control the consequences of your actions?"

"Right."

"Will you go over what he said about ideals again?"

"Well, that was after his third margarita, so . . . All that really made sense to me is that sometimes you have to dump some of your ideals in favor of upholding the most important one. After that he rambled on about guilt and atonement and symbolic acts. I wasn't raised religious, so it didn't really mean much to me."

I *had* been raised religious, but in view of Perry's atheism, it didn't mean much to me, either. Unless I could find a context in which to place it . . . "Thanks, Kurt."

"Uh, sure. Anytime." His tone was somewhat bewildered, as if he'd been expecting some sort of explanation for my questions.

Next I called Rae at All Souls. "Any word on Hank?" I asked.

"Nothing."

"If you hear, will you call my house, leave a message on the machine?"

"Okay. Where are you?"

"Out in the field," I said vaguely. "I need your help for a couple of minutes. You know that stack of back issues of the papers in Hank's office? Would you go in there and get yesterday's *Chron*—the one with the story on Tom Grant's murder?"

"Hang on."

As I waited for her to come back, I glanced across the newsroom at Goodhue's cubicle. The anchorwoman was already there— freshly made up and dressed in dry clothes. She picked up the phone receiver, consulted the yellow sheet on the desk in front of her, and began to dial.

Rae's voice said, "Shar? I've got it. What do you need?"

"First, Grant's date of graduation from the University of Colorado. I presume it will be in the obituary."

"The obit . . . here it is—they ran it as a sidebar to the story. Class of fifty-nine."

"Okay. Now University of Illinois Law School."

"Sixty-two."

"Bastard lied all over the place. Any mention of what he did immediately after law school?"

"Uh . . . no, it just talks about his 'rather unique law practice.' But it doesn't say when he first hung out his shingle."

I'd suspected as much.

"Shar, what's this—"

"I'll tell you later. Thanks." I cut off her protesting "Hey!" by replacing the receiver.

As I crossed the newsroom, Goodhue motioned to me. I went into the cubicle.

"I reached Harry Sullivan's service and convinced them it was an emergency," she said. "He's supposed to call me."

"Good. When you talk with him, ask him to check with me before speaking with the police. There may be a way I can keep you

352

out of this entirely. And give me your home number in case I need to get in touch."

She wrote it on a card. "Why are you doing this for me?"

"I like people with guts. You've overcome a great deal in your life and shouldn't have to suffer for one mistake. Besides, I'm doing it for myself, as well—my need to get at the truth."

"Well, I can't tell you how much I appreciate it. But I sure didn't act as if I had guts tonight. Hurling myself into the bay, like Anna Karenina under the train. Whimpering and sniveling and probably causing us both to get bad colds."

"We all do some whimpering and sniveling," I said. "Just be glad you got yours over with early in life."

"You know, I think I'm going to put my past behind me now and get on with that life. My mother killed herself, and my father wouldn't acknowledge me. Their problems had nothing to do with me as a person. My mother's family didn't want me, either. Fuck 'em—it's their loss."

I gave her a thumbs-up sign and left the studio.

On the drive to West Marin I thought about

various scraps of seemingly unrelated information that I'd collected over the past five days. Some pertained to Tom Grant: the things Cal Hurley had told me; Grant's fabrications about his past; Luke Widdows's insights into certain aspects of the sixties. Others had to do with Perry Hilderly: the things he'd told Kurt; what I thought his "most important" ideal was; a police inspector who normally went by the book but now seemed to be covering up something.

And I thought about dreams, and how they sometimes can take the form of clever visual puns, prompting the dreamer to become aware of things she already knows . . .

By the time I reached Inverness it was after ten. The hamlet was shut down, except for the Czech restaurant. I continued along the shoreline, past dark cottages, then wound up through the conifer forest. Fog drifted from pockets between the hills; the night was moonless. On the barren headland the mist thickened, coated my windshield. When I put on the wipers, the glass smeared. Beyond it the headlight beams looked to be reflected off a solid white wall. All I could make out were the fence posts along the road.

The wind blew strong, pushing at the little

car until its tires strained to hold the pavement. I slowed to twenty, opened my window to help the feeble defroster. As I rounded the sharp curve above Moon Ridge Stables, I saw that the fog was lighter on that side of the headland—blowing back out to sea. Abbotts Lagoon was a black stain on the landscape; beyond the beach, a white line of surf moved restlessly.

I couldn't make out any of the ranch buildings down in the cypress-ringed hollow, but there was a pair of lights moving across the cattle graze. I turned into the rutted access road, rumbled down the hillside. The lights came my way, moving fast. I crossed a cattle guard beyond which the land dropped off on either side, and suddenly the other vehicle rounded the curve some twenty yards ahead.

I slammed on my brakes, stalling the MG; yanked on the wheel, fighting a skid. The other vehicle—a Jeep—slewed sideways. For an instant it hung on the edge of the road, then lurched nose-downward into the ditch. Its motor stalled, and the night became very quiet.

I jumped out of my car and ran toward the Jeep. Its driver's door opened and a tall, rangy figure got out. Libby Ross.

"Goddamn it!" her husky voice shouted. "What the hell're you doing running me off the road like that?"

"Are you all right?" I called.

Ross stopped halfway up the incline, recognizing me. "I thought I told you to stay the hell away from here. Now you've gone and made me wreck my Jeep."

"Doesn't look wrecked," I said. "You've got four-wheel drive, should be able to get it out of there easily."

"No way. I hit a rock—one of the tires is going flat." Ross kicked the Jeep's bumper. "Shit! Not my day. Or week. Or year." She kicked the Jeep again, then looked back at me. "What're you doing here?"

"I need to talk with you."

"Can't. I've got to get over to Taylor's. Some trouble with D. A." She glanced speculatively at my car.

I said, "Climb in, I'll take you."

Ross came the rest of the way up the incline and strode to the car, folding her rangy body into the cramped passenger seat.

I backed up and turned around on the other side of the cattle guard. "What kind of trouble?" I asked.

"Don't know. Mia was practically incoherent when she called. Panicky. She'd

356

walked down the highway to the phone booth outside of Nick's Cove."

"How long ago?"

"Maybe fifteen minutes. Something about D. A. and that island. Nobody's there at the restaurant but her, so she called me."

I didn't like the sound of that at all. When I turned onto the main road, I put on speed in spite of the limited visibility.

Ross glanced at me. "What're you thinking?"

"The same thing you are."

She bit her lip, turned her face toward the side window.

"It's time you leveled with me," I said. "You pretended you had no ongoing relationship with D. A., that Mia's jealousy was unfounded. But not long after that I saw the two of you kissing down on the beach."

"Where were you when this supposedly happened?"

"At the stables."

"I thought I told you to leave when I rode off."

"I stayed to look around your tack room."

"You had no right—"

"I found the photograph of you, D. A., Perry, and Jenny. Who took it—Andy Wrightman?"

". . . Yeah."

"Why'd you keep it?"

She sighed. "You wouldn't understand. You probably think I wouldn't want a reminder of those days, not after the way things turned out. That was what Glen—my husband—thought. It was him that didn't want to be reminded of my past, so I always kept the picture out in the tack room. *I* didn't mind remembering. Those were the best days of my life, back when we were young and going to change the world. Since then, nothing's been . . . anything."

"When did you first figure out Wrightman and Grant were one and the same?"

"I'd never even heard of Grant until you came here the first time."

"But when I described him, you suspected who he was."

No reply.

"D. A. did, too."

More silence.

I said, "Why did you lie about your relationship with D. A.?"

"Because it's too damn hard to explain a relationship like that. What little we have isn't taking anything away from Mia. It's just our way of keeping the past alive."

"D. A. did come to see you Wednesday

afternoon, then. He'd been brooding about Andy Wrightman, hadn't he?"

She shifted in the cramped seat, shoved her hands between her bent knees.

"Did you tell him where to find Tom Grant?"

"In a way I guess I did. I told him what you'd said about where he lived, that he'd done well for himself after—"

"After what?"

Ross stared out the window at the buildings of Inverness. The lights of the Czech restaurant briefly washed over her dark blond curls.

"What you started to say was after Andy Wrightman went back to his true identity. Tom Grant was the man's actual name. Wrightman was just an alias he used."

Ross glanced at me. Her eyes glittered in the headlight beams from a passing car.

"Grant graduated from the University of Illinois Law School in nineteen sixty-two," I went on. "It's my guess that he was recruited by the FBI; many law graduates are. He adopted the Wrightman name when he was sent to Berkeley to infiltrate radical student organizations. There were a lot of undercover agents on the campuses during those days. A man I know says most of them

359

weren't very successful: they either didn't fit in and weren't trusted with any real information, or they fit in too well, became unreliable. Grant was effective for a while, but by fathering Jenny's child, in a sense he also joined forces with the people the Bureau perceived as the enemy."

I stopped at the intersection with Highway One. There were no cars coming from either direction. I eased the clutch out and turned north, over the bridge and into Point Reyes Station. It was livelier than Iverness: lights shone in most of the houses, and a group of people congregated on the sidewalk in front of one of the bars. Ross was silent until after we came out on the other side of the little town.

"Do you have proof of all this?"

"No, but there's a San Francisco homicide inspector who probably does, whether he knows it or not. And I think you and D. A. realized it a long time ago."

"Yeah, we always suspected Andy informed on us, D. A. and I. Why else would the feds have let him just walk away from Port Chicago? I saw that at the time. He just jammed his gun into D. A.'s hand and melted into the scenery. And why was his girlfriend the one they made the deal with, rather than either of us? If they wanted to make an example of somebody, the daughter of a rich family would have been a better choice. Except they didn't want that; it would have blown Andy's cover. And Andy probably urged it; he must have been scared to death that the depth of his involvement with her would come out and screw up his career."

"You and D. A. never said anything about him to the authorities?"

She shook her head. "It seems incredible now, but at the time we didn't know. Or maybe it was that we didn't want to believe what he was. Our rationale was, what if we were wrong? We'd have been informing on one of our own."

"Andy left Berkeley when Jenny told him she was pregnant, didn't he?"

"Uh-huh."

"He probably requested assignment to another campus. If it came out that he'd fathered a child by her, the Bureau would have terminated him. But he couldn't stay away from her—maybe he did care for her on some level, maybe he was curious about his child. He came back a few years later, and when you all started planning the bombing, he saw an opportunity to make some real career points."

We were passing through Marshall now. The boarded-up oyster restaurant was a dark monolith. Tendrils of fog curled around the small cottages and drifted across the wet road.

I asked, "When he came to see you Wednesday afternoon, did D. A. say he wanted to confront Grant?"

". . . He wasn't making sense. D. A. rarely does."

"When you told him where Grant lived, you must have known he'd go there."

"I never thought he would."

I wondered about that, but I let it go for now. "What about the next afternoon on the beach—did he mention Grant?"

"No. He was in bad shape, had been doing booze and pills. I tried to slow him down, but when D. A. goes off on a jag . . ." She shrugged. After a while she asked, "How come you're so sure D. A. was there at Grant's house?"

"That night, D. A. supposedly took Jake's truck and went barhopping. Mia told me he'd been in a fight, lost his jacket. A witness saw a truck like Jake's outside Grant's house just before he was killed.

362

There would have been a lot of blood on the jacket if D. A. beat Grant to death—enough that he'd want to get rid of it."

"God, then it's true."

"You suspected all along. You should have told me."

"I know, but my protective instincts kicked in. I've been trying to save D. A. for so long now that it's automatic."

"You ought to know by now that it's a lost cause. The man doesn't want to be saved."

"No, but here we both are, trying to save him one last time."

We neared Nick's Cove in a few minutes. I asked, "Is Mia still there, or did she walk back home?"

"Said she'd meet me at Taylor's."

I accelerated up the hill.

Ross said, "Thing that bothers me about Grant—there was nothing in the paper about him having been with the FBI."

"I thought you said you didn't take a paper."

"I saw the headline when I was shopping in Point Reyes yesterday, so I bought it. Picture didn't look much like Andy, but I recognized the name Grant from your visit."

As I recalled, the story and picture had

appeared on an inside page—a place Ross wouldn't have been able to see from a casual glance at a newspaper rack. I decided to let it go for a moment, however.

She added, "Why all the secrecy about him being with the FBI? Given the political climate in this country today, you'd think he'd have written a book about his experiences, gone on talk shows. Man could have been a hero."

"I think the FBI has restrictions on that sort of thing. Undercover agents' activities are classified information. But even if they weren't, I don't think Grant would have gone public with the story. He had reasons for not wanting his past too closely scrutinized."

"You mean because of Jenny's baby?"

"That, and other things." But I couldn't go into them at the moment because ahead I saw the outlines of Taylor's sign, and the entrance to the crushed-shell driveway. I turned the MG and coasted down into the parking lot.

My headlights washed over Mia Taylor. She stood in front of the restaurant, backlit by its beer signs, wearing a blue sweater that was many sizes too big for her. Before I brought the car to a stop she ran toward it.

"What're you doing here?" she exclaimed, her startled face appearing at the side window. Then she looked across me, saw Ross. "Oh."

I shut off the engine and we got out. "Where's D. A.?" I asked.

"Gone. To the island. He took my babies with him."

I felt a sudden chill.

Ross came around the car. "He's got little Mia and Davey?"

She closed her eyes and nodded.

"Why? Why would he take them out there?"

"I don't know."

I asked, "Have you called the sheriff?"

Her eyes flew open in panic. "I can't! Like I told you, there's been lots of trouble with D. A. I'm afraid after this Salcido business, they'll shoot first, kill him, maybe the kids, too."

She had a point. Ramon Salcido, a Sonoma Valley winery worker, had gone on a drug-and-alcohol-induced rampage the previous spring, leaving seven people dead, including his wife and two of his three young daughters. Area sheriffs' departments were now understandably more nervous than usual when it came to hostage situations involving children. And the situation with Taylor—a known substance abuser—was entirely too reminiscent of the Salcido case.

"Is D. A. armed?" I asked.

"The twenty-two we keep behind the bar is gone."

Ross was looking around. "Where is everybody? What happened to Jake and Harley?"

Mia said, "They're over to Occidental— big dinner for this lodge they belong to. Just as well—there's nothing they'd like more than to blow D. A.'s head off."

I glanced at Ross. She shrugged. I asked Mia, "Is there a boat we can use?"

"Outboard tied up to the dock. D. A. took one of the rowboats. Does that sometimes, the damn fool, rowing around in the dark. I heard him cast off, went out to see what was going on. Then I heard my babies crying."

"And you're sure he went to the island?"

"He had a Coleman lantern. I could see it until he got there and then it disappeared into the trees."

I asked Ross, "Can you pilot a boat?"

"Of course."

"Good. Once I get those kids away from D. A. I'll want you to bring them back to shore, while I try to convince him to give himself up." Quickly I glanced at Mia, regretting the way I'd phrased it. But she was staring off at the bay, probably searching for light from D. A.'s lantern. When I touched her arm, she started.

"We'll need some things," I told her. "Flashlights—the most powerful you've got. Blankets. A first-aid kit, if you have one."

She nodded and set off for her cabin at a run.

Ross moved closer to me, said in a low voice, "What do you think our chances are?"

I looked out at the dock, where a pair of lights shone fuzzily through the fog. Imagined the expanse of water beyond them, and the uncharted terrain of Hog Island. And wished for my gun, which I'd locked away that morning—hoping never to need it again after last night's shooting.

I said, "Not real good, but we've got to risk it."

Twenty-Five

I killed the stuttering motor as the boat scraped bottom off the island's shore. Ross jumped over the side, sloshing in the shallow water. I moved toward the bow, stepped out onto a flat rock, and together we hauled the boat up onto the beach. There was another vessel to our left: a blue rowboat that had seen better days. Ross reached for one of the powerful torchlights Mia had given us and went toward it.

She held the torch up, moving it from bow to stern. Then she bent, reaching for something inside the boat. She turned, her face furrowed with concern, and held the object aloft. It was a fuzzy white slipper, child-size.

I grimaced and reached under the seat of the motorboat for the other torch, then raised it and studied the fog-swept terrain. The island's rocky beach rose to jagged outcroppings; then the thick and tangled cypress and eucalypti started, covering it all the way to the top. I could see no light anywhere. All I could hear was the soughing of the branches, the lapping of small waves. Ross still stood by the rowboat clutching the slipper, scarcely breathing.

The engine's racket had prevented all but minimal conversation on the way over. Now I asked, "Have you ever come out here?"

Although I'd spoken in a low voice, the

sound carried, echoing. Ross jerked, said, "Ssh!"

"For God's sake, he knows we're here by now. No way he couldn't hear that engine."

"Sorry, I'm jumpy." She moved closer to where I stood. "No, I've never been here before. When I first came up from the city, D. A. was always trying to get me to come with him. But there was something about the way he talked about the place made me not want to do that."

"What about the kids? Did he ever bring them?"

"Plenty of times, before these past few months when he got so strange that Mia told him he couldn't. They know the island as well as D. A. He said they would clamber all over it like little goats."

"Well, that's something, anyway. It's not unfamiliar territory to them."

"But in the dark . . . D. A. told me that it's rocky all the way to the top. There're trails, but some of them come to dead ends. Further up are big rocks, sort of like steps that were built for giants. Where he liked to go was a flat rock at the very top. He could look out through the trees, see the whole bay. He said . . ." She paused, shivering.

"He said?"

"He said he liked to lie on the rock and . . . imagine what it would be like to be dead and at peace."

A chill that had nothing to do with the wind off the bay enveloped me. "Then that's probably where he went. Let's see if we can find the right trail."

The tide had gone out, but not long ago. The rocks underfoot were slick. I trained my torch downward so neither of us would slip. There were two trails starting at that part of the beach—one paralleling the shoreline, the other snaking up into the jagged rocks. We took the latter.

As we climbed, the smell of cypress and eucalypti became more pungent; the ground was carpeted in needles, making it easier to lose one's footing. I became aware of night noises now: a scurrying to one side; branches rubbing together; the rustling of birds in their nesting places. The wind was not as strong as it had been on the beach, but still cold. It brought with it the odor of brackish salt water and the fresher scent of the open sea, not too many miles away. At the base of a high outcropping I stopped, wiping fog-damp off my face with one hand, holding the torch aloft with the other.

Nothing but a sheer rock wall.

Ross came up behind me. I said, "It looks as if this is one of the dead-end trails."

"Shit! Better go back to the beach. We can try the other."

We retraced the path we'd climbed on, Ross tripping once and nearly pitching headlong into a declivity. Passed the beached boats and began moving along the shoreline. Small waves sucked at the island's edges, lapped at the rocks, and washed up into the hollows between them. I lowered my torch once more, illuminating the treacherous ground.

And saw her . . .

Little Mia Taylor lay in a rocky depression that was partially filled with water, curled into a fetal position. She wore white pajamas printed with red and yellow and blue and green circus clowns, and one foot was bare. The other was encased in a fuzzy white slipper, the twin of the one Ross had found in the rowboat.

Behind me Ross gasped. She tried to push around me, but I held her back. Briefly I closed my eyes, bracing myself for what could easily be the worst discovery of my entire life. Then I stepped across the rocks to the child.

Mia didn't stir as I approached her. I

squatted beside her, touched her arm. Her flesh felt cold and clammy. A gust of wind ruffled her fine black hair.

And then I heard her suck in her breath —a quick tremulous intake that was filled with grief and terror.

Relief washed over me. I placed my hand on her head, smoothed her hair, touched her neck. Her artery pulsed strongly. I said, "Mia, it's okay now. Libby and I are here."

"Sharon?" Ross called.

"She's alive. Go back to the boat and get those blankets."

Ross's footsteps moved swiftly away over the rocks.

Mia began to whimper. I started to move her—carefully, in case any bones were broken. She didn't cry out or wince; once I had her in my arms, she coiled her body even more tightly.

"Daddy," she said.

"Mia, what happened to your daddy? And Davey?"

"Gone." Her voice was muffled against me. "Daddy let go of my hand. I fell. I called him, but he didn't hear. Davey screamed for him to stop. But they went away and left me."

D. A. probably hadn't even noticed he'd

372

let go of her. Too drunk or stoned to realize or care that she was gone. Anger flared within me, and I held Mia more tightly.

Ross returned with the blankets. We wrapped the little girl in them. I said, "Take her to the boat. I'll go after D. A. and Davey."

"You'd better not—"

"For God's sake, Libby, you can't leave her alone in that condition! I'll be okay."

Without a word Ross hefted the swaddled child. I stood, focused my torch on the trail, and set out alone.

After a few minutes I was reasonably sure I'd found the trail that would take me to D. A.'s flat rock at the top of the island. It zigzagged steadily upward, around trees and jagged outcroppings, past deep declivities. The wind grew stronger as I climbed; fog drifted in and out of the encroaching branches. Silence lay heavy all around me, but I knew it was deceptive; there was danger in the void that held an unbalanced man with a gun.

Soon my ungloved fingers began to stiffen from the chill; I flexed them. My throat was scratchy, and I kept swallowing to relieve it. I'd lost my bearings, didn't know which side of the island I was on now, or how far I'd traveled toward the top.

Finally the trail came out onto a ledge. I stopped, breathing hard. Through rents in the fog I could see the eastern shore of the bay—faint lights winking here and there on the hillsides, others strung out along the water. I checked my watch, was surprised to find I'd only been climbing a little over ten minutes. I'd lost my sense of time, too.

After I went a few more yards, the trail split. I took the arm to my left, but soon found it was descending. I retraced my steps, took the other arm uphill. The terrain quickly became more rugged, the vegetation sparser. I came up against a rock ledge, raised my flash, and realized I'd come to the "giant steps"—three feet or more in height, set one atop the other. A light glowed beyond the highest step; I was very close to the place where Taylor liked to lie and imagine the tranquility of death.

My heart beat faster. I stood still, strained to hear. No sound up there but the wind.

I began climbing the steps, boosting myself up, remembering the old schoolyard game of Mother, May I?

Mother, may I take a baby step? A banana step? A giant step?

374

One more giant step. Then another. Light glowing brighter now. One last step, higher than the others. Rest before you climb it.

I looked up, saw a ring of eucalypti faintly illuminated by the lantern rays. Their branches and ragged, curling bark were etched against a high-drifting fog. Nothing else moved up there. No one spoke. Did anyone still breathe?

A sick dread of what I might find filled me. And then I heard a sound . . . a sob. Davey.

A soothing voice said, "Hush." Then it began to sing. The voice was D. A.'s, the words in another language. Miwok? The cadence was that of a lullaby.

Slowly I pulled myself over the last step. The ground above it sloped upward; my sight was blocked by a fallen tree. I flattened, wriggled forward on my stomach. Peered over the tree trunk.

The slab of rock sat in the middle of the clearing. The lantern stood at its far side. Taylor lay on his back, one denim-covered knee bent upward, his left arm flung over his eyes. His right arm—the one closest to me—encircled Davey. The pajama-clad little boy lay with his head on his father's shoulder. He'd stopped crying, but his dark eyes darted around the clearing. I saw no gun, no other weapon.

Cautiously I raised myself above the tree trunk. Davey spotted me instantly, and his eyes flashed with recognition.

I shook my head. Pantomimed that he should pretend to sleep. For a moment he looked confused. Then he shut his eyes.

Taylor's singing trailed off in a minute or two. Resumed. Trailed off again. He sighed deeply, and then his chest moved up and down in a regular rhythm. After a bit his mouth sagged open and he began to snore.

Davey opened his eyes, looking at me. I shook my head, waited another couple of minutes before I motioned for him to come to me.

He sat slowly, watching his father. Slipped away from his encircling arm. Stood and moved quietly across the clearing. I pulled him down beside me on the other side of the tree trunk.

Putting my lips close to his ear, I whispered, "Everything's going to be okay now. Mia's down on the beach with Libby. Can you get back there on your own?"

". . . If I have a light."

"Come on, then."

We wriggled back to the first giant step,

and I boosted him over it. Handed him my torch. He glanced around at the encroaching blackness, but when he looked at me again, his gaze was steady, resolute. In it I recognized the strength and pride his father had possessed so long ago.

"Be careful," I whispered. "Tell Libby I said to take you and Mia home. Then she can come back for your daddy and me."

For a moment he looked longingly upward, to the misty light coming from the clearing where his father slept. Then he turned and let himself down the next step.

I remained where I was, giving him a five-minute head start before I went to rouse D. A.

Taylor took a great deal of rousing. He thrashed and mumbled and jerked violently away from my outstretched hand. I got a firm grip on his shoulders and hauled him to a sitting position. He hunched over, black hair down in his eyes. For a moment his emaciated frame shuddered. Then he looked up at me.

Beneath the shaggy fringe of hair his eyes were as burnt-out as the first time I'd looked into them. He stared at me without recognition.

I said, "D. A., it's time to go home now."

He didn't reply, merely moved the focus of his gaze to the lantern and then around the clearing. He put a hand on the smooth rock and stroked it.

"Do you know where we are?" I asked.

"I know."

"Do you remember coming here?"

He considered, shook his head. "I often do."

"You brought your children with you this time."

"My children."

"Mia and Davey—"

"I *know* who my children are." Now a puzzled expression crossed his face. He continued to look around the clearing. "I was singing to them . . . Where are they?"

"On their way home."

He nodded, as if he'd suspected as much.

I sat cross-legged on the end of the rock, looking about for the gun Mia thought he'd taken. There was no sign of it. "D. A., why did you come here tonight?"

"It seemed time, I suppose." He was entering one of his periods of lucidity now; I could tell by his expression and the tone of his voice. "But I'm not all that clear on it, to tell you the truth. There were some pills, and some wine."

"I see. What's the last thing you *are* clear on?"

"You'll have to refresh me as to what day this is."

"It's Friday, near midnight."

He looked down at his hands, making an effort to recall. "As near as I know, this began a couple of days ago."

"On Wednesday, when you went to San Francisco to see Tom Grant."

His fingers clenched spasmodically.

"How did you know where to find Grant, D. A.?"

". . . There was a map, drawn for me. It showed where his house was."

Although it didn't surprise me, anger at Libby Ross rose, forcing me to choke back a curse. After I got it under control, I asked, "Why did you go there?"

"Just to see. I wanted to know what had become of the man who betrayed us."

"And you saw . . . ?"

"He was afraid. Oh, there was something about someone just having attacked him, and a bump on the head, but I knew I was the one he really feared. He hid behind scorn and ugly words and threats—just as once he hid behind Andy Wrightman. But in the end, he was very afraid."

I bit my lip, remembering the blood-spattered workshop and the ruin of what had once been human.

"Tell me about the ugly words," I finally said.

Taylor made a motion with his hand, brushing the request away. "They were very unpleasant."

"Did he tell you about Jenny—about how he drove her to suicide by working on her guilt over turning you and Libby in, and gave her the gun?" It was the only explanation I'd been able to come up with for Grant going to such lengths to keep his past from coming under scrutiny. He'd rid himself of a woman who was a great liability, but he'd done it by providing her with a weapon that he should have turned over to his fellow agents when they'd searched the flat on Page Street.

But Taylor shook his head. "He didn't need to. Libby and I knew; we've always known. Jenny could only have gotten that gun from the man who knew where the weapons were kept in the flat. No, what he said was worse than that. He said it was Perry who betrayed us."

380

Again I wasn't surprised.

Taylor added, "I couldn't listen to him say those things. Perry was the man I looked up to the most. If he betrayed us, then . . . there were no heroes."

D. A. bowed his head again. A sudden gust of wind swirled through the clearing. From below I heard the faint noise of a motor—the overworked one on the boat I'd piloted earlier. Davey had reached safety; Ross was taking them home.

The lantern flickered, getting low on fuel. I stood. "D. A., come back to shore with me. We'll work this out."

He shook his head.

I went over to the lantern, turned it down lower. "Come on," I said. "You'll be okay." I stretched out my hand.

He didn't seem to see or hear me. His gaze moved around the clearing, stopping here and there, as if the trees and rocks and plants were cherished objects. Then his eyes met mine—their always fleeting light extinguished so totally that not even the rays from the lantern enlivened them.

"What happened to all the heroes?" he asked.

I had no answer for him, because I suspected there had never been any heroes—

not in the world he was longing for. That was a world all too often re-created not from fact but from wishful fantasy, and none of us could ever know where the truth left off and the lies began.

I turned, bent to pick up the lantern. Behind me I heard Taylor make a sudden movement.

Then I heard the click.

I froze, skin acrawl; the click was the unmistakable one of a safety being flipped off an automatic. I glanced back, ready to run. And saw that the .22 he'd had concealed somewhere on his person was not pointed at me.

Taylor held the gun in both hands, muzzle in his mouth.

As I lunged at him, screaming for him not to do it, he pulled the trigger.

Twenty-Six

I left D. A. Taylor finally at peace on the slab on top of his island. Climbed back down, feeling sick, the lantern guttering and going out when I reached the easy section of the trail on the beach. There I rested until

I heard the irregular stutter of the returning motorboat.

Ross was piloting it. I slogged through the shallow water and climbed aboard.

"D. A.?" she asked.

"Dead. He shot himself."

She compressed her lips, turned the boat around. I made no effort to speak to her on the return trip. When we reached the dock behind Taylor's, I jumped from the boat as soon as it bumped against the pilings.

"Wait!" Ross said.

I turned, looked coldly at her. "Before he killed himself, D. A. told me about the map you drew him. What did you do—go down to the city and case Grant's property before you sent D. A. out to exact revenge for you?"

The faint light from the restaurant's windows showed her face, surprise altering its set lines of strain.

"You knew what would happen," I added. "You're an accessory—more guilty than D. A., to my way of thinking."

". . . What do you intend to do about it?"

"Nothing. You'd only cover up with more lies. Besides, enough people are going to be hurt by this without me compounding it."

She raised her hands, then let them fall

383

limply to her sides. "Everybody I ever cared about is dead. Everything that ever mattered to me is over."

"And now you'll just have to live with what you did, won't you?" I strode up the rickety dock, away from her self-serving deceptions, out of her wasted life.

From the phone booth outside Nick's Cove I called the sheriff's department. Later, when I was finished dealing with them, I made two other calls.

The first was to Goodhue, relaying what had happened and saying that I would be able to leave her out of my version for the authorities. "There's something I want you to do in exchange, however," I told her.

"Certainly. What?"

"Since Taylor's dead, his share in the Hilderly estate will be divided between you and Libby Ross. The same with Tom Grant's. I want you to give the amount you receive beyond your original inheritance to Taylor's wife and children. They're going to need money to start a new life."

Goodhue agreed without hesitation.

Next I called Greg at home. I asked him to meet me at the Hall in an hour, said I wanted McFate there, too. Greg didn't ask many questions; he was used to peculiar requests from me and, besides, he probably relished dragging McFate out of whatever bed he might occupy at that hour on a weekend morning.

By the time I parked at the nearly deserted curb in front of the Hall of Justice my anger had built to full pressure and I was primed for a confrontation. As I passed through the echoing marble-walled lobby, I glanced at the clock. Twenty minutes to four on Saturday morning—a week after I'd become involved in the case that for me had stripped away what little remained of the mythic charm of the 1960s.

I still valued the legacy of those years. A war had been stopped, the will of the people had prevailed, society had been altered in profound ways. But there was a darker side to the legacy, and the personal cost had been high on both sides.

I'd been right on Monday night when I'd told Rae that what the sixties had been about was rage—but that was only part of it. What they'd also been about was the same as any other decade: winning and losing. Winning the war against communism in Southeast Asia; winning the war against the Establishment in the streets at home. Losing the country because it had become bitterly divided over the Asian conflict; losing yourself because the conflict in the streets had left you bitter, broken, alone.

That was another legacy of the sixties: trophies and dead things. Nets to catch the wind . . .

McFate was the first person I saw when I entered the squad room: standing near Greg's office, looking pressed and combed and clean-shaven, even on such short notice. He glanced at me—took in my mud-stained clothes and dirty face and disheveled hair— and sneered. The pressure of my anger soared, and then I totally lost it.

I strode over to him, put my grimy hands against his pin-striped chest, and gave him a shove. "You son of a bitch!"

Greg came to the door of his cubicle, eyebrows raised.

"You fucking pompous jerk!" I shoved McFate again, making sure I left a dirty handprint on the front of his pale blue shirt.

McFate shoved me back, said to Greg, "You saw that! She assaulted a police officer! What are you going to do about it?"

"Shut up, Leo," Greg said wearily. "Get in this office. You, too," he added to me.

McFate did an about-face and went in there, brushing fussily at his shirt. "I don't know why you let her get away with things like this," he told Greg. "If you ask me—"

"Nobody did. Sit down, Leo. Sharon, close the door."

I closed it, then moved the second visitor's chair as far from McFate's as possible, and sat.

"You could at least make her apologize," McFate said.

"Unfortunately, she's not very good at that." Greg turned to me; I could tell I was putting a heavy load on his patience. "Will you explain why this is necessary, please?"

I took a deep breath, gathering the vestiges of my shattered self-control. "The man who killed Tom Grant shot himself tonight —on Hog Island in Tomales Bay."

Slowly McFate turned his head toward me; his pupils narrowed to pinpoints. Greg merely waited.

I filled them in on what had happened, making it sound as if I'd gone up there on business about Hilderly's will and walked in on a family crisis. When I finished, I said to Greg, "That's one of the reasons I'm so pissed at him." I jerked my chin at McFate. "If he'd told me about Grant's early career

387

as a federal undercover agent, I would have realized who had motive to kill him, and Taylor might not have died."

McFate said, "Doesn't sound as if he was worth keeping alive."

I turned on him. "Shut up, you! You don't know anything about . . . anything."

Greg sighed and rolled his eyes.

"Okay," I said. "I'm sorry. But he can be such a pain in the—"

"If I may be heard," McFate said. "I withheld that information for two reasons. First, I do not feel required to share the details of my investigations with civilians. And second, the identities and records of undercover agents are classified information. I was not provided with full details of Grant's activities, so I could hardly be expected to connect it with the other persons named in Hilderly's will."

Greg said, "He has a point, Sharon."

"Half a point. I mentioned the probable connection with Hilderly to him—and more than once. If he had followed up on that, shared what he knew with me . . . Just yesterday didn't you say it's making the collar that counts—not who makes it?"

Greg nodded.

"Then as a corollary, I'd say it's utilizing

the available information that counts, not whether the information was uncovered by a civilian or a member of the department."

McFate said, "I still could not have been expected to make the connection—"

"I think you could have, given the other information you got from the Intelligence Division—but conveniently neglected to put in your reports."

McFate stiffened slightly. Greg leaned forward, interested.

I said to Greg, "Yesterday you also told me you were annoyed at how Leo kept disappearing."

"That's right."

"On at least one of those occasions—and I'm willing to bet quite a few others—he was over at his old detail."

"So?"

I glanced at McFate. He was sitting very still now.

"I suspect what he was doing there was going through back files on radicals they spied on in the sixties, looking for information on Hilderly and his other heirs—just in case the lead I'd given him was valid after all. One of the things he discovered was the circumstance that twenty years later caused

Hilderly to change his will—which in turn triggered Grant's murder."

"Why *did* Hilderly change his will?"

"Hilderly was never a part of that collective, at least not in the sense its members thought he was. He was close to the people, and they assumed he was using his job as a reporter to further their propaganda efforts. What he was really doing was gathering information for a story, perhaps something along the lines of 'Inside a Weather Collective.' But when they began to formulate plans to bomb Port Chicago—plans that were certain to result in the deaths of innocent people—he became disillusioned and concerned."

McFate said, "Why would he? He was a radical. None of them cared—"

"Hilderly cared. He valued human life above anything. Even above his loyalty to his closest friends. I think he went to the ID—their activities were well known even in those days—and warned them about the bombing plans. He knew he'd done the right thing, but his guilt over the betrayal more or less soured the rest of his life. Then last May he ran into Tom Grant, who handed him an untrue story about *his* ruined life, and Hilderly decided to atone for what he'd done—by leaving money to three of the people he'd harmed, plus to the only living heir of the other."

Greg looked at McFate. "Is it true that Hilderly went to the ID, Leo?"

It was a moment before he replied. "Yes. I don't know about the business with the will; I don't know how she can surmise all that. But Hilderly did talk with the ID. They, in turn, contacted the FBI. When the Bureau got back to them, they said they already had the situation covered and that arrests would be forthcoming. Hilderly needn't have felt guilty about anything; he didn't even try to turn them in to the agency with jurisdiction."

McFate spoke as if what had happened was amusing—a joke that Hilderly had led a guilt-ridden life and then attempted to atone for something he hadn't actually done. I frowned at his callousness, saw Greg was frowning, too.

"How *did* you put all that together?" Greg asked.

"I'll explain later." I was *not* going to tell him in front of McFate about my dream of the previous morning—the sly visual pun on the word "intelligence," in which a gilt suit of armor stood for "guilt" and a gnawed

391

diploma indicated its possessor had "ratted on" someone.

"All right," Greg said. Then to McFate, "Why wasn't I apprised of any of this, Leo?"

"I didn't find it relevant—"

"Bullshit! The reason you didn't report it to me is that you were protecting your pals at the ID."

"Lieutenant, twenty years ago it was acceptable for the division to maintain surveillance on groups who could be deemed—"

"Yes. But it hasn't been acceptable since nineteen seventy-five, when the commission adopted rules against such activity. And recently the ID has taken a lot of heat for having ignored those rules. They like to maintain a low profile over there these days; I'm sure your pals made it clear they'd appreciate being kept out of something like the Grant case—even though their involvement was a long way back and very peripheral."

"I . . . well, I . . ."

"Funny thing about this, McFate: Sharon—this civilian—shared most of the details of her investigation with me. I knew a lot of the facts you didn't deem 'relevant.' If you'd reported properly, I would probably have worked out the solution to your case, and Taylor would still be alive." Greg was as angry as I'd ever seen him.

"Lieutenant, I—"

"Oh, get the hell out of here. We'll discuss it tomorrow."

McFate left the cubicle without looking at either of us.

"You know," Greg said when he was gone, "I'm pleased that one of my last official acts on Homicide will be making sure he's reprimanded for this. I damned well want it to go in his file."

"The captaincy came through, then?"

"They're announcing it Monday."

I felt an odd tug of sadness. "Congratulations."

"Jesus, you make it sound as if I'd just told you I had a fatal disease."

"Oh, Greg." I stood and moved toward the door, suddenly needing to be out of there. "It's only that it'll seem strange for you not to be here, where you've been ever since I've known you."

"Wherever I am, I'll always be there for you."

"I know, but . . . everything's changing." I actually felt as if I might cry.

As soon as I closed my front door behind

393

me, I realized how weary I was—and that I was also coming down with a cold. I took a handful of vitamin C with a big glass of red wine, then showered and washed my hair and bundled up in my white terry-cloth bathrobe.

And thought, My God, I haven't checked on Hank in nearly ten hours!

I hurried to the phone, but before I could dial the hospital I saw the red light was on on my answering machine. Quickly I reached for the rewind button—five calls.

My mother: "Are you there? I read in the paper about Hank getting shot and you chasing after that sniper like a lunatic. Oh, Shari, why can't you get a decent job where you won't always be—"

I thought, Oh, Ma, I love you, too. And fast-forwarded through the rest of the message.

Luke Widdows: "I heard about the shooting. Are you okay? Call me anytime."

Jim Addison: "You didn't return my last call, but don't bother. I've been reading about you in the papers. You know, I always thought you were a gentle person like me, but this thing with the sniper . . . what you did was like police brutality. Sharon, you're just too violent for me. Violent women are unnatural—" The beep cut him off with a satisfying finality.

I smiled, remembering how I'd worried about Jim's potential for violence. Now *he* was put off by *mine!*

The fourth call was the one I'd been hoping for, Anne-Marie: "Well, God, he's okay. Surgery went fine. I think that on Sunday he'll be able to have a certain visitor he's already asking for. I'm going home to sleep now, so check with me sometime after noon tomorrow."

I stopped the tape, replayed the message. Hank was all right; soon I could visit him. I'd take him a stack of magazines, a care package from that bakery on Twenty-fourth Street whose blueberry muffins he so loved . . .

I'd almost forgotten that there was one more message. I switched the tape on. It was from George Kostakos.

I played it all the way through. Reversed the tape, listened to it again. His wife was fully recovered from her breakdown, and they'd begun divorce proceedings. She'd taken the Palo Alto house, and he'd moved to a condominium on Russian Hill. He still cared for me. If I felt the same, he'd love to see me. His new phone number was . . .

At first I felt a stubborn resistance. All

those months he'd been silent, left me wondering where we stood, and now he thought he could simply walk back into my life. But then I felt a softening: it couldn't have been easy for him, either. Besides, on some level I'd always known where we stood, known he'd eventually return.

I pictured George: his rough-hewn face, his changeable hazel eyes, his gray-frosted black hair, his tall, lean body. I put my hand to my lips, imagining how it would be to see him after all this time. Imagining how we would be together.

The pain and anger and disillusionment of the past week fell away from me. Their vestiges would return, I knew. Bad memories would recur—probably for the rest of my life. But I would take comfort in moments like this, when I felt temporarily safe, warm, insulated. I stretched, yawned. What an embarrassment of riches I'd come home to!

Restlessly I moved about the silent house, testing the doors and windows, even though I knew they were all locked. I prowled through the parlor, straightening a book on the shelf, dusting a cobweb from the mantelpiece. In the kitchen I checked to see if the pilot light on the stove was lit. Snooped at the ice cubes in the freezer, felt the bread for freshness, looked to see if there were enough eggs for breakfast. But finally weariness drove me to the bedroom, where I dropped my robe to the floor and crawled naked between the sheets.

As I hugged my pillow and closed my eyes, I resolved to wake by noon and return four of the five phone calls. I would reassure my mother. Thank Luke Widdows for the information that had aided me in my investigation. Ask Anne-Marie if I couldn't visit Hank sooner than Sunday. And tell George yes, I felt the same, wanted to see him.

And after that I would initiate a call of my own. I couldn't go on fooling myself: it was high time I told Ted to drop Ralph and Alice off at their new home.